S0-AYA-258

AULD ACQUAINTANCE

RUTH HAY

About This Book

Auld Acquaintance by Ruth Hay is the story of a woman in her 60s who has lost her confidence through life events, including a divorce. Anna has a part-time job in a library, and a group of good friends, but she is sinking into a depression.

Unexpectedly, she receives a legal letter informing her that she has inherited a piece of property in Scotland. Her first instinct is to ignore this letter as she has no knowledge of the person named as the owner.

Anna's friends persuade her to travel to Scotland and stay until she can decide how to dispose of the farm house near Oban. So begins an adventure which opens up prospects for Anna and introduces her to a new environment and new people who help her.

Will Anna adjust to living in a farm house with the minimum of amenities? Will she solve the family mystery of the unknown relative who has bestowed this legacy on her? Will she leave Canada for Scotland or return to her homeland and her safe life there?

Chapter One

The letter that was to change Anna's life lay buried in the pile of yesterday's bills and flyers on the hall table.

Anna was running late. She grabbed her bag, checking the contents while she donned her coat: flat shoes for the miles she would cover while tracking books; keys, wallet, Ziploc bag with peanuts and raisins for a snack; brush to fluff up her hair after the wool hat came off in the staff room. Yes, all present and correct.

A chuckle escaped her lips as she closed the door behind her, narrowly avoiding trapping her winter coat in the door frame. 'All present and correct' was one of her father's favourite sayings. He had passed away twenty years ago, but Anna thought, not for the first time, how the time-worn phrases of her parents lived on through her unconscious repetition of them.

Bitter January cold startled Anna as she picked her way through ice and snow towards her Toyota. No point in rushing now and breaking a leg. 'Better a moment at the curb than a month in hospital', as her mother used to say. As a teen, Anna would sigh in disbelief when her parents came out with one of these antique sayings. Years later she found out they were handed on from her grandmother in Scotland. Since Anna had never seen either her grandmother or Scotland, she was left with the distinct impression that both were somewhat outdated.

Sweeping the piled snow from the driver's window, Anna carefully opened the door far enough to let her sit inside and start the engine without flooding the interior of the car with snow that would melt uncomfortably during the drive downtown.

With the car windows cleared, she negotiated her way from the apartment building's parking lot, through the subdivision side streets, to join the inevitable, post-snowfall traffic crawl.

Nothing I can do about this now. I really must buy a cell phone, at least I could call ahead and warn Andrew I'll be late.

Anna knew she was a bit of a technophobe and coping with a cell phone might be difficult, but, in fact, there were few people in her life now who she needed to contact. Simon lived out west with his wife, two grown children and grandkids. She was only rarely a part of their busy lives. Still, a single woman, living alone, travelling around, should probably carry a phone as a safety precaution. Everyone seemed to have one. As she surveyed the lines of cars crawling toward a distant red light, Anna could see several people chatting or texting happily.

The Toyota was warming up nicely now after its icy night outdoors. Thank heaven for small mercies, she thought, and instantly she was standing in her mother's kitchen as she delivered these hurtful words to a daughter who had just confessed that her marriage of thirty years was about to end.

"What on earth do you mean by that Mother?" Anna had gasped, her heart still thumping from having to make the dreaded confession.

"Well, dear, I have always been thankful that you and that man never had any children.

I can't say I'm sorry to hear about your divorce. You know how I feel about Richard.

I'm only sorry it took you so long to realise that I was right about him all along."

A shiver went through Anna that had nothing to do with the weather outside the car.

What was wrong with her today? Normally she could avoid thinking about the past.

She usually tried to concentrate on positive events rather than the failures she had accumulated in almost six decades of living.

Enough of this. Anna gave herself a mental shake and began to tally a checklist of the good stuff in her life. Yes, she lived in a small apartment since the divorce, but she was saving for a deposit on a darling little house on the outskirts of town where she could have a garden with the cats and dogs she had always loved.

Her job at the library was part-time, but she had a government pension that covered the basics and a small inheritance from her parents that she had never touched.

She was independent and needed no one's permission to do anything or go anywhere.

She could watch television or read all night and snack on chocolate chip cookies to her heart's content if she so desired. She had a posse of girlfriends to call upon for dinners out with gossip for dessert, or movie nights followed by intensive analysis of the film over coffee and donuts.

All in all not such a bad life compared to a lot of other people these days.

At last Anna reached the front of the line of traffic and surged ahead as soon as the lights turned green.

Green for go. Forward thinking. The future, not the past.

It sounded like a useful mantra so she repeated it all the way to work.

It had been an endless day. One of those days when everything was just a bit out of balance and the unexpected cropped up with more than the usual regularity.

Arriving late was a bad start and finding out that three of the office staff had called, either sick or snowed in, did not help. At least Andrew was relieved to see Anna. He just managed to restrain himself from pushing her forcibly toward the front desk, although he was delivering instructions at top speed before she could get her coat off.

The line of patrons waiting to check out books or ask research questions, was already

snaking through the reception area. As she scanned books with a facility born of many hours at this task, Anna estimated that all these library users must have walked through the snow from downtown homes and were stocking up with more than the typical number of items to see them through a possibly serious snow storm.

Thank goodness Maya was available to help. They quickly divided those needing research help from the checkout line and Maya firmly steered her group towards the bank of computers. The student Pages who were of great help with computer skills would not be appearing until after high school finished for the day, so Maya would have to do her best on her own for now.

Anna glanced over the entire library area from the slightly elevated platform behind the main desk. Experience had taught her that problems were better prevented than cured.

A quick survey of the stacks, tables and seating, showed her that Old Jasper and his buddy Sam were drying off their sodden clothes near the heating vent. They were no trouble and Anna always felt they deserved a little comfort after spending the night in some doorway.

She knew Jasper would never go to the shelter in a nearby church.

"They steal stuff when you're asleep!" he had confided to Anna more than once.

She would have to keep an eye on the two old men as they would give out rather pungent aromas once their clothing warmed up. The public were known to complain about such inconveniences.

A slight sound caught Anna's attention in another direction. Moving quietly toward the sound she soon identified the source. There were three young lads hunched over a computer in a far corner giggling and nudging each other. Anna guessed they were skipping school and looking at something inappropriate. The library's programs had various protective devices to prevent pornographic sites from being accessed, but kids today had skills to circumvent almost any restriction.

Anna made sure the teens saw her approaching and judged they would scatter before she was close enough to see what was causing such mirth. It took only a moment to switch the computer to more useful purposes.

There was always demand for programs linking library users with government employment web sites these days. Andrew always asserted that a public library was the first line of defence for society in a recession, and because of that he could assure both his permanent and part-time staff, they would not be subjected to the layoffs that were inevitable in other service industries.

Anna was reassured by this thought. Working in the library was something essential to her wellbeing. It gave shape and purpose to her days and knowing she was needed there was far more valuable than the small salary she earned. On days when she was not working, she would think about book displays and catch up with periodical reading so that she could advise patrons where to look for material they were seeking.

It constantly amazed Anna how fast the day went when she was at work. Whichever shift she was required to fill, the time just flew by. There was always something to do to keep the backlog of materials from overwhelming the staff, and on some days the phone would ring incessantly as if there was a conspiracy to prevent any books or videos from being returned to their respective shelves. On those days, Anna had a habit of scattering returned materials on a large table with a sign issuing the challenge: 'What's on the Minds of Londoners this Week?'

It was surprising how many people came up with a response and happily accepted a bookmark prize. Even Andrew had to admit the unconventional method usually worked.

After an hour or so the table was cleared and the materials signed out to new borrowers.

Amongst themselves the staff called it, 'The Anna Factor'.

Anna always laughed silently when she heard the phrase. She often wondered, on sleepless nights, how she could be so creative in her professional life and so helpless in her personal life. When it came to her marriage to Richard, all the confidence and independence of her teaching career had vanished in tears and heartache whenever he turned that cold, disapproving glare in her direction.

One glance, and she knew that no matter what she said or did to appease him, she would remain frozen out of his love until days of silence had passed. The thaw would eventually occur, but the worst of it was that Anna could never figure out what prompted the melt so that she could shorten the lonely period. After years of this conditioning, she was just so grateful Richard had decided to restore his affection, that she smiled and said nothing about what his cruel treatment had cost her.

After the divorce, Anna had developed enough distance from the pain to recognise the emotional blackmail Richard was employing, perhaps unconsciously. She had read enough to see herself in the role of eternal pursuer while her husband retreated from her needy behaviour. This insight came too late.

The failure of her marriage was a secret shame she carried deep inside.

Her only consolation was that no one else knew how badly she felt and how it had affected her relationships with men. Even her Samba group of friends were unaware of the true depth of her despair. She put much effort into concealing that fact.

Susan, (Samba's 'S'), would, from time to time, set up a date for Anna.

Susan had the best of intentions but Anna had such fear of rejection that she would inevitably jeopardize the slightest chance of a connection to the man, with her nervous manner-isms and solemn disdain.

Before the 'Hi, how are you?' and the 'So what do you do?' were over, she would have retreated behind her defen-sive barriers and the poor guy would flee.

Anna would report back to Susan, "He was a very nice man, but they just didn't hit it off for some reason."

Susan never presented to Anna the nice man's version of events, but there was no second date. To Anna's profound relief, Susan would not make another matchmaking attempt for months.

Being single was a much safer option. Anna's post-divorce reading sources had advised her to create an impervious ring of protection around her heart. This would, supposedly, give her confidence that no one could breach the barrier without her specific permission. Her heart would remain immune from emotional attacks.

Anna thought this was a fine idea in theory, but in spite of several tries at forging this mythical barrier, she would find herself just as vulnerable and unprepared to move ahead as she had been since Richard's departure.

In her most honest moments, Anna knew this lack of

confidence was holding her back from living fully. It was one thing to realise this intellectually, of course, but it was quite

a different thing to act on the knowledge and risk more failure in her relationships.

When the depression of this realization hit, Anna had two choices.

One was to work all the harder and find oblivion in the immediacy of daily tasks.

She would approach Andrew and ask if she could volunteer her time to sort out some backroom mess or other, and often he was only too glad to get the extra help.

The other choice was to call on her oldest and best friend, Alina.

Their friendship went all the way back to childhood and no one knew Anna as well as Alina did. They had been there for each other through the good and bad times.

Many tears had been shed on each other's shoulders over the years and the sad secrets of their hearts and lives were shared, and lessened, in the sharing.

Only Alina knew the strong, independent young woman Anna had been before Richard.

Only Anna knew of the teenage rape attempt that had thrown her bright, pretty friend into a tailspin for years and resulted in a life choice devoid of male companionship.

Each was damaged emotionally, and sometimes Anna feared they were each incapable of providing the help the other needed to get out of the pain rut.

And yet, there was deep comfort in knowing no words were necessary to explain their feelings in the bad times. Often, they would talk quietly and then sit in silence together and that was enough to heal the misery for another while.

As years went by, the sharp pains had faded into the background of their lives. The bitter residue still lingered, however, and Anna wondered what it would take to restore her confidence again.

· · ·

By six thirty Anna was heading home from work. The pristine snow of the morning had turned to dismal grey but the roads had been plowed and the traffic was moving smoothly again.

It had been a busy day downtown despite the snowfall. It seemed as if everyone wanted to get shopping done in anticipation of more snow. Surprisingly this anxiety of preparation extended to reading matter also. The library had been thronged with students seeking research materials for homework assignments as well as the usual complement of avid readers insulating themselves with a comforting stack of novels for the weekend.

Anna had spent time with patrons recommending titles from her own extensive reading background and enjoyed the challenge of requests.

"Another one like this but not so long and set in another time period perhaps?"

"I saw it here last month. It had a red cover I think."

"Any more by this author?"

The returned books had piled up again and Andrew asked Anna to add a few extra hours in the next week to tackle the backlog. The library Pages who were supposed to arrive after the school day ended, had not turned up because of the weather. Anna knew that her diversion trick with the books would not work with this huge and growing pile of materials. Chaos could ensue in a remarkably short time if the books were not dealt with promptly.

The only benefit of such a busy day, thought Anna, as she flipped her long, lank hair to the back again, was the lack of time to worry about one's own life problems.

Anna could not wait to shut her own door behind her and divest herself of both her boots and the work day. A supper of toasted cheese with tomato sounded enticing and there was some frozen cheesecake in the freezer that would respond to a few seconds in the microwave. Then, a couple of hours of non-news television, and a comfortable bed beckoned with her own book extracted from the newly-purchased selections not yet available to library patrons. One of the perks of the job thought Anna with a contented sigh.

Keys, gloves and purse landed on the console table in the tiny entrance hall in her apartment. Coat, hat and boots were quickly stowed in the hall closet and as Anna bent to retrieve her cosy slippers, she bumped into the table sending the pile of mail cascading onto the floor.

Anna had discovered long ago one of the advantages of living alone. Nothing moved from its place during her absence and nothing was in anyone else's way if she chose to be untidy. Leaving the letters and magazines where they lay, she stepped into her living room, switching on the lamps as she moved to the window and closed the drapes against the night.

Home sweet home, at last.

Chapter Two

"Wat on earth is this?"

Anna read the paragraph again without any further understanding.

...............therefore, we are apprising you of the transfer of owner-ship of said property and wish to hear from you at your earliest convenience regarding your instructions for sale or other disposal. Please accept our condolences on the death of your relative and feel free to consider our firm your representative in Scotland, should you be requiring of our services.
Sincerely,
George L. McLennan.
Thompson McLennan and Baines.
Oban, Scotland.

The envelope, thrown into the garbage can next to the sofa a moment ago with all the other superfluous mail items, was hastily recovered as Anna checked the address.

The letter appeared to be for her but did not make any sense.

It is too early in the morning to cope with mysterious stuff, she thought, with a shake of her head.

Who was this relative and what property was referred to in the lawyer's letter?

Another reading revealed the name of the deceased as Helen Dunlop, spinster, aged 87 years residing alone at McCaig House Farm on the outskirts of Oban.

Anna had never heard of this Helen Dunlop and had no clue where Oban might be in Scotland or how she could possibly be the sole inheritor of a property there.

Check the information, she told herself, reaching for the telephone and almost knocking over her rapidly-cooling cup of coffee in the process. Anna carefully dialled the numbers of the legal firm but was interrupted by a voice message stating that she had misdialed and would she please check the number again.

"Wait just a minute! This must be some kind of confidence trick."

Anna's skeptical side jumped to her defence as she considered that a phone call could be an attempt to extort money in some way. She had heard of such schemes where an older person was duped into sending cash to obtain an inheritance where no such inheritance actually existed.

'When in doubt, do nowt.' Her father's oft-repeated advice seemed apt to Anna at this moment. She walked to the apartment window and took a deep breath to still the shaking of her hands as she looked out at the snowy scene below. There was no rush. Things could be checked out. There were people who could assist at such times and Anna had a friend or two who would be happy to help get to the bottom of this mystery that threatened to disturb her quiet Saturday morning.

Anna's next call quickly reached Susan on the other side of town where she lived with husband Jake and two huge dogs. Susan had been a legal secretary before she retired and was the legal eagle for Anna's entire Samba circle of friends. It was Susan who had steered Anna through the minefield of divorce ten years before and it took her quick mind only a minute to grasp the current dilemma.

"Get in the car and head over here right away, Anna," demanded Susan in her forthright manner, "and don't forget to bring the letter, the envelope and any family information you have from your parents. Don't worry, we'll sort this out in no time. I'll put on the coffee and tell the dogs you are on your way!"

Oscar and Dominic greeted Anna at the door in a flurry of wet noses and waving tails. The two Labradors, one brown and one black, were large for the breed and would have been a handful in Susan's one-floor house if it were not for the wider doors required by her husband Jake's wheelchair.

"Come in, come in!" said Susan, "You made good time. Just as well it's the weekend and the traffic is a lot lighter."

She took charge of Anna's coat and hat, produced slippers, sent the dogs to their beds in the corner of the kitchen and poured coffee for Anna and Jake in the time it took for Anna to take a deep breath. Susan was the kind of capable and reliable friend who created confidence in those around her. Anna knew that Jake's ability to cope so well with his MS was a direct result of his wife's no-nonsense attitude that extended to the medical personnel they both had to deal with.

"Right! Let's take a look at this letter, Anna."

Susan cleared a space on the kitchen table and studied the envelope first, then the letter.

"Looks authentic enough. I can easily check the firm in a legal index. Your problem phoning was likely to do with the international codes. I think you have to drop this zero when you call from Canada."

Looking up, Susan fixed Anna with the gimlet gaze that had scared many a young lawyer.

"Who's this Helen Dunlop? Can't say I've ever heard you mention her."

"That's just it," explained Anna with a sigh. "I have no clue. I never even heard her name before this and I can't imagine why she would leave anything to me, never mind a house of some sort!"

"Hey! Look on the bright side, lady! You could be the new owner of a residence in Scotland. I hear the property values there are far higher than they are in Ontario.

You could be a woman of substance, my dear!"

Susan's unexpectedly positive response to what had seemed to be a huge problem to Anna, turned the situation upside down in a moment.

A property of her own. A chance to make a new start in a new place. Somewhere far from the failures Anna had been dogged with since her divorce. Could it be....?

Almost as soon as these thoughts crowded her mind, Anna's pessimistic and practical side took over and the dream crashed with a thud.

Susan had been watching Anna's face closely and saw the frown between her blue eyes deepen.

"What are you thinking now?' she accused.

"Well, I can't imagine this is a simple matter of claiming a property. There are bound to be all kinds of ownership requirements including a raft of papers to be signed and possibly residence qualifications and who knows what else. I couldn't just up sticks and take off across the Atlantic and ......"

"Why on earth not?" demanded Susan. "It's about time you had an adventure Anna. You can't let life pass you by any more. The past few years have not been easy, I know, but this could be exactly what you need to shift you out of the boring groove you're in these days."

"Hey! Less of the insults, Susan! I am not so boring. I have a perfectly comfortable life and I'm not sure I really want to change it for something so uncertain."

An image of all the ornaments in her apartment flashed before Anna's eyes. There were precious memories there.

What would happen to all her stuff if she took off on this 'adventure'? Who would she know in a strange place? How could she afford to do such a risky thing?

With a shake of her head to erase these uncomfortable thoughts Anna stood up abruptly and pushed back her chair.

"Susan, I'm just not ready to discuss this any more today. I have a lot of thinking to do.

Keep the letter and feel free to see what you can find out for me but I am not promising anything. I don't feel happy about all this turmoil just when my life was beginning to fall into place again. Please don't push me Susan."

Anna had seen the determined look in Susan's eye. Of all Anna's friends, Susan was the one who wanted to fix everyone's problems for them. Not that she wasn't capable of doing so with some amazing results at times, but Anna did not want that kind of help at the moment.

She extricated herself from Susan's house with a quick goodbye and drove off down the snowy street, her head in such chaos that it was obviously not a good time to be driving.

A Tim Horton's appeared at a street corner so Anna took refuge in its steamy interior and settled by a window with a large double double, taking a deep breath to calm her racing mind.

Why am I in such a state about this, she fumed? I can easily turn my back on the whole stupid idea and forget the letter ever arrived. The farm house could be sold perhaps? It would never work anyway. I am way too old to be thinking about something so crazy at this time in my life. Woman of substance, indeed!

A few sips of coffee later, Anna felt calm enough to look around her. The café was nearly empty at this time in the afternoon with only a few customers lined up at the counter and a young girl swabbing the melted snow off the floor. At a corner table, a man and woman were sampling donuts and talking excitedly about flyers or brochures in front of them.

They're probably thinking about buying a house or a car, mused Anna. Nice to see such enthusiasm. She smiled as the woman clapped her hands in delight and threw her arms around the man.

When did I lose that kind of enthusiasm for life, she wondered? I used to be the kind of person who welcomed any diversion, loved the next episode, longed to see what was at the end of a road not travelled before. What happened to me?

A sigh so deep it brought tears welling up in her eyes, shocked Anna.

I'm not so unaware of my problems, she told herself. I do know what happened to me. Life happened. Disappointment happened. Things did not turn out the way I always hoped. The husband, children and cozy domestic scene I thought I could count on, just didn't work out and now here I am, alone in a coffee shop trying to face my fears and find the woman I used to be before all the disasters ruined my neat little life plans.

I know it started with Richard, or else it ended with him. It seemed like a good match; two people in their twenties with careers just beginning and ambitious plans for travel and a house in the suburbs with 2.5 children and a garden. Years of hard work to raise enough money for the dreams to come true became the daily grind that wore down the stamina and the resolve to make those dreams a reality.

The little annoyances of living with a partner who was just as weary as you were, began to chip away at the love Anna and Richard had cherished at the start.

Of course it didn't dissolve the marriage right away. It took a long time for the real damage to show.

Richard worked long hours and was often on the road serving clients for his family's insurance firm. When he came home again he didn't seem interested in Anna's lonely days, or notice the housework she had done, despite her own fatigue, so that their time together would be uninterrupted.

Instead, he collapsed on the sofa and expected Anna to listen to his complaints about clients and crazy drivers while providing meals on a tray in front of the TV where Richard invariably fell asleep after an hour or so.

Anna fell into the habit of unloading her frustrations after a week or two of this.

She longed for a baby, but Richard no longer saw this as a priority and it inevitably meant a fight.

Anna rubbed her neck, sipped her cooling coffee again and grimaced towards the window. She tried not to relive the ugly scenes that contaminated her marriage but with time she knew that both partners were to blame and she could not escape the guilt.

Perhaps she had never learned from her silent parents how to fight effectively.

That was what the self-help books the library constantly circulated, had taught her, in the long sleepless nights after Richard left.

Their own fights had escalated in just a few anguished minutes to full-scale attacks with shouting and accusations totally unrelated to the particular trigger that had started it all.

The atmosphere in the kitchen or bedroom where these scenes usually took place, was poisonous. Anna knew it, but employed some form of magical thinking that led her to believe 'This time it will be different. This time he'll see my point of view and not blame me for everything wrong since the beginning. This time he won't beat me down with words.'

It was quite ridiculous, Anna acknowledged. She was an intelligent woman, respected in her profession, whose advice was often sought by her teaching colleagues. She was competent in so many ways, yet she could not hold her own when it mattered most. Interviews for demanding jobs were a breeze for her but she collapsed in tears when challenged unfairly by the man she loved.

"Doesn't do any good to go over all this again," Anna

murmured to the window, then swiftly looked around to see if anyone was near enough to have heard her. Crazy old lady talking to herself would be the verdict for sure, she thought.

The end of the marriage was inevitable, although Anna was the only one who could not see it coming.

Her staunch pal Alina had tried to warn her more than once, but Anna was deep into denial by then, unwilling to admit the death of her dreams.

Richard's work hours continued to increase until their home life was little more than an armed camp. He took to sleeping in the spare bedroom so as not to disturb Anna when he came home late.

The final death knell rang clearly when a neighbour returned from a family trip to Toronto and told her friend that she had seen Richard outside a hotel in a very warm embrace with a young woman who was definitely more than a work colleague.

The ensuing fight tore down all Anna's defences and when Richard left, she was a quivering wreck for months until Susan took over and steered Anna through the divorce settlement.

The worst part was the aftermath. Anna's confidence was shattered. She constantly mourned the lost decades and blamed herself for wasting so much time.

Then came the slow rebuilding period, with extensive reading, self-examination and support from Samba, Anna's long-time pals, named for a combination of the first letters of their names.

"All in the past. All over. I am a new person now!" Anna asserted again, to her reflection in the window.

She wiped away the stray tear with a paper napkin, stood up and fastened her coat.

The coffee queue was building up now as the end of the afternoon approached.

"It's time for me to go home to a safe, secure place of my

own where I can lick my wounds in peace. I have a lot to think about now."

By the time she reached her apartment Anna could feel an acid churning in her stomach from all the coffee she had drunk that day. She shuffled into the kitchen and stared inside the fridge for inspiration.

"Could this be an ice cream day? No, a bit too chilly for that treat. Chocolate? That's a never-fail comfort food. Now where did I stash the chocolate the last time I had a bad date?"

A few minutes rummaging around in the kitchen cupboards and her bedroom drawers revealed nothing sufficiently satisfying for the current crisis. Anna was about to give up when she remembered the gift bag in her closet where the emergency supply of goodies was stored. Retrieval required some digging into the back of the closet behind the summer shoes and clothing. Just as she spied the bright red gift bag with its hoard of chocolate bars, another familiar smell stopped Anna in her tracks. Bent double with very little light to see with, she could still identify this scent and trace its source inside the storage box she had once thrust far out of her sight.

"Well," she sighed in despair, "isn't this just typical! How much worse could this damn day get?"

Anna dragged the offending box backwards out to daylight, grunting through gritted teeth.

"'In for a penny; in for a pound'," as mother used to say. "I might as well dive to the bottom of this well of desperation. It's the only way to burst this particular boil of bad feelings. Now there's a bag of mixed metaphors!" Anna chuckled to herself, glad that she could still laugh at what had once been a very painful journey.

The smell of Richard's deodorant assailed her nostrils as she threw aside the box lid and saw the contents folded neatly inside. This was all that remained of her marriage. Items she had kept because the memories they revived were mainly happy ones.

Richard's favourite old, brown, sweater came out first. It was so worn in the elbows, it was almost transparent. Anna had removed it finally from Richard when she won a bet with her husband that she could find a replacement in the exact same colour and pattern.

Maria had come to the rescue that time, and after hours of shopping and lots of laughter about men and their dress disasters, she had unearthed a duplicate sweater from some antique store she knew.

Anna had proudly presented the substitute sweater to Richard and confiscated the offending item, little thinking that it would provide such a sentimental memory for her one day, redolent of evenings reading together by the fireside that ended with a sleepy embrace as she and Richard went to bed arm in arm.

Below the sweater, Anna uncovered some framed photographs that had once stood proudly on a bookcase shelf in their home. The engagement picture on Valentine's Day at the outdoor skating rink; red noses to match Anna's cap and scarf; left hand held up to the camera with the diamond glittering in the sunlight, almost as brightly as the smiles on their faces.

How long has it been since I looked that happy, thought Anna, and when did I last have the courage to wear red with this dull, grey hair of mine?

The wedding picture on the beach at the Caribbean resort; tanned skin against white veil

floating lazily in the tropical breezes. The ideal setting for a lifelong dream of love.

We looked like such a perfect couple, mused Anna, but all the good wishes showered on us that day couldn't prevent the bad times ahead. I wish ....

"No point in wishing now," Anna said decisively. "The past can't be changed. Learn the lessons and move on".

Thrusting aside the velvet jewellery box and a collection of elaborate hairclips she had once worn when her hair was full, long and brown she grabbed the lid of the box, impatient to bring to a close this useless trip down nostalgia lane.

The lid refused to fit back on the box despite Anna's firm push. She saw a cardboard folder jutting up from the contents and blocking the lid. She took out the folder intending to replace it flat on top of the box, but something about the faded paper cover made her stop and open it up.

"Where did this come from?" she puzzled. The sepia-toned photograph of a group of people in a formal pose, taken in a studio many years ago was vaguely familiar to Anna.

She felt as if she had seen it somewhere but had not really studied the figures long enough to establish any connections.

Anna leaned back against the closet door and angled the photograph toward the fading light from the bedroom window. One of the women held a small posy of flowers and now Anna saw that all the men and women had carnations in the lapels of their suits.

"Could this be a wedding photo, or is my imagination tying my wedding picture to this one? Certainly doesn't look like a wedding. No white dress here, it all seems rather sombre. Not even a real smile on any of the faces."

As she looked again at the faces, something stirred in Anna's memory. The solemn young couple in the centre wearing dark suits and hats had a slightly familiar appearance. The angle of the man's head and the tilt of the woman's eyebrows struck a chord.

"Wait a minute!" she exclaimed. "That's Simon's head shape and my eyebrows. This must be our mum and dad's wedding picture!"

The shrill ring of the telephone broke abruptly into Anna's

thoughts. She extricated herself from the closet but kept hold of the photograph as she dived for the bedside table. The answering service was not switched on and Anna detested missing a call in case it was something important. She untangled the phone cord and dropped the photograph in her hurry but managed to lift the receiver on the fourth or fifth ring.

"Yes, who's calling?" she asked in some agitation.

"Sis, is that you? It's Simon. Are you OK? You sound anxious."

"Oh, Simon, I'm sorry, it's just that I have had a strange day and I was deep in old memories when your call came. How is the family? Is Michelle all right?"

"Sure thing, everyone's in fine fettle here. The grandkids are revelling in the snow. They're always asking when Great Auntie Anna is coming to visit."

"Actually, Sis, I'm calling about a letter I received a couple of days ago. It's from a solicitor in Scotland of all places and I don't know what to make of it."

"Not you too!" interrupted Anna. "This is positively weird! I have just discovered an old photograph and I was wondering if it was our parents' wedding picture."

"Well, fine Anna, but what has that to do with the letter I got?"

"Right! I'm getting ahead of myself, Simon. My letter from Scotland informed me I am the owner of a farm house belonging to Helen somebody who has recently died. Was your letter the same?"

"No, but the same Helen, Helen Dunlop, I think, has apparently left me some money."

"Really? That's amazing! Simon, who is this person and why are we hearing about her for the first time?"

"Anna, I am no wiser about that than you seem to be. You said you had an old wedding picture of our parents? Do you recognise any of the wedding party? Our folks never spoke about family much. All I know is that they met and married in Scotland before emigrating to Canada. Maybe there's a story here. Could be, the house is worth a fortune

and there's a family feud at the heart of it all!"

"Ha! I seriously doubt it Simon. You always did have a vivid imagination!"

Anna was reluctant to mention that Simon's theory was the second version she had heard that day, so she rushed on to a more sensible topic.

"Give this Dunlop name some thought, Simon, and see if you can come up with an explanation or find something in Mum and Dad's papers. Didn't you inherit a bureau that used to be in Dad's office when the old house was sold? Perhaps there's a clue in there. Anyway, we'll talk soon and try to figure this out. Give my love to Michelle, the kids and the grandkids. Bye for now."

"All right, I'll do that! Don't fret Anna. We'll get to the bottom of this and at least we have a handsome cheque at this end to help us pay off the Christmas bills! Take care of you."

As soon as the phone was replaced on the bedside table, Anna felt the exhaustion of the day overtake her.

"Enough already! I have to eat something and collapse into bed before I expire!" she shouted to the empty rooms.

No wonder they say living alone is bad for your health, Anna thought, as she headed for the kitchen. Talking to yourself is the first sign of mental stress and I've been doing it all day. I guess there's not so much distance between me and those two homeless men in the library after all.

With this chilling conclusion, Anna placed the old wedding photograph on her bedside table for later consideration, and dragged herself into the kitchen for scrambled eggs and toast with a large mug of hot tea.

Chapter Three

"**B**ev, it's Susan. I'm calling a Samba meeting for next week. Anna needs our help. Nothing serious, she's OK but requiring a little of our brand of gentle persuasion.

You know what I mean, eh?

I'll explain everything when you call me back with a date. Talk to you soon."

"Maria, I know you're at work and I didn't want to call you at the Mall. I'm trying to get a date for a Samba meeting next week. Anna's had a great opportunity dropped in her lap and I'm afraid she'll miss out if we don't encourage her to accept it. Don't say anything to Anna yet. Call me back at home tonight if you can."

"Alina, I think this is one of your volunteer days but I need to talk to you about Anna.

If she has already told you about Scotland, you'll know why we need a Samba meeting soon. Give me a buzz when you get home from school."

. . .

"Right, that's the gang alerted. Now I need to tackle Anna and see how she feels after a couple of days to think things over."

"Hold it Sue! You are rushing things here." Jake's calm voice always soothed his wife but a massage on her tense shoulders did an even better job. Jake manoeuvred his wheelchair into position with accustomed ease and started the treatment.

"I know, I know, honey, but this could be Anna's big chance to recapture her energy and drive. You know how I have worried about her for years now."

"Yes, I do understand. Some might say you are interfering in your friend's life, Susan, but I have watched you move mountains for your buddies and they are so lucky to have you fighting in their corner. I have first-hand experience of how valuable your persistence can be!"

"Thanks, Jake. That means a lot to me." Susan reached back to touch Jake's warm hands on her shoulders and gave them a squeeze. He was in a good period of health at the moment with only minimal muscle weakness. It was so like him to want to give comfort to her when he could. She knew it was his way of saying thanks for all the hospital visits and physical help she gave when things were bad.

"I'll try to slow down a bit but I do have some new information to share with Anna about the inheritance."

"Can't say I'm surprised about that. You were still at the computer when I woke around four this morning."

"It was worth it Jake. I connected with the website in London, England, where births and deaths are registered and I found out more about who Helen Dunlop might be.

I was pretty sure she must be related to Anna and I think I have found a clue. Complete strangers don't leave property to just anyone.

I searched Anna's parents' marriage certificate. They were married in a Glasgow registry office in 1940, listed as Marion H. Jarvis, shop assistant and Angus T. R. McLeod, engineer.

Kyle Purdy was a witness, and an Amy Warren also signed the document."

"How does that help find Helen Dunlop, Susan? I can't see any connection."

Jake had stopped the massage and wheeled round to look at his wife's notes on the office desk.

"Neither did I, at first. I checked the list of births, deaths and marriages rather than the certificates because I was curious about the initials in each name. Sometimes middle names derive from family links and can lead to other sources."

Susan's excitement was obvious in the tone of her voice now and the dogs, sensing her emotion, rose from the doorway and pushed their wet noses onto their mistress' knee to provide comfort in case it should be needed.

Jake signalled silently to the Labradors and they settled at his feet with the promise of a walk soon. Susan had hardly noticed this interruption as she was intent on the pages in front of her.

"Look here, Jake. Anna's mother's middle name is Helena!"

"So? That could be entirely coincidental, Susan. It doesn't prove anything and you know it."

"Of course I know it, but you must admit it is a little strange and that got me thinking about Anna's grandparents. Helen Dunlop died in her late eighties so she would be a contemporary of Anna's mother and father, although her name is different. What if the answer was in the previous generation?"

"Now you're getting into the realm of outright supposition. Was Anna's grandmother or grandfather a Dunlop?"

"Unfortunately not, Jake. Their married name was Knox."

"Hmm! A dead end then?"

"I suppose so. I ran out of steam at that point, I admit, but I have a feeling there's more to it. I am not giving up just yet."

"I never expected you to Susan. Why don't you have a

nap and I'll take the dogs for a run in the dog park. The sidewalk snow should be cleared by now.

Don't forget you have to tell Anna about all this. She may not be quite so enthusiastic especially when she realises you have been poking around in her family business without her permission."

"True. I'd better not get too far ahead without reporting in to Anna. I'll need to see her as soon as possible and I'd better be well rested for that little encounter, judging from the reception I got yesterday."

"Susan, it's Alina returning your call. What's going on with Anna, you've really got me wondering? Don't panic, I haven't called her yet but I am due to hear from her any day now. It's been a week since we last spoke. I put it down to the weather but now I'm thinking something's up. I can meet any evening this week, or next if need be…the sooner the better as I am getting worried now. Anna is my oldest friend and needs gentle handling Susan. Just let me know the where and when and I'll be there. Bye for now."

"Maria here. I'm working nights till 10:30 this week Susan, but I can switch shifts with someone if necessary. Is Anna sick? I tried to get her on Thursday but her phone was busy or off the hook all day. I'm sending you an e mail and a text to Jake. Get back to me ASAP."

"Hi Susan, it's Bev. I've got a big accounting job on this week. It's the best chance I've had all month to make headway on the mortgage so I can't risk it. I'll be glued to my home computer day and night until the work's done but you know where I am. Call me when the time and location for the meeting are set and I'll drop everything. Who needs sleep anyway!
Love ya for caring, Sister Susan."

Susan sighed as she came to the end of her messages. It was supposed to be easier to get together with friends when most of them reached retirement age but, honestly, this group seemed to be busier than ever, what with Maria at the Mall and Bev working from home, not to mention Anna's erratic hours at the library. What happened to the nice image of little old ladies in rocking chairs on the front porch with tea and scones?

Scheduling a meeting with this lot was worse now than when they were all working full time, although both Maria and Bev were younger mums with kids at home.

I have to solve the problem of getting Anna to agree to meet without alerting her to the kind of intervention I have in mind. I'd better start working out the details.

Lunch is out. With most of us busy during the day, that could only happen on a weekend

and I don't know if this can wait so long.

An evening meal might be possible if Maria gets enough warning. A restaurant could be neutral ground for what I have in mind but not so good for the sort of enthusiastic atmosphere I need to create. In any case we can't have Anna storming off if she doesn't like my suggestions.

Susan turned to her laptop and decided to send an e mail to the Samba group filling in some of the detail about Anna's situation and asking for advice about a meeting place.

As Anna was the only one of the group without a home computer since she used the library e mail, there was no chance she would see the messages, and the information would allay Alina's fears for now, giving everyone a chance to think of how they could persuade Anna to take the chance of a new start in life.

I still have to deal with Anna of course, she realized. She won't be impressed by all this cloak and dagger stuff behind her back but I really feel this is an amazing opportunity for her.

Perhaps I won't mention my plans to Jake just yet though.

Susan, you are such a good friend to do all this for Anna but you must know you are treading on dangerous ground. She is only just recovering from the last bad episode of blaming herself for Richard and I don't want to send her off on another downward spiral.

Be sure you handle things as diplomatically as possible.

I'll be there whenever and wherever. We can do a pot luck at my place if you like but what will the occasion/excuse be?

Alina.

Susan anything you decide is good for me. Just give me a bit of notice so I can clear the work, and my mind. Can't offer my place as it would require a major clean up that I just don't have time for right now. Kudos to you for setting things in motion. Anna deserves some good luck.

Bev.

"Anna, it's Susan, here."

"Oh, I've been meaning to call you Susan. I want to apologize for my behaviour on Saturday. I left you so abruptly when you were only trying to help me. I ....."

"Wait! It's perfectly OK Anna. Don't worry. I know you were upset and I jumped in without thinking about your feelings. You know me, I never hesitate to rush in where angels fear to tread."

"Susan, you don't need to apologize to me. You have been such a good friend. I could never repay your kindness to me. I feel like such a fool letting myself be thrown by a silly letter like that. It's nothing to be concerned about, and I'm sure it will all work out once I contact that lawyer."

"That's what I'm calling about, my dear. I did do some investigation and found out some more. Remember I asked you to see if you had any family information?"

"Yes, I did find an old photograph that might be useful and that

reminds me, Simon got a letter from the same lawyer and a sum of money from the Dunlop lady."

"Ah, that's interesting! I want to see that photo Anna. Listen, it's about time the Samba group got together again. Why don't we meet at your place and put our heads together to see what we can figure out? I've told the girls the rough outline of events and they're all dying to get in on the mystery. I'll order a big pan of lasagna and bring some Italian bread so you don't have to do a thing. Does Wednesday evening suit you? It looks like the weather has calmed down for now."

"Wednesday? Well, if you think the girls would be free it's all right I suppose, but I really wonder if it's worth everyone's time and trouble Susan. It's a bit of a storm in a teacup I think."

"Don't be too sure, Anna. I'll send messages right away and if you don't hear from me before Wednesday, we'll be on your doorstep around 7:00pm. I am so looking forward to a good chat and catch up. Bye for now!"

Anna put the phone down and tried to figure out what was going on. Susan was a force of nature all right. When she got an idea in her head she was like a whirlwind and sometimes she left people spinning in her wake. Anna felt like she had been spun around and she wasn't quite sure what direction she was facing.

A simple get together for food and gossip, or a plot of some kind? What was behind Susan's request? It can't be anything drastic Anna told herself as she automatically tidied up papers and dishes, casting her eye over the apartment as it would be seen by her friends in a day or two.

I won't have long to wait before I find out. I'll do a spot of cleaning this evening and maybe I'll make a start on that sherry trifle all the girls love.

Anna spent most of Wednesday at the library. The February

'Loving Reading' series was about to begin and Anna's talent for eye-catching displays was in demand.

"I can't imagine how we could do this every year without you, Anna," gushed Andrew.

"Your ideas are the foundation of our print and TV ads and Tony will scan them into the web site. That combination you created of teen sci fi book covers and futuristic business non-fiction, is outstanding, and will appeal to our reader demographic.

Tony has some kids standing by to do personal reviews of the new titles and we have persuaded some local reviewers to do critical pieces tying together the economic theme and science fiction as a predictor of future trends. It's a perfect match and I can't thank you enough."

"Not a problem, Andrew. I really enjoy this kind of thing. It reminds me of my teaching years and I always loved science fiction for my grade 7 and 8 students even although some of them thought I was too ancient to know what it was about."

"I doubt that Anna!" Andrew laughed aloud. "I've seen you with a group of our teen readers around you. What was that series they were all talking about; Scott Westerfeld,

an Australian author?"

"Well, now my secret's out, Andrew. I only come here to get advance notice on the next hot authors!"

"Perfect match, then, so just keep coming Anna".

The rest of the day was a blur of conferencing with Tony on the colour ads while Anna proofed the text and made adjustments to the script to suit different media, all the while watching the main desk for library patrons who expected her to recommend titles each time they visited. It was 6:00pm before Anna realized the time and made a hurried exit.

She wanted to get home and make some last minute preparations before the Samba group arrived.

Luckily the traffic was lighter than usual, and by 6:30 she

was unlocking her apartment door when a familiar voice hailed her from the direction of the elevator.

"Miss Mason, I'm glad I caught you!"

"Oh, Joseph, don't rush like that. Remember your asthma. Please take your time!"

"No worries, Miss M. I just wanted you to get this as soon as possible. It's an Express package. I had to sign for it or they would have returned it to the main office and goodness knows when you would have seen it again. I thought it might be something important."

"Thank you so much, Joseph. I'll just take the package inside. My lady friends are arriving shortly, so if you see them at the door downstairs just let them in for me, will you?"

"Sure thing Miss M. It'll be that nice bunch of ladies who make you laugh, I suppose?"

"That's right. We'll probably have some food for you later, if you want it."

"Always welcome! Always welcome for an old widower like me".

"See you later then, Joseph".

Anna turned away deliberately so that the apartment manager would get the message that she was not about to reveal the contents of her mail delivery.

She saw Joseph move slowly towards the elevator, glancing back in case she was overcome with the same curiosity that drove him. He told his residents that it was concern for them that made him want to know what was going on in their lives.

Most of Joseph's renters understood it was a way to fill the lonely hours since his wife had died, although on one occasion he had prevented a robbery by knowing the consistent habits of an older couple who had been staying with family when a stranger arrived with a key to their apartment and began moving furniture into a van.

Anna kicked off her shoes inside the door and leaned back to close it behind her while scanning the Express envelope.

The name was correct at least, although she could not imagine who would be sending her urgent material.

Turning the package over, she was astonished to see the sender's name and address.

It was the same solicitor in Scotland who had sent the original letter informing her about the legacy.

Anna had put the entire incident out of her mind after her previous reaction to the very thought of the responsibility of disposing of a property gifted by a stranger.

Now, at the worst possible moment, the entire situation was looming again.

I am not going to deal with this right now, she told herself. The girls will be here any minute and Susan will know what to do. I'll wait till they arrive and then we'll see what's in this package and what, if anything, can be done about it.

Anna put the package on her dressing table in the bedroom and went out again, shutting the door firmly behind her.

"Out of sight; out of mind," she murmured with a grin. "Now that's an old saying that is both practical and easy to understand. My mother would approve."

Chapter Four

✦

Anna opened her apartment door to a gaggle of chatter and laughter. Maria had evidently regaled the group in the elevator with another anecdote from the bottomless reservoir of funny incidents provided by her large Italian family.

Anna caught the tag line, "....and then he dumped the entire bucket of mortar on the garden path and the aunts had to put the brick wall together by themselves or have a solid heap of cement lying there forever!"

The volume of laughter rose again as Maria shrugged expressively and Alina collapsed in giggles.

"Hush up!" whispered Susan. "The entire floor will be out of their doors in a minute to see what the fuss is. See! Anna's heard the commotion already."

"Get in here you crazy women," exclaimed Anna, hustling them inside and collecting coats, boots, dishes and hugs as they trooped in.

"It's so good to see you all. What happens to us in winter? We never seem to have time to get together."

"Must be the weather, Anna," responded Alina with a special smile for her best friend. "We do talk to each other but the thought of venturing out after dark is not appealing to me, even for you guys."

"Cut the cackle you two," interrupted Bev, "the smell of this lasagna has been driving me crazy all the way here. I am so busy at the computer this month that I never cook a decent meal and my boys are useless in the kitchen despite my best efforts to encourage them."

"Don't complain. That's what keeps you so slim!" Anna hugged Bev affectionately and ruffled her short, dark, curly, hair before announcing to the group,

"There's salad and bread sticks on the table and wine for those who aren't driving.

Help yourselves to plates and glasses, buffet style, and sit wherever you can.

I'll heat up the extra servings and if you are very, very good there will be dessert to follow."

"Honestly, Anna," sighed Susan, "they call *me* the bossy one, but you have never lost that teacher manner. I'll bet the library patrons are scared to death of you."

"You'll be the scared one, Susan if you don't get the sherry trifle. You know it's your favourite."

"Yes, ma'am! I'll be good." Susan's mock humility did not fool anyone.

"That won't last long," chortled Maria and the entire group laughed again.

When dessert and coffee had been circulated and the major part of the gossip shared,

Susan looked around the group and an expectant hush descended.

"Anna, you probably realize there's a hidden agenda tonight. We all want to help you with this business of the inheritance. I hope you don't mind, but I've filled the girls in on the basic details."

"What details? You must know more than I do then, Susan. I have very little information and very little idea of what to do other than the obvious solution which is to sell the property for as much as I can get and be done with it."

"Of course, I know we are treading on thin ice here, Anna. The decision is yours but we are your friends and we want what is best for you. Give us a chance to tell you what we think."

"You had better bring me up to date first, Susan. The last I heard, you were not entirely sure about the validity of the offer. What did you discover in such a short time?"

"Well, the firm of solicitors in Oban is legit, so presumably the offer is also. The real mystery lies in the relationship issue. I did a little digging in the Scottish records of births, deaths and marriages and I might have found a clue, although Jake says it is a fragile link at best."

"What sort of clue? This is getting more interesting by the minute."

"Pipe down, Maria. Your family has more than enough mysteries to keep you satisfied for decades."

The tension broken by shared laughter, Susan resumed her account.

"As you will know, Anna, your mother's middle name was Helena. Did your mother ever tell you where the name came from?"

"No, she never said anything to me about it. It could be a complete coincidence that she had a middle name similar to Helen and that doesn't explain where the Dunlop surname came from. I certainly never heard that name mentioned at all."

"It does seem a stretch, but as it was the only connection I could find, I went back another generation to your grandparents to see if there was anything there. Your mother was Marian McLeod and her maiden name was Jarvis, isn't that right?"

"I believe so." Despite herself, Anna's initial resistance to this invasion of privacy was now morphing into curiosity.

Susan certainly knew more about her family now than Anna had ever been told.

"Your grandmother on your mother's side was Aileen Jarvis but the records revealed that she had been married once before to a Patrick Knox who died in the influenza epidemic of 1918."

"Good heavens, Susan! I had no idea. Was there a child of that marriage? What's the Wilson/Dunlop connection? Did my mother have a half-sister? Why did I never hear about any of this?"

There was a collective gasp from three eager listeners as these possibilities were revealed.

"I can't answer all your questions, Anna, but at least there's now a start to finding the answers and your guess is a good one."

"Anna, this is so exciting!" breathed Alina, her bright blue eyes sparkling with delight. "Your mother and father were very reserved. I was rather afraid to talk to them on the few occasions I went to your house after school. I never heard any talk about family members or even saw photographs around the place. Is it possible you had relatives in Scotland who would know this Helen Dunlop?"

"I suppose that's possible, Alina, but I wouldn't know where to begin. Susan has uncovered already, so much more than I was aware of, but I do have an old wedding picture and also an Express mail package from Scotland that just arrived tonight and hasn't yet been opened."

All the voices shouted at once, encouraging Anna to get the items and bring another bottle of wine as well.

"This is better than a movie," said Bev, "and I still want to hear what you meant Susan when you suggested Anna's guess might be on target."

"Wait till Anna comes back and I will reveal all," stated Susan in her best spooky voice.

"Please just remember girls, this is Anna's life we are

messing about in and proceed with caution." Alina's anxiety could be clearly heard in her tentative manner.

"Oh, Alina, you are like a mother hen when it comes to Anna. She's made of much tougher stuff than you think, despite all the bad luck she has had lately. She'll take charge when she's ready to."

"Well, I hope you are right about that Maria. I can't help worrying about her. We have been such good friends for so long and, frankly, I would not want her to leave Canada."

"Who's talking about leaving Canada?" exploded Anna, as she came back into the living room with her arms full. "That's about the last thing I would want. It's taken me years to get myself settled in a good job with some savings for the future and good pals to help me spend the money and the time."

"Calm down Anna," soothed Susan. "Pass that bottle around and I'll get some more coffee. Nobody is making any decisions for you. We wouldn't even try. Am I right ladies?"

Laughter broke the tension once more as Anna handed the wedding photograph to Alina and opened the mail package to reveal a letter and an aerial photograph of a small building.

Bev and Maria crowded around Alina while Anna read the letter first.

"Who's in the photo, Alina? Is that Anna's parents? Would you look at the style of them! That's a long way from your Theresa's white crinoline dress. Am I right Maria? How things have changed in the wedding department!"

Susan took the chance to draw Anna aside and glance over the letter. It was from the solicitor who had contacted Anna just a few days ago.

Dear Ms. Mason,

As I have not received a reply to my previous letter regarding the estate of my client, Miss Helen Dunlop, I am taking the liberty of sending more information by Express Post Courier.

Enclosed, please find a recent photograph commissioned by my office, showing the McCaig Estate Farm House property. The boundary lines extend to the foot of the hill to the rear and on the west as far as the line of scots pines. The eastern boundary is several hundred yards beyond the small burn marked by the large boulders. I can assure you that the property is without liens and that you, Ms. Mason, are the sole beneficiary other than the sum of money forwarded to a gentleman who I presume to be a male relative of your own.

My former client, Miss Dunlop, trusted my firm with her affairs for many years and was most insistent that you should be the inheritor of her property despite, as far as I can tell, never having met you. I would not wish to place any pressure upon you at this time, Ms. Mason, and I understand the difficulty of making decisions when you reside at such a great distance from Scotland, but I am obliged to request the favour of a reply with respect to your intentions.

The McCaig Estate Farm House has been unoccupied for some 18 months since the illness of its owner required a move to a local nursing home and I fear the empty buildings may be an invitation to some unscrupulous persons.

I await your response, and reaffirm the willingness of our solicitors to act as your representatives in Scotland should you so decide.

Sincerely,

George L. McLennan

Thomson McLennan and Baines

121 George Street

Oban

Argyll and Bute PA56 8SE

Scotland.

Phone: 01631 5632280 | Fax: 01631 563 2281

Email: www.tmboban.com

Anna's gaze was fixed firmly on the photograph of the farm while Susan re-read the letter. The buzz of talk from the rest of the Sambas faded as she saw for the first time the property that lay at the heart of the decision she had to make.

There were the boundaries mentioned in the lawyer's letter and Anna could see clearly how green and luscious the land looked with grass or shrubs ascending almost to the top of the hill that seemed to shelter the little house far below.

What remained an unknown quantity, was the farm house itself. The roof could be seen from the air and possibly a chimney but any detail of the house was obscured by the roof's overhang. Similarly lacking in detail, was a shed or outbuilding to the east and stones near the stream, if that was what the letter named as a burn. There might have been a fence or wall around the house, enclosing a green area but at this point Anna realised she was guessing wildly.

What was for sure, was the sudden attraction she felt for this unknown place, out on its own, with no road or hydro poles in view. At the same time, her practical side told her she was being a romantic fool. Didn't her father always say, 'Never buy a pig in a poke,' whatever that meant, but it certainly indicated caution until you knew all the facts and factors involved. Anna was too long in the tooth to let foolish notions guide her decisions.

"Anna, let's see the photograph!" Alina was tugging on Anna's arm and still holding the old wedding photo in her other hand. "But, first, see if you agree with me about the wedding party here. I think it's your Mum and Dad alright because I can see the resemblance. The girls disagree with me but they didn't know you when you were younger like I did. What do you say?"

Anna dragged her attention back to her living room and the eager faces of her friends.

"Yes. Well, I do think it's my parents but I just don't recognise the other two."

"You know," Maria said thoughtfully, "it's a crying shame

people don't write the dates and names on photographs. It would make life much easier for the next generation.

I have a stack of old family photos from Italy, and God knows where else, and hardly a clue who is who. The first thing I do this weekend is start labelling a whole box full of the Canadian family's pictures and send them off to everyone and see if it sets off a chain reaction."

"You're crazy Maria!" laughed Bev. "No one has print pictures any more. It's all digital now and who knows how long *they* will last. The best you can get is a date on them. Anna, just ignore Maria and let's see the colour photograph."

Anna handed over the photograph almost reluctantly and heard the gasps and exclamations of delight from the group.

"It's a country estate, Anna!"

"You lucky dog! I'd give my right arm for a place in the country. I could run away and my boys would never find me."

"As if you would, Bev. Anyway, the boys would track you down as soon as they got hungry!"

"Now that's the honest truth!" agreed Bev, with a deep chuckle. "Doesn't it look peaceful, though? I wonder how far it is from a town or even a road?"

"Get real, all of you." Susan's practical manner brought them all back to reality with a bump. "Stop dreaming! It's only our winter weather that's got you all drooling.

You know what they say; Britain is green for a reason. That's because it rains there a lot. You can't tell a thing from this angle. It could be a swamp. In any case, this is Anna's decision so back off and let the girl think."

"Probably a good idea, Susan. Truthfully, my head is spinning. I do need time to think about this and get back to the solicitor before he sends out the army. I want to call Simon as well."

"Right! We are out of here. Call me tomorrow afternoon Anna. I have a doctor's appointment with Jake in the morning."

Susan's statement was a signal to everyone. As the tallest among them, she commanded attention just by standing up and smoothing her skirt with the elegant, capable hands that were her best feature.

In a trice, the apartment was emptied leaving a cleared table, plumped up cushions,

lasagna in the fridge and very few dirty dishes in the kitchen. Susan was a master organizer but the Sambas all knew their roles on occasions like this. Nevertheless, despite the rapid exit, Anna was left with kisses and promises of help with anything she might need, from coffee to consolation.

It is too late in the day to be thinking of any of this, thought Anna with a yawn. I need to sleep on it and see how I feel in the morning light. That is, if I can sleep at all after all this excitement.

By the time she had donned pyjamas and brushed her teeth, Anna was already half asleep.

Turning out the bedside lamp, she pulled the covers over her shoulder and, with a sigh, thankfully closed her eyes.

Her final, drowsy thought was..............why did Helen Dunlop choose me?

Chapter Five

Despite her fears, Anna slept soundly and awoke just in time to switch off the alarm.

The bright light sneaking through the drapes, combined with a lack of the usual morning sounds, alerted her to another snowfall overnight.

The ensuing rush to get to the library, left no time for speculation on the events of the previous evening until Anna found herself alone in the staff room, taking a late lunch with the first chance in the day to catch her breath.

The whole thing seemed ridiculous. It was most unlikely that people like Anna had unknown relatives appear out of nowhere with property offers. Nothing like this had ever happened to her, or to anyone she had known. It seemed more like a novel than something that would occur in Anna's fairly dull life.

Her first instinct to wash her hands of the whole matter and turn it over to the lawyers was altered by the unexpected arrival of the photograph. A sense of reality had crept in to the fantasy with the view of the McCaig Farm House. Admittedly, the detail was almost non-existent. There was no clue as to the size or condition of the actual farm house. Had George

McLennan's letter not stated that the place had been unoccupied for some time while the owner was in a nursing home? Heaven only knew what it would be like inside.

The housewifely side of Anna's nature began to speculate on buckets and brushes and cleaning solvents and lots of elbow grease.

"Enough of this dreaming!" Anna shouted out to the empty room. "Get a grip on yourself and make a decision right now."

With her customary discipline, Anna faced facts. The solicitors needed a response soon.

What was it to be? Sell the property and put the money towards her savings for the purchase of a country home in her retirement years, or ....?

Anna's practical mind knew there was no real alternative, but somehow the issue was not as cut and dried as she believed. Something was niggling at the back of her mind and preventing her from sending a dismissive e mail to Scotland and getting on with the rest of her predictable life.

Perhaps that was the problem. Predictable.

How long had it been since the unexpected or exciting had happened to her?

Anna could not even summon an example. Since the divorce, most of her life had been a struggle to keep on an even keel and damp down the unexpected, in fear of emotional turmoil surfacing and unbalancing her carefully-constructed, safe little existence.

Could this be an opportunity rather than a problem; a fresh start somewhere completely new with no bad memories in the past? Could the little place in the country that she longed for be in Scotland instead of in Ontario?

Immediately a host of objections rushed to mind. What would all this cost? The apartment would have to be emptied and sub-let. She would be leaving her Samba pals behind and giving up a very satisfying job. Her only family was in Canada although Simon was out west and not exactly close by. She would be venturing into the unknown with no support system for emergencies and little idea of the kind of life she would be living.

Did she want to change her life at this point? Could she change her life?

Into the swirling jumble of questions and concerns that filled her mind, sprang a scene from her childhood.

Anna was playing with school friends in her neighbourhood. Dusk was descending on a summer evening full of warmth and the dusty streets that were the territory of the young and carefree.

Mothers would be calling their broods in for supper soon and the moment of decision had arrived. Anna was first in line to climb the old apple tree and jump to the branch of the dead tree that almost touched it. Six faces watched avidly as she made her way upward. Would she chicken out of the dare and be laughed at in the school yard the next day, or would she brave the risk and be a hero?

Edging her way to the very end of the nearest branch, Anna took a deep breath and launched out over the heads of her gang and grabbed the dead tree in a fireman's grip. Before her weight could crack the old limb, she scrambled to the trunk and made her way down to solid earth with the cheers of her friends ringing in her ears.

Anna's mother never knew why her daughter's arms and legs were scratched and bleeding but Anna never felt the sting. The sheer euphoria of the successful challenge; the triumph of risking all, overcame any pain.

Anna blinked and found herself in the staff room again. Where had that vivid memory come from? She hadn't thought back to her childhood days for so long. Why had this particular incident come to mind at the point of decision in the present day?

Another image presented itself unbidden. Anna was walking alone in the dark with tears

falling fast. Another fight with Richard had driven her

from their home. The reason for the fight was not clear to Anna. It rarely was. What hurt the most was Richard's ability to shut out her concerns and her pleas for understanding. He only saw, and only justified, his own needs, no matter what she said.

Anna wandered through the park talking to herself, crying out her frustration, feeling utterly helpless to change the deteriorating situation in her marriage, chilled by thoughts of a hopeless future.

It took a gulp of coffee and a deep breath to shake that sad memory from Anna's mind. She had chosen to put all those dire days behind her long ago. What a strange trick her mind was playing on her today. Two entirely different incidents from her life juxtaposed like that. What was going on?

A moment's deliberation while she refilled her coffee from the percolator made it all clear. It did not take a psychologist to decipher this.

Once upon a time Anna was a brave soul who was not afraid of anything. Somewhere in the intervening years much of that courage had been siphoned away, but deep inside the spirit of adventure, of independence, might, possibly, still linger.

"What the hell! I'm going to take control of this!"

The young staff members who opened the door hoping for a quiet coffee break were just in time to hear this outrageous statement from the usually decorous Mrs. Mason and stopped on the threshold in alarm. Anna brushed past them with a beaming smile and rushed off to find Andrew. It was time for action at last.

"Hi Susan, Anna here. No, don't say anything yet. I need to thank you for Wednesday night. I woke this morning determined to get some more information about this Helen Dunlop so I called the solicitor in Scotland.

Yes, it was quite difficult, but fortunately I started early so Mr. McLennan was still in his office.

No, I wasn't thinking about the time change in the United Kingdom but I will remember the next time.

Well, yes, there should be a next time as Mr. McLennan was very helpful. He is going to contact the National Archives of Scotland in Edinburgh, the capital city. Apparently there's a General Registry Office there and he is going to apply for information on an adoption.

Right, I am jumping ahead a bit Susan. I'll start at the beginning.

I came to a decision on Thursday to stop thinking of this inheritance as a problem and start thinking it could be an opportunity.

Don't cheer yet! There's a long way to go before I know for sure what I will do.

It was something you said that got me thinking, Susan. I woke up today with the certainty that I can't make any decisions until I understand this relationship, if there is any, between Helen Dunlop and me. I figured the solicitor would be the only one who would know so I just tackled him with the question as soon as I got through to his office.

Oh yes, he was quite startled to hear from me but he caught on quickly, probably because I was calling long distance.

He said Helen Dunlop was alone in the world with no relatives that he knew of.

She lived on the farm for many years and in all that time she never spoke of family members other than once when Mr. McLennan visited her to get a signature on a document applying for social assistance with a heating allowance or something, and she shared the information, over a pot of tea, that she had been adopted.

Well, perhaps the adoption papers will give us a clue about the child's birth name and parents. At least it's a chance to find out more.

He said I could expect a call in a day or two if he is successful in the search.

I know, Susan, I do feel more hopeful about things now that I've taken control.

Listen, I must call Simon and bring him up to date on events.

By the way, how did Jake's check-up appointment go?

Really? He is doing well this winter. Of course it's the fabulous nursing care he gets at home. Give him a gentle hug from me.

Thanks again Susan. You have been such a help with this, as always.

Don't worry I'll keep in touch.

Take care."

Now that she had set events in motion, Anna found every-thing around her had changed in some subtle way.

She had called Andrew early on Friday morning before tackling the call to Scotland, to say she wouldn't be coming in to work. She did not supply any further details but promised to clarify her reasons as soon as possible.

Anna could not expect to hear from George McLennan again until at least the next week but already she was thinking as if the decision had been made. She realized this was illogical behaviour, yet the habit of preparing for eventu-alities was strong in her nature. Probably a lingering part of her mother's conditioning. 'Always think ahead,' she used to say, followed inevitably by the old adage, 'A stitch in time saves nine'.

Looking around her apartment with a view to moving, she could see a series of problems.

What would she do with all this old stuff? What did she really want to keep and what would happen to all the rest of it? Storage? Furnished sub-let? Charity? City garbage dump? It was clear that some organization would be required first. Even if nothing happened in the end and Anna stayed where she was, it would not be a bad idea to get started on some tidying up and it would occupy some time on the weekend.

With the nervous energy created by an undercurrent of

excitement at future prospects, Anna grabbed a handful of trash bags and decided to begin on her bedroom clothes closet.

Throwing open the bi-fold doors she surveyed the scene inside with new eyes.

When did this get into such a mess, she wondered? The closet was stuffed with sweaters and purses on the top shelf and boxes, shoes and plastic bags spilled out at Anna's feet.

In between was the real problem. Every inch of space was crammed with clothes on hangers. Fall, winter and spring clothes were jumbled together and every hanger seemed to have two or three garments on it. The left and right sides of the closet were the worst offenders with older and out of season clothes crushed against the walls. Anna realized that she actually used only a small section in the middle of the closet where her current wardrobe hung and she seldom ventured into the dark recesses.

"Right! It's high time this closet got a good clear out."

Armed with energy and ambition she hauled out the boxes, bags and purses, stacking them beside her bed for further consideration after the clothes were dealt with.

"That's better!" she breathed, "Now I can see the problem. There's way too much stuff in here and it needs to go, whether or not I am moving. It would have to be done some time for sure."

Anna had watched the shows on TV where peoples' houses get cleared out by professionals and she understood the basics. Divide the items into three categories;

Stay | Recycle | Discard. Not too different from weeding out in the Library, she thought, and as she had lots of experience at that job it shouldn't take too long.

I'll work for an hour or so and then have a break for coffee, she decided.

She started off well with three large green garbage bags on the floor. The winter suits and shirts in the centre of the closet were moved to the bed to allow access to the summer wear. A number of summery dresses, skirts and pants went into the discard pile when Anna remembered that she had not taken the time to deal with them at the end of last season.

Just when she was thinking this was going to be easy, she came across a section of hangers laden with clothing she had almost forgotten and which required frequent detours to the bedroom mirror as she tried on clothes to decide whether or not they still fit.

An 'Undecided' pile began to grow in front of the wall mirror.

It soon became clear to Anna that this was like most household tasks which seem to take much longer than you expect, but with a sigh she soldiered on into the depths of the closet's darkness and here she almost came to a dead stop.

On padded hangers were the clothes she had brought from the home she had shared with Richard. Each outfit was drenched in memories which enveloped her as soon as she brought the clothes into the light of day.

Here was the lilac silk dress and jacket she had lovingly chosen for her honeymoon outfit.

The shopping expedition with her mother when they had roamed the stores chatting about Anna's new life as a married woman sprang into mind at if it were yesterday.

Anna had hardly heard most of her mother's advice about fit, style and comfort.

Her only focus that day was on clothes to make her even more attractive to Richard on their honeymoon.

Her mother's practicalities were the furthest thing from her mind as they accumulated shopping bags from a dozen Toronto stores and laughed at the difficulty of getting through the door of the cafe where they stopped for lunch.

What was this relic still doing here? Anna had sold her wedding dress long ago and this fragile silk outfit would never fit her today. What on earth had possessed her to hang on to this and what other spectres were lingering in the dark?

With some trepidation, she pulled out the next hanger. A

garment bag shrouded the clothing but as soon as she unzipped it, another evocative scene emerged intact:

their first visit to the riverside restaurant that would become their favourite place for celebrations. Anna had worn this beautiful long dress that was so clinging at the top that she had worried the zip might break. The full skirt swirled around her legs as they were escorted to a table on the veranda lit by candles in the dusky night.

It was Richard's idea to reserve this table although they could not really afford the extravagance as they had just signed a contract to purchase their very first home together.

It was a magical evening, laced with such promise and excitement that Anna's heart beat faster at the very thought of the love and longing that suffused the memory.

It must be the scent that made it so vivid. Anna saw the evening bag suspended by its gold chain from the hanger. She knew, before she unclipped the clasp, that a small bottle of Richard's favourite gardenia perfume must be scenting the entire outfit.

These were good memories. Happy times from the past that she had wanted to cling to as proof that she had not wasted the years of her devotion to Richard.

Sudden emotional fatigue overwhelmed Anna and she sank onto a tiny corner of the bed that was not yet mounded in clothes.

The shrill ringing of the telephone brought her back to the present with a thump.

"Anna, are you all right? What happened? We were supposed to meet this noon to catch up with things. We haven't had much time together lately."

"Alina! You would not believe how happy I am to hear your voice. I completely forgot our date! I am so sorry to worry you. Can you come to my place right now? I am in the middle of something and I really need your help."

"Of course! I'll come at once Anna. You sound upset. Has something happened?"

"I'll fill you in when you get here. Don't be long, OK?"

"I'm on my way. The A Plus can fix it whatever it is Anna!"

Her pal's use of the old label 'A Plus' brought a smile to Anna's face. It was the name the kids in high school used to call them because they were seldom apart and both had the same first initial. Alina was the bright spark of their class who often achieved the much-envied A+ on her schoolwork. Anna often studied at Alina's house where her ambitious parents had set aside a room equipped with the latest encyclopedia and a typewriter that Anna's family could never have afforded. The shared time and resulting benefit to Anna's homework brought the two girls even closer together in a friendship that would outlast many changes in their lives. There were no secrets between them.

To strangers in their schooldays they may have looked like an odd pair: Anna with long brown hair, light olive skin and dark blue eyes and Alina, tiny and neat with a short fair bob that complimented her clear complexion and bright, green eyes. In those days, Anna was the outgoing one, taller and more athletic, who had the daring ideas and fast-talking style while her friend was more reticent, preferring to think carefully before speaking or acting.

Yet, of the two of them, Alina was more popular with the guys and more susceptible to their adolescent charms. Several times over the years Anna had to warn off the Charlie-Charming types who were up to no good before they could damage her pal's tender feelings.

"I can't believe I haven't had time for a heart-to-heart with my best friend! Don't the kids today say 'BFF'? That's what we are. Forever. How could I be contemplating a move to another country leaving Alina behind? It's just not possible."

Shaking her head in disbelief, Anna surveyed the disaster

zone she had created in her bedroom. With no space left to sit down, she moved dejectedly to the sofa to await her friend's arrival. If she could not face more turmoil from the simple job of clearing out a closet how could she cope with all the rest of the decisions required to make a huge change in her life?

Chapter Six

❧❀❧

Alina provided chocolate croissants, a kiss and several hugs, together with a sympathetic ear, as Anna filled her in on current developments.

It was obvious in her friend's depressed voice and distracted manner that things were getting to be too much for her, but what disturbed Alina the most was Anna's appearance. Dark circles under her eyes, bedraggled hair and not a scrap of makeup at noon were not Anna's style at all while the old robe clutched around her was doing nothing for her reputation as a classy dresser.

Alina could not suppress a sharp intake of breath when she beheld the scene of chaos in Anna's bedroom.

"What happened here, an earthquake?" she gasped. "Where did all this stuff come from Anna? There are clothes here I haven't seen in thirty years. Have you been hoarding, or is this apartment a subsidiary of the local Goodwill?"

"Oh, Alina, you are just the breath of fresh air I need right now. I am trying to clear out my old life but it's not as easy as I thought it would be. I am at a complete standstill!"

"Right, my dear. You go off and have a nice hot shower and I'll heat up some soup for us and start organizing this mess. Don't worry! I won't throw out anything till you say so."

With this assurance, Anna disappeared and Alina was left to contemplate the mess of clothing that had been a tidy bedroom the last time she had seen it.

"I know these apartments don't have a lot of storage space," she murmured under her breath, "but this is ridiculous! What has Anna been hiding from me?"

She started with the bags and boxes littering the floor at the side of Anna's bed.

Arranging the purses upright in colour and seasonal groups took only a few minutes and then she moved on to the boxes, most of which were labelled in Anna's clear print and were mainly photographs and souvenirs from holidays and the other lives we all accumulate with the passing years.

The clothing was the real problem. There was so much of it that Alina could not immediately see a way to organize it. Discarding the idea of sorting the piles into dark and light clothing, she decided to use a radical approach and take the risk of dividing the garments into possible and impossible. The latter group would be outfits that were so far out of style that neither Anna, nor anyone else, should be wearing them. She realized this was stepping on Anna's toes somewhat, but relied on their long friendship to soften the blow.

The sound of the shower had ceased, so Alina hurried to complete the task.

The 'impossible' pile was almost toppling over but Alina knew the padded shoulder jackets and granny-length skirts were never going to be worn again and she trusted this would be obvious to her friend when she saw the evidence in front of her.

Anna emerged from the bathroom towelling her hair and looking quite refreshed.

She greeted Alina's efforts with a sigh of relief and began to move toward the closet announcing, "I'll just get dressed and then we can decide where some of this stuff should go."

Tentatively Alina suggested, "Just put on the underwear basics for now, Anna. I think we should have a dress-up session unless you agree with me that this whole pile should go to a charity shop right now." Alina gestured to the heaped 'impossible' collection.

"What! This is more than half my wardrobe, Alina. There are some good things here. Look, I wore this suit to a business dinner a few years ago and this dress is my favourite peri-winkle blue colour that you always said suited me so well, and what about the white culottes and the matching linen jackets? I can't throw these away!"

Recognizing an impasse, Alina backed down and offered an alternative strategy.

"Fine. Let's deal with the easy part now. We can take the recycling away this afternoon and dispose of the rejects but I really think we need some professional help for the big pile. What do you say about giving Maria a call? She would soon sort this out for us. You know how savvy she is about clothes with her own store to manage in the mall."

Anna could only agree. At least she would be delaying the process and saving some energy. The entire clear-out project that had seemed so possible a short time ago, had now unexpectedly depleted her physical strength. A chatty lunch with her friend and the prospect of seeing the ever-cheerful Maria later was a much more appealing prospect.

While Anna set out bowls of soup and defrosted cheese bread, Alina took the chance to call Maria.

"It's Alina. I'm so glad I caught you between customers. I won't take up your time, but I have a bit of a crisis here at Anna's place."

"For goodness sake, what's happening now? I got a call from Susan telling me things were more positive with Anna and she was on the verge of making a decision!"

"Yes, I think she may well be heading that way but this

wardrobes crisis is something only you could settle, Maria, if you could possibly come over here later this afternoon.

I know this is a busy day at the mall..........."

"I could manage a couple of hours, Alina, if you really think I can help. I am stocktaking this evening so one of the girls is looking after sales for me."

"That's excellent news! Just come when you can. I'll be staying with Anna all day and we both look forward to your expert help. Bye for now, Maria, and thank you so much."

"No problem. Always happy to help! Samba solidarity!"

Maria pocketed her cell phone wondering what kind of wardrobe crisis Anna could be involved in. Her friend was not exactly a fashion-forward type of person, preferring a more conservative style. Maria had occasionally thought Anna could benefit from some younger, more modern clothes but she hesitated to suggest this. It was a standing joke with Samba that Maria wanted to boost her sales results by pitching out all her friends' clothing every season for the current 'new look'.

"Well, I'll discover the problem soon enough," she mused. "Meanwhile, I'd better attend to business."

Spotting a regular customer admiring the spring cruise wear display in the store windows, Maria moved smoothly into selling mode and prepared to assist her client in parting with some money in exchange for a superb new wardrobe to dazzle her fellow passengers on board ship.

By the time Maria arrived at Anna's door, the A Plus pair had spent a pleasant afternoon together and Anna was in a better humour. Alina had carefully prepared the ground and her friend was ready to accept Maria's advice on what suited her.

With no delay, the trio moved into the bedroom where Maria could see immediately what was required of her.

"You know what needs to be done with this pile, don't you?' she began. "Open the window and toss the lot out. Some homeless person will come by and make a mattress out of it!"

Anna's shocked response was obvious and Maria could see at once the warning look in Alina's eye. There was no use challenging this pair, she knew. They stuck together like glue whenever one of them was threatened.

"All right, all right! I'm only joking!" Maria made to back away with her hands held up in defeat. "I can, however, prove my point without any trouble, ladies. Anna, give me twenty minutes of your time. I want you to choose four favourite outfits from this pile and model them for us with the appropriate accessories."

While Anna retired to the washroom with an armful of clothing and a shopping bag of shoes, scarves and purses selected in consultation with Alina, Maria simply withdrew a digital camera from the pocket of her smart, new jacket, and waited for the first outfit to be presented.

"This is a very expensive suit, Maria. I bought it in the states and it still fits me very well, I think, although the skirt could possibly be shortened a little."

Anna was prepared to defend her choices, but Maria merely glanced at the dark green, wool jacket and pleated skirt without comment and snapped four pictures of Anna from different angles.

Three more outfits were treated in the same way. Anna felt as if she was vindicated since Maria had nothing derogatory to say. In fact, Maria was on her way back to the mall in no time at all. Her only comment was that Anna should retrieve the photographs from her e mail on her next day at the Library.

Alina began to suspect what Maria was up to but she refrained from spoiling Anna's good mood as she bid her friend farewell, donned her coat and boots and joined Maria in the elevator.

"We'll talk soon, Anna. Let me know what you think about the photographs," she called out as the elevator doors closed.

Anna returned to her bedroom and started to clear floor space by re-hanging some of the clothing in her closet. At least, she thought, there's a little more room to show for my efforts today. Not a bad day's work. Tomorrow I'll tackle the boxes after I get home from the Library.

The usual frantic Saturday at the Library absorbed all of Anna's attention and it wasn't until the end of the day that she remembered to check her e mail and set the printer to copy Maria's digital photographs. Before the download was completed, Anna was called to the office phone to answer a complicated reference question about Egyptian dynasties and she had no chance to examine the photographs until she reached home.

Fortified with a piping-hot pepperoni pizza from the oven and a glass of red wine, she settled down on the sofa and opened the folder intending to glance over the copies and then slide a video into the VCR from her collection of chick-flick romances and enjoy a relaxing evening.

The first set of images was enough to jolt Anna out of her contented mood. What she saw now was not what her mirror had revealed. The woman in the green wool suit looked old and bedraggled. Neither the colour nor the style did her any favours. The double-breasted jacket was boxy and simply too small, while the pleated skirt added inches to her hips and reduced her legs to thin white pins emerging from worn flat shoes. The ghastly yellow blouse with the bow at the neck just emphasized Anna's flabby chin and the untidy twist of greying hair caught up with a brown clasp was unflattering to say the least.

Anna's hands flew to her hair and with a deft, automatic movement she re-coiled her hair and tightened the clasp.

Who was this shabby old person? How had this happened to the smart young woman she used to see in the mirror?

Shuffling through the other prints Anna could not find one view that fit her own image of herself as an older version of her once trim and stylish figure. Each of the four outfits she had selected as the best of the bunch was worse than the one before.

No wonder Alina and Maria had suggested disposing of this rubbish. Anna felt a blush of shame colour her face as she thought of the way she had defended her ancient clothing.

The evidence before her was incontrovertible. The clothes would have to go for a start but Anna was beginning to suspect that a complete overhaul would be required.

If there was to be any chance of a new life, the time was ripe for a bolder, revitalized Anna to emerge from the fog of the past.

This thought impelled her into the kitchen to grab another handful of garbage bags.

The despised clothing that littered the bedroom was swiftly thrust into bags and followed in quick succession by anything Anna could spy that was not a recent purchase.

The clothes from her life with Richard were discarded without a second glance and this act seemed to energize her even more. Purses and sweaters flew into another bag for recycling and old shoes and sandals were tossed into the garbage can.

In a remarkably short time the bedroom floor was cleared and the closet had only a fraction of the number of clothes that had once lingered there. Anna could not bear to keep the discards around for another minute so she called Joseph and asked him to store her stuff in one of his basement lock-ups until she could deal with them after the weekend.

When she returned to her apartment from the elevator trip, it was as if she saw things through different eyes. None of her 'stuff' had the same hold over her feelings as before.

Nothing here was so important that it couldn't be replaced

or renewed. It was as if a breath of winter's icy cold fresh air had blown through the building and blasted the cobwebs from Anna's mind.

"What an old fuddy-duddy I have been! I can't believe I have let myself get into this condition. I'm still alive and healthy and not ready for the scrap heap yet by any means."

With this assertion ringing in her ears Anna picked up the phone.

"Alina, it's me. No, I'm fine, don't worry. I just had to call and tell you what I have done this evening. I tossed out all that old stuff from my closet and I feel so much lighter it's like I have lost a kilo for every garbage bag I filled!

Well, I'm sure you have already guessed what prompted this change of heart. I saw the pictures Maria took of my so-called fashion show. I am so embarrassed, Alina, I truly had no idea I looked so ghastly in those outfits.

No, you will not be seeing the pictures soon, or ever. When I have apologised for wasting Maria's time last night I will be ceremonially burning the evidence and trying to wipe the images from my mind. By the way, can you get me an appointment with your hairstylist next week? I am thinking of getting my hair coloured.

No, really, I feel better than I have in years. This was just the incentive I needed and you, my dear friend, were just the person to make the magic happen.

Dinner's on me soon in a nice restaurant but not until I have a new hairstyle and perhaps some new clothes!

That's right! I really have turned over a new leaf. Who knew!

Talk to you soon.

Bye, Alina."

Chapter Seven

Sunday flew by in a whirlwind of activity as Anna continued to clear up and clean out her apartment. Mismatched, cracked or chipped china and kitchenware was boxed up and with the oldest of the furniture, moved to the hallway for Joseph's attention. He had a friend in a seniors' building nearby who was always grateful to have supplies to pass on to his single, male residents who sometimes arrived with little or no household goods of their own.

Anna was past the point of worrying where her rejects wound up. She was just glad that she had made the decision to divest herself of her past encumbrances. As an unexpected bonus, she found the extra space to be conducive to clearer thinking.

After she had calculated that a call from Scotland would not be likely before 1:30pm on Monday, due to the five hour time difference, she determined to make use of the morning hours to continue on her quest for change. Andrew was willing to reschedule her hours at the library for the week, although Anna could hear in his voice rising curiosity about this uncharacteristic flightiness in her most predictable part-time worker.

I really must put Andrew in the picture soon, she thought, as she put down the phone, but what would I tell him? I don't have a clue what I will do in the end only that I am embarking on some kind of a journey of self-discovery on so many levels and that sounds way too 'new age' for me. No one would believe me. At least, not yet!

With this conclusion, Anna made a series of calls, setting up appointments for the morning hours, leaving her afternoons free to wait for a call and then to work the late shift at the library. Fortunately the weather had settled into a normal February pattern with light snowfall every day or two and slightly warmer temperatures causing the snow piles to diminish in between, making travel around town more convenient.

Monday. Travel agent. A very helpful young girl gave Anna prices and times for the most economical flights from Toronto to Scotland. She also supplied a map showing Glasgow airport, where she would presumably arrive, and the routes north to Oban which was on the west coast of Scotland and did not seem far from the airport, although Anna surmised that could be because the entire British Isles seemed so tiny in comparison to the vast distances in Canada.

Anna emerged from the bustling travel store where the focus was on sunny southern destinations as a relief from the unrelenting winter cold of the north. She realised she had no clear idea at all of basic climate conditions in Scotland, or much knowledge about the country in general.

Refusing to allow herself to get excited at the prospect of venturing into the unknown, Anna determined she would not treat the travel information as a commitment to anything. She was strictly on a fact-finding mission at this point, a type of research such as she would have done for any patron in the library.

. . .

Tuesday. Hair Design and Spa. Keeping firmly in mind that hair will grow again no matter what is done to it, Anna subjected herself to the ministrations of a series of salon associates who discussed her face shape and hair condition in terms Anna could barely decipher. Now that she had placed herself in their hands, literally, she tried to relax and trust the results would be some kind of improvement and eradicate the dreadful images she had seen in Maria's photographs.

The treatment began with serious pampering. Foot massage and pedicure were followed by a manicure and a gentle lecture on nail care from a charming Asian girl.

While her newly-washed and conditioned hair, augmented by a semi-permanent colour wash, was wrapped in a warm towel, Anna experienced for the first time in years the delights of a facial. As she reclined in comfort in a quiet room, a technician examined her cleansed skin under a lighted microscope and found a number of imperfections that she swiftly removed. She then proceeded to cover the area with a thick layer of cooling, healing ointment. This was followed by a period during which Anna was admonished to "Close your eyes and let the mask do its work." As this was accompanied by classical music playing somewhere nearby, Anna was delighted to comply and soon drifted off to sleep.

She sensed the lights being turned up and the music turned down as the aesthetician gently peeled off the mask and finished the session with a make-up lesson consisting of a light foundation over a rich moisturizer and some expert re-touching of eyebrows and lashes that left Anna completely bemused when she saw the final results in the mirror.

By this point she was so thoroughly relaxed that she was not about to complain when the hair cutting began and the long strands fell to the floor. A razor was deftly applied, a large brush was swept through the newly-bronzed tangle and a number of 'products' were applied with the aid of a rapid hair dryer.

The vision that met Anna's dazzled gaze at the finale of

this performance was in no way recognizable, but at the same time infinitely superior to the sad, old lady who had entered the salon. Floating home on a wave of euphoria Anna wondered what on earth Andrew and the team at the library would say when she appeared in the afternoon. She also determined that if there was no phone call from Scotland she would arrange to see both Maria and Alina that evening before the glory diminished, as who knew what she would find the next morning after laying her head on a pillow for the night.

Maria was busy with a customer when Anna presented herself at the store. She broke into a stream of Italian as soon as she recognized Anna then looked hastily around to see if anyone had understood her expletives.

"I can't believe it! You are transformed Anna. Turn around and let me see the full effect. The shorter hair is miraculous! The colour lifts your whole face. I swear you look twenty years younger, *cara mia*. Come over here into the change room. This new you demands an appropriate style of clothing. I'll be right back with a selection for *madame*."

With a swish of curtains, Maria vanished and Anna laughed out loud relishing the energy her friend always left in her wake. It was going to be interesting to see what Maria would choose for her now that she was open to a brand new look.

The first outfit consisted of a brown jacket and pants with a pale gold sweater. Anna had expected something more adventurous but she soon discovered that the clothes she was mentally labelling as 'dull' were anything but. The jacket was seamed in such a way as to define her waist and the collar's proportions framed her face and balanced her shoulders making the slimming pants lengthen her entire body.

"I am amazed that such a simple outfit can make me look so good" she enthused, as she turned and looked in the mirrors admiring her figure from all angles, "and this dropped waistband is much more comfortable and a style I would never have chosen for myself."

"Ah, it's the tailoring, Anna." Maria advised. "The colour suits your new hair style and just a touch of pale gold at the neckline throws brightness on to your face. This is a good business outfit but let's try something more daring for your future travels."

Before Anna could protest that future travels were not at all certain, Maria had disappeared through the curtains again for all the world like a genie of the fashion trade, and as Anna surveyed the results of her magic she could only admire her friend's skills.

The next outfit was quite unexpected.

"Oh, I never wear red, Maria, it's far too bright for me!"

"Just try it on. I want to see how this shade works for you. The material is uncrushable and has lycra for stretch and it comes with a skirt making it a very useful three piece ensemble with multiple mix-and-match possibilities. The jacket can be worn with a darker skirt or pants if you don't like too much colour at once. I'll be back with a couple of blouses."

Having heard this impassioned recommendation, Anna could hardly refuse to try the red jacket at least. To her surprise, the comfort outweighed the distasteful colour almost at once. Perhaps it was the stretch feature but it seemed to be the perfect size for Anna's body and felt immediately like something she had always worn.

Maria, returning with an armful of tops, sighed with satisfaction. "Just what I thought.

This is your colour, Anna, and the high-fastening neck works for you. Come out to the daylight and see the difference that makes."

Still wearing her brown skirt from the previous outfit, Anna could see the impact of the new jacket. In daylight from the mall's skylights the red tone was muted to a softer shade. Coral? Flame? Anna did not know how to describe the colour yet she could clearly see how flattering it was. Despite the fact that it had no lining, a feature her mother had always said marked a quality garment, the jacket's lapels and cuffs were faced with a silvery-grey fabric indicating alternate ways to wear it in different seasons or temperatures.

"I have no idea the cost of these items, Maria, but I think I'll take them, along with whatever accessories you choose. I have one request though. Please take a photograph of me wearing the outfits before I decide. I have learned, recently, how deceptive a mirror can be!"

Anna wore the brown suit to work that afternoon and basked in the positive comments from her colleagues and regular customers. Even Tony, web site guru and youngest member of the admin team, was effusive in his praise of the new-look-Anna saying,

"Bad! I mean cool. Very cool!" with an appreciative nod.

Andrew seemed satisfied that a make-over was the reason for Anna's schedule changes so he asked no more questions. She was happy to leave him with this conclusion for the present time.

Anna found a renewed energy and optimism as she went about the Library's tasks.

A shelf unit in the office filled with books that had routing slips in them, received the filing categories that had been awaiting attention for some weeks. She caught sight of her reflection in glass windows as she moved around the Library and was momentarily halted as she realised how improved her appearance now was.

A late date for a meal in a downtown restaurant with Maria and Alina was accomplished very easily. Alina, a skilled handcraft worker, sold some of her creations in Maria's store and had a scheduled visit to deliver a batch of crochet scarves in rainbow colours for one of Maria's displays.

Anna's quick call to Alina arranged the restaurant meeting place and Maria was sitting comfortably with Anna in front of the fireplace sipping a nice red chianti when Alina arrived bearing a large, patchwork cloth bag, another of her craft ideas.

At first, Alina did not recognise the elegant stranger beside Maria but when Anna spoke a greeting she did a double-take and broke into a whoop of delight.

"Anna! This is wonderful! What a transformation. If I hadn't seen you a couple of days ago I'd swear you had lost major weight. What have you two been up to?"

"Come and sit down, Alina. You have scared the waiters with your yelling! We will tell you all about it but you must take some responsibility, you know. By contacting your hair salon and making the appointment you set all this in motion."

"Thank you, Anna. It was no trouble at all. But wait! I have the perfect thing to set off your beautiful new suit." Bending down for a moment, Alina withdrew a long, narrow, silky scarf from the bag at her feet and looped it expertly around Anna's neck.

The gold, bronze and silver strands complemented Anna's outfit and the intertwined hint of turquoise in the scarf added the perfect jolt of colour.

"*Bella! Bellisima!*" exclaimed Maria, clapping her hands in delight and offering Alina a glass of wine so they could share a toast.

"To our dear friend Anna who deserves all the good fortune in the world and who now looks ready to claim it."

On Wednesday morning Anna awoke and stretched lazily. I feel like the cat that got the cream, she told herself. Despite the busy and exciting day she had on Tuesday, she felt invigorated and ready for the challenge of an early appointment with Bev to discuss financial and banking matters. Even the thought of the amount of cash she had spent the day before could not dampen Anna's enthusiasm. She rarely spent money on herself and judging from the positive reactions of yesterday, she should be doing so more often.

Anna stretched again, burying her head in the soft pillows and then she remembered the new hairdo. Jumping up she fled to the mirror to see what a night's sleep had done to her coiffure.

The new shorter style seemed intact although somewhat flattened at the back. Anna was afraid to disturb it with a brush or comb so she shook her head vigorously and miraculously it fell into place at once. The bronze strands framed her face and covered her high forehead with a delicate fringe while the effect of cutting off the straggly length seemed to have added much-needed volume to Anna's hair. It was skilfully cut so as to curve slightly inward at the back of her head and every hair shone like silk.

"This must be what a good hair cut does," she lectured the mirror. "Why did I wait so long?" The thought of the maintenance this short style would require whenever she washed her hair did not deter Anna as it might have done in the past.

"One must suffer to be beautiful, even if it is an expensive inconvenience!" was her final comment to the mirror.

Some of the glamour of the previous night had disappeared when Anna washed her face so she added a trip to the drugstore to buy cosmetics, to the day's tasks.

"I'll ask one of these gorgeous girls who shows you how to apply products to advise me, then I can arrive at Bev's in splendour."

With this decision made, Anna selected a pair of black pants and a sweater and laid them on her bed with the new carmine jacket. Her black winter boots would look suitable but her old winter coat might need to be replaced soon.

"I can't spoil the effect with that worn old coat I bought ten years ago," she admonished herself, chuckling as she acknowledged the change in perception that had occurred so recently. To counteract the winter coat she chose a pair of splendid silver earrings Susan had given her last Christmas.

The desk under the living room window revealed stored bank statements and budget records which Anna transferred to a briefcase. With one last admiring check on her appearance she was out the door with a spring in her step that had nothing to do with the season.

A gusting wind heavily laden with snowflakes met her in the parking lot and the first thought in her head was that a stylish hat might be required when the new winter coat was purchased. Pulling up the coat collar to protect her hairdo, Anna rapidly started the engine to defrost the windshield and quickly cleared the snow from her car.

The strip mall with a Shopper's Drug Mart was only a couple of blocks away and there was some covered parking there. The young woman behind the cosmetics counter was more than pleased to advise Anna and was discreet enough to avoid layering products on Anna's face, electing instead for a few items for 'senior' skin that provided a more subtle effect. As a result, Anna happily purchased the creams, blush and mascara that had been demonstrated and promised to return for further instruction if required.

Heading back to the car she wondered when she had abandoned all but the most basic skin care. Was it when make-up became a high-tech science with multiple choices to be made or when her skin began to age and she despaired of ever looking young and fresh again? Or was it after Richard, when looking in a mirror only reminded her of how rejected and worthless she felt?

Bev's neat little semi-detached home was in a sub-division on the north side of town.

As Anna pulled into the driveway behind Bev's battered blue Volkswagen, she noticed the front porch was swept of snow and the piles of snow at the road had recently been cleared so that exiting cars could more easily see oncoming traffic.

"Bev's boys are using their muscles, I see," she observed.

Being a single mother to two teens had not been easy for Bev after her husband died on a Canadian peace mission in Bosnia. Anna had met Bev in Susan's law office when she was setting up education policies for her boys with funds supplied by the armed forces' insurance.

The two had struck up a friendship then, recognizing in each other an unspoken, deep sorrow. Anna's divorce was in process but the raw feelings were still painful. Sympathizing with this devastated young mother helped her to put her own tragedy in proportion and was the beginning of a friendship that had spanned the decade since then.

Anna had watched James and Eric grow into responsible young men in a society where it was all too easy for kids to go off the rails in pursuit of the fast high and the latest gadgets.

Bev's decision to work from home had to be a large part of her family's success. She was always there when the boys came home from primary school to ask about their day and supervise homework. She welcomed their friends but was a listening ear whenever doors were locked or arguments got out of hand.

In time, James realized that their standard of living depended on the late hours his mother spent at the computer and he tried to relieve her stress by helping out at home with daily tasks and watching over his younger brother's progress in high school, vetting his friends in a way Bev could not have managed. It seemed trite to say that James took over his father's role, but Anna, who had never met Bev's husband, knew the kind of responsible, caring man he must have been, through watching his sons grow up.

Bev opened the front door before Anna could ring the bell

and ushered her into the hallway out of the cold. "I think it's turning bitter outside," she said, shivering. "Come in, come in, I have coffee on."

It wasn't until Bev was helping Anna take off her coat, that she recognised the improvements in her friend's appearance. Over steaming mugs of coffee in Bev's cozy, bright kitchen, Anna related the events since the Samba group's evening at her apartment a week before, and Bev was astounded at how fast things were changing in Anna's life.

"You know, the one thing I miss about working from home is the chance to sit down for a good old gossip like this. You have really brightened my day already Anna.

I'm not sure how I can help you at this point but fire away and I'll do whatever I can."

"Well, this is strictly a fact-finding mission, Bev. I just want to know what problems there would be for me if, and it is still very much an 'if,' I should decide to take off for Scotland for a few months to see what the situation is there. I don't know much about banking transfers or what the costs might be. You know my finances better than anyone and I have valued your advice about investments since we met."

"Right, I see you have brought current bank statements Anna. Let's start there and consider the possibilities."

The next hour was filled with discussion about accessing Canadian bank accounts from abroad and about how much liquidity Anna's funds presently had. A number of questions about currency values and international communications emerged which Bev agreed to investigate.

"My feeling is that you might be best to use the legacy from your parents for this venture," she concluded. "That would avoid major adjustments to your finances and you could take international money orders with you rather than cash, to accommodate expenses for at least a month or two."

Anna felt doubtful about this at first. She had always considered the small endowment from the sale of the family home to be a down payment on the country place she was hoping to buy one day.

"Look at it this way, Anna. You might have a country house waiting for you in Scotland instead of in Ontario. It's a sensible way to spend the money and if the idea doesn't work out you could sell the property and probably realize extra funds from the higher real estate prices in the UK. Either way you can afford to take this risk without endangering your current situation. In fact, I am pleased to see you have spent a little money on yourself recently. You have been a bit too frugal of late."

"Bev!" Anna exclaimed in surprise, "I certainly did not expect to hear that advice from you considering the state of the world's economic climate."

"Ah! I have an ulterior motive, my friend. If this plan works out, I will be bringing the boys to visit you. I've always wanted to see Scotland!"

On the drive home, Anna thought about Bev's comments and began to speculate about how she could accomplish the need to investigate what she thought of as the 'Helen Mystery', while arranging a long-overdue holiday for herself and possibly providing a way to thank her friends for the invaluable help they had so freely given in the years since Samba had become her support group.

"I wonder if the farm house is big enough to accommodate a whole series of visitors?" she asked herself, while mentally calculating what furnishing several bedrooms might cost.

In this positive frame of mind she arrived back at her apartment intending to fix some lunch and watch daytime trivia television for an hour or so before setting out for her shift in the Library.

When the phone rang, she assumed it was Bev with the

answer to one of the questions they had discussed, and was surprised to hear a male voice instead.

"Ms. Mason, or may I address you as Anna, as I feel we are acquaintances by now?"

The polite manner and Scottish accent, reminiscent of her father's voice, alerted Anna to the identity of the speaker.

"Certainly, George! I am delighted to hear from you so soon and your timing is perfect. What have you discovered about Helen Dunlop?"

"I did the research in Edinburgh, as I had suggested to you previously, and, with help from the professionals, I was able to unearth what I believe to be some useful information."

In an attempt to hide her impatience at the scholarly manner George always chose to employ whether writing or speaking, Anna encouraged him in as gentle terms as she could manage.

"Excellent George! What exactly did you find out?"

"Well, as we suspected, there is a family connection but it is a sad one that goes back to your grandparents' generation."

"Really? I am afraid I know little or nothing about my grandparents. My parents never spoke about them at all and I regret never questioning my mother or father about family.

They were always reluctant to discuss family matters and I guess I just gave up in time."

"Yes Anna, not uncommon in that generation, I believe. I will, of course, fax you the appropriate document copies for your perusal at leisure but I can provide an outline of the facts now, if you wish."

"Yes, George, I do wish. Please go on."

"Your maternal grandmother, Aileen Wilson, married a Patrick Knox in 1916. He was a volunteer in the Black Watch Regiment and was sent to the front lines in World War I."

"Oh dear! Don't tell me he was one of the many thousands of young men who died in the trenches in Europe?"

"No. In fact, he was injured and returned to Scotland to recuperate."

"So he survived?"

"I am afraid not. Patrick Knox succumbed to the influenza pandemic that swept the world in 1918 but his wife bore a daughter just three months after her husband's death."

"Ah! This confirms something my friend Susan uncovered. She must have accessed some of the same sources you used, but I hadn't heard about a child. What was the daughter's name? Was it Helen?"

"The child in question was christened Aileen Anne after her mother, but it is at this point the trail becomes cold. In 1925, Aileen Knox married a Samuel Jarvis....."

"But that's my mother's maiden name," Anna interrupted.

"Yes, their child Marion, your mother, was born two years after that marriage but the certificate of marriage states that Aileen was a widow and no child was listed in the details."

"Wait a minute, George! What happened to Aileen Anne? Would a child be included in a certificate of marriage in normal circumstances? Did my grandfather adopt her later?

And who on earth is Helen?"

"I do realise how frustrating this all is, Ms. Mason."

Anna recognised the change of tone as evidenced by the lawyer's use of her formal name so she tried to calm her impatience once again.

"George, I apologize. This is so fascinating to me and I am rushing things, I know.

You told me previously that Helen had been adopted. Are you aware that here in Ontario adoption records have just been opened to inquirers for the very first time? I do think you have done extremely well in such a short period and isn't it fortunate that Scottish records are open to the public?"

"Indeed, it is fortunate. Now, before I continue, I must caution you that this phone call is likely to be expensive. I can, of course, curtail my remarks and send documents instead if you wish."

"'In for a penny; in for a pound' was a saying of my mother's George. I can't bear to stop now. Please go on."

"I did pursue the question of Aileen Anne's fate but I could not find any record of her subsequent adoption by Samuel Jarvis. She *may have died in the intervening period before the marriage, but I could not find a death certificate in her birth name or under the name of Jarvis. At this juncture, I began to follow alternative strategies."*

"What does that mean, George?"

"When your grandmother re-married, Aileen Anne would have been six years of age.

I then attempted to trace adoption records during the six to eight years of her early life."

"George! I am amazed! How did you manage to do all this so quickly?"

"Ah, I am afraid I was not able to complete my research. There are, as you can imagine thousands of records to examine, and what makes the task more difficult is that many children from Scotland were sent to Canada and Australia during this period from Barnardo's and Quarrier's Homes for poor or abandoned families."

"Are you suggesting that my grandmother abandoned her own daughter?"

"Not at all, Anna, but you must remember the times. In the early part of the last century there was much poverty in Britain following the war years.

Perhaps your grandmother did not have the benefit of family support and found it impossible to earn enough money to maintain a home for herself and a young child and was forced to give her to a charity or to an agency that could provide food and shelter."

"My God! Do you think that is what happened to Aileen Anne?"

"I cannot tell. I was obliged to turn over the search to a genealogy expert who is pursuing enquiries for me. I must remind you that this, also, is a costly business."

"To hell with the expense, George! Forgive me, I am forgetting my manners.

Please give me some time to digest this news. Fax the papers to my London Library number and I will look them over. In the meantime go ahead with any developments, no matter the expense, and I will talk to you again in a few days. I can't thank you enough George. You have done sterling work for me."

"Thank you, Anna. It's my pleasure. I must admit to increasing curiosity about this situation. I may be just as anxious as are you, about the results of the search. Goodbye, for now."

"Goodbye, George."

Anna put down the phone and exhaled. She felt as if she had been holding her breath for minutes, afraid to miss one word of the saga. Her mind was far away in an unknown land and time, wondering about the fate of a child who would be an aunt of hers; older sister to her mother Marion.

"Why did I never hear about this aunt?" she challenged the air. "Even if she did die as a child, someone, somewhere, sometime, should have cared enough to remember her in some permanent way."

Sinking back into the chair cushions, Anna stared out of the window and found a little comfort in watching the endless snow drift past. She could not imagine any circumstances that would make her give up a child of her own........... if only she had ever been so fortunate as to have a child of her own.

George proved to be as good as his word, and Anna found a large document file awaiting her when she arrived at the Library. There was no time to read the items and even a glance revealed that the hand-written cursive script would not be easy to decipher.

Anna put the entire issue out of her mind for now, although she had to admit that the fate of poor Aileen Anne lingered as a shadow in the background.

As the hours wore on toward the 9:00pm closing, the library patrons were thinning out. Snow had fallen steadily all day and the downtown regulars had decided to stay home rather than face the onslaught of wind-created snow drifts.

Andrew sent most of the evening staff home early, but Anna decided to stay and close up for him and take the opportunity to do some private research on the library's super-fast internet.

It was hard to know where to start. There were so many unanswered questions.

Foremost among these was the identity of Helen Dunlop and the possible, or improbable, connection to Anna and her family.

Anna clicked onto Google and on an impulse typed in the name Helen Dunlop.

The rush of responses indicated that it was not an uncommon name. Anna was faced with dozens of pages of information. She refined the search by locating the name in Scotland and providing a time frame. For this she had to refer to George's folder where she tracked down the certificate of death. Not much help there. She still found a dozen pages of Helen Dunlops.

Looking around the Library area to confirm that she was not needed at the desk, Anna rolled up her sleeves and tackled the entries one by one. She had no idea what she was looking for at first. Details about memberships and author-ships scrolled by but not much in the way of personal infor-mation of the type Anna needed. 'Her' Helen did not appear to be notable in any way that was important to Google. She was just about to switch to tourist information about Scotland as a light relief when something unusual caught her eye.

It was the word 'adoption' in an entry on the next-to-last page.

Helen Dunlop, daughter of a distant cousin of the famous Dunlop family.
In her teen years, Helen was the subject of a huge police search in Scotland that lasted three weeks. A kidnapping was suspected but

*no ransom note ever transpired. Helen was found safe, miles from
her exclusive Dundee home after apparently hitchhiking across
Scotland.*

*There was speculation in the press that Helen was unhappy at home
and had attempted to trace her real parents. No confirmation of this
supposed adoption was ever provided, and the family refused all
interviews.*

Could this be the Helen Dunlop she was seeking? Anna's
pulse was racing as she considered the possibilities. Adoption. It was a giant leap of faith but something drew Anna to
make a connection to the forlorn little child, Aileen Anne,
who had disappeared from the records some time in her
childhood. Was it just the recent phone conversation with the
solicitor in Scotland that made these two unrelated events
seem linked?

Was it even possible that Aileen Anne and Helen were one
and the same? What were the chances that such a coincidence
could occur? At this thought with numbers in the range of
millions to one zooming into her consciousness, Anna pushed
back her chair in an attempt to separate herself from this
futile speculation.

"What am I doing?" she accused herself out loud. "This is
craziness! It's time I went home and got some sleep."

A timid voice from behind her announced, "Well, if you
could just check out these books before you go, I would be
very grateful."

Anna recovered her balance after nearly falling off the
chair in shock and rushed to help the young student with her
research homework.

The swift return to reality gave her the energy to turn off
lights and check that doors were locked before setting the
alarms and heading to the underground parking building.

During the slow drive home through snowy streets that
would not be cleared until overnight sno- removal plows
came out, the exhaustion of a very eventful day began to

catch up with Anna. She felt more and more weary as she neared the apartment building.

Dragging herself into the elevator, she decided that she really needed time to think.

So much had happened so quickly. She must not allow events to escalate out of her control.

It was time to take stock, review the past week and make some decisions but, first, sleep was a priority and giving no thought to hairstyle or makeup, Anna collapsed into bed with a grateful sigh.

Chapter Eight

Thursday morning dawned bright and clear. "A good day for decisions," yawned Anna, as she pulled open the drapes and admired the fresh white snow mounded over bushes and cars in the parking lot.

"Coffee, then I'll read those papers George sent and do a lot of thinking, hopefully without interruptions."

She brewed a whole pot of coffee and savoured the aroma that soon filled the room.

Before she could finish the first full mug, papers were scattered on the floor in front of her chair and Anna had to resort to sketching out a tentative family tree on a large piece of paper in order to make sense of all the new information George's research had provided.

A feeling of annoyance surfaced again as she contemplated a family history of which she had never previously been made aware. Stepping carefully over the document copies, she fetched the photograph of her parents' wedding from her bedside, as if to accuse them face to face of keeping secrets from her.

Such young faces met her gaze. Once more she realised the gaps in her information.

Why had this young couple left Scotland to settle in Canada? Why had they never returned to their homeland for a holiday or to contact relatives? Did they know about the first marriage of Marion's mother and the story of Aileen Anne? Could they have solved the mystery of Helen Dunlop for their daughter and if so, why did they never mention her?

Side by side with these unanswered questions came the personal challenge that could not be ignored. Why had Anna neglected to ask the questions about family that might have prompted her mother's or father's confidences?

Surely there were occasions during her schooldays when families were discussed in class.

What responses had Anna made? Did she resort to fabrications to avoid being singled out for lack of knowledge? Why did she remember nothing of this? Had she blocked it out altogether?

Anna realized suddenly that she knew more about Alina's family background than she did about her own. She had met Alina's aunts and uncles many times and shared a cottage holiday on Georgian Bay in Northern Ontario one summer with Alina and a tribe of cousins. They had happily accepted Anna into the fold and she was welcomed by the adults as one of the extended family group.

Swimming, canoes and fishing, interspersed with explorations in the deep woods and along the rocky shores, were still vivid in Anna's memory. She could almost feel the sunburned skin and itchy blackfly bites and the glorious freedom of endless hours of unsupervised play. They roamed around as a group with the older boys and girls warned to keep an eye on the smaller ones on pain of death.

One hot afternoon when the grown-ups were dozing on the deck, the cousins had bounced into a far clearing in the woods and found themselves three yards from a black bear cub. Jaws dropped in amazement and eyes popped as they stood transfixed absorbing every detail of the cub's appearance from his wet brown nose and tiny eyes to his shiny fur and huge claws. When the spell was broken by the cub's plaintive mew, it was Anna who took charge and signalled to the pack to keep silent and back out slowly. Somewhere she had read that cubs were always accompanied by an adult female and the wrath of a threatened mother bear was not to be taken lightly.

By mutual agreement, Alina's cousins promised each other to keep this incident secret, fearing the adults would never let them out of their sight again all summer.

Ever after this, the code words 'Black Bear' whispered between them signalled an unbreakable bond of silence that excluded all adults.

Anna had to smile remembering that summer. It was decades since she and Alina had invoked the Black Bear code but it was just one layer of the bond that made their friendship so strong.

Somehow Anna could not recall such happy memories of her own small family group.

Simon and she were comfortable enough and fortunate to have a bedroom each.

Perhaps because of this, and because Simon was three years older, they did not share many hobbies or friends. Simon was into hockey from a young age and spent early morning hours practising in the arena with his dad, while Anna hated the cold atmosphere and refused to accompany them to games, preferring to spend her time with Alina in her fashionable home only a short walk away. Alina's mother always seemed to be at home with cookies and milk at the ready and they had a beautiful backyard pool where Mrs. Barlow supervised their play on hot summer days.

Thinking of Mrs. Barlow relaxing with a book by the poolside while her only daughter splashed and laughed with her best friend, Anna began to wonder why her own mother was absent from the picture. So many memories of her childhood revolved around the Barlow household that Anna had trouble conjuring up a cozy chat with her mother at the kitchen table, or a cooking lesson, or girl talk about boys. Where was her mother all those hours when Anna was with the Barlows?

A blush of shame rose into Anna's cheeks as she remembered the reason why her mother was not available for after-school or summer vacation activities.

"What a selfish little monster I was," she admitted to herself, "rushing off to Alina's house instead of helping out at home."

Her mother had worked long hours of shift work as a registered nurse at the Children's Hospital, a large complex of buildings on the outskirts of town. By the time she arrived home in the evenings, she was often exhausted and not capable of much more than a cursory attempt at family interaction with her own children after a day dealing with the life and death crises of her young patients.

No wonder there was little time or opportunity for long reminiscences about Scotland and a life that must have seemed as if it belonged to another era altogether. As an adult, Anna could see that her parents' primary concern must have been to establish a new home in Canada for their family and that this concern outweighed all others.

Her father was an engineer but he was required to re-train by repeating some of his Scottish courses to meet Ontario standards. During this period he worked as an apprentice in machine shops while studying at night school for his qualifications.

There was seldom enough money for expensive gifts or treats. Simon and Anna, like most children, did not appreciate that having a roof over their heads and food on the table was achieved through the sacrifice of their hard-working parents.

Not for the first time, Anna wished she could go back and make amends for the careless way she had accepted the sacrifices of her parents without acknowledging the personal price they had paid.

Delving into past memories brought the thought of Simon to the forefront of Anna's mind.

It's about time I called Simon again, she decided. It's just possible that he can shed some light on all this.

Michelle answered the phone and after some light banter about the weather and their adult children's latest purchases followed by the inevitable wonders of the grandkids, she called her husband to the phone.

"He's been working in the garage on an old beat up motor he found. I think he hopes it will magically transform into a new lawn mower by the summer!"

While she waited for Simon to pick up the receiver, Anna thought how much like their father he was. Fiddling around with an engine was always the most relaxing thing both men could find to do whenever problems confronted them.

"Hi, sis! I've been hoping you would call. I haven't been able to get our last conversation out of my mind. It's brought up so much stuff from our childhood that I had forgotten."

"Me too, Simon. I've just been sitting here thinking about mum and dad and what a tough life they must have had when they came to Canada. I really didn't appreciate everything they did for us."

"You're right, of course, but does one generation ever appreciate the efforts of the one that came before?"

"Ah, there speaks a parent!"

"Don't laugh! It's no joke, believe me."

"Listen Simon, here's why I am calling. I have been trying to fathom this Helen Dunlop connection and I am stuck in some family history that was news to me. Did you know that our grandmother was married twice and that our mother once had a half sister named Aileen Anne?"

"What! Where did this come from?"

"I take it you are no wiser than I was? It's a long story. I'll forward documents to you by e mail in the next few days, Simon, and you can catch up with the research the solicitor in Scotland has been doing on my behalf. I have a sheaf of papers spread out on the floor in front of me at this moment."

"Wow! You have been busy, Anna Banana."

"Don't you dare call me that, Simon. I mean it! If the grandkids get wind of that name, I'll never forgive you."

"No danger of that, sis! The grandkids are skiing in B.C. with their parents this week."

"Good for them! I've often wished I had learned to ski."

"Seriously, though, sis, I did find out some stuff about the more recent past from an unexpected source right here at home."

"What do you mean? What source?"

"Well, remember when you asked me to check in the old bureau of dad's for family information? Honestly, I had never really investigated it before. It's been stuck upstairs in the spare bedroom with other old furniture and I haven't even glanced at it for years."

"What did you find Simon? Get to the point! Please!"

"OK. Calm down, I'm not sure it will help us find Helen, but when dad died there was a letter detailing his funeral arrangements and a bequest or two to various charities.

I remember reading the letter as executor and taking care of dad's wishes but, I have to confess Anna, I did not read right to the end of that letter. I stuffed it back in the bureau with other family papers and forgot about it."

"Typical male! Curiosity was never your strong point, Simon. So what vital information have I missed?"

"You know, it's more sad than instructive, sis. The letter was about dad's regrets in life; a kind of last message to me about things he wished he had done differently."

"For example? What regrets did he have? You were there when he died Simon."

"He said he was sorry that he hadn't spent more time with us when we were children and that he could have been a better father and husband despite the pressure to earn a living for us and provide money for our education, but what surprised me was the part where he claimed he had disappointed our mother by doing something in haste that he later deeply regretted."

"What on earth was he referring to? I can't recall mum saying anything like this."

"It didn't really resonate with me either until you called today with that question about our grandmother. Now, I'm beginning to think there might be a connection."

"Simon, if you don't tell me right now what you are talking about I swear I'll strangle you over this phone if necessary!!"

"Easy, Anna! I'm just putting it together in my own mind for the first time. Dad wrote that our mother got a strange phone call a day or two before they were leaving for Canada. It was from a woman who claimed she was an aunt who was trying to trace her family."

"Interesting, but what did this have to do with our dad's regrets?"

"He warned mum not to have anything to do with this woman in case she was a confidence trickster and only after money. He told mum they had no time to deal with the matter since they were far too busy with packing and other details of the move."

"So mum never found out who the woman on the phone was?"

"No. Later on, she did write and ask her own mother about this, but was told to forget the whole thing as it was likely a wrong number."

"Why did dad regret this incident so much that he wrote about it at the end of his life?"

"I can only tell you what dad wrote. It seems that our mother suffered greatly from homesickness in the first years of their life in Canada. She often talked about the strange call and wished she had been able to pursue the woman's claims. Something about the voice and the woman's emotion struck a chord in mum that remained with her through the years. She blamed dad for turning away the chance to meet a relative who could have been a real friend. Apparently it was a bone of contention between them for years."

"How sad! Of course mum had very few relatives that we know of. So, our mother had no clue who this woman might be?"

"No. It seems she gave no name or contact number. She was to call again but, of course, our parents would be gone on their way to Canada by then."

"Hmm! Simon, are you thinking what I'm thinking?"

"Perhaps I am? You go first."

"Is it possible that the woman claiming to be an aunt was, in fact, the Helen Dunlop who left money to you and a farm house in Scotland to me?"

"It sounds crazy, all right, but I suppose it's not impossible."

"Think about it, Simon, and don't stop digging through that bureau. I'll be searching for more evidence at this end and I just might have a place to start."

"Good luck, Anna. Isn't this a strange business? All these years in Canada never hearing much about our Scottish roots and suddenly, out of the blue, a voice from the past brings a possible family history to life."

"History or mystery, Simon, I am not sure yet, but I'll be working on the answers.

By the way, see if you can find any reference to this Aileen Anne anywhere. It seems she is a lost child."

"I certainly never heard of her, Anna, but I'll start looking in earnest now. I'll send on to you anything I find that might be helpful."

"Thanks, Simon. I have to go now. Love to all the family."

"Right! Take care and keep warm, sis. Bye."

Well, now, the circumstantial evidence mounts up, thought Anna, as she replaced the receiver and sat back in her chair. She turned to the paper where she had started a family tree and tried to insert the new information, or perhaps new invention was a more accurate term at this point, she admitted to herself.

Using pencil to signify the temporary nature of the notes, she scrawled the name Aileen Anne beside her grandmother Aileen's name and added a question mark. Another larger question mark followed the name Helen Dunlop and the initials AKA for 'also known as'. Feeling like some detective on a TV murder mystery show, Anna sighed with frustration.

How could she prove Aileen Anne and Helen were the same child?

She knew there had been an adoption. Helen's admission of this to George McLennan was proof enough, but the link from Helen to Aileen Anne was a pure fantasy of Anna's and not even tangible enough for Anna to have mentioned it to her brother.

What significance could be placed on the phone call Simon had uncovered from a possible unknown relative to Anna's mother so long ago? It seemed strange that her mother had clung on to this incident and even blamed her husband for what could only be termed unfortunate timing. Was her mother so homesick that she would grasp at this slender link to family so tightly? Did this mean that her mother missed the few family members from her years in Scotland? Anna knew her mother believed she was an only child. Perhaps there was some reason that deprived her mother of family connections and this was one of the factors that contributed to the move to Canada.

Once more Anna felt annoyed and frustrated. More questions than answers presented themselves. Everywhere she turned there were unknown elements and few people who could be expected to know the answers.

The inevitable conclusion seemed to be that an expedition to Scotland might bring her closer to the source of the information Anna sought. But, was that realistic or magical thinking again?

Who was left alive in Scotland who could help solve the mystery? George had actually known Helen. Were there others who knew Helen when she was younger or who might have shared confidences with her in the nursing home in Oban?

Anna thought back to her meeting with Bev. A month or two in Scotland was not beyond her means financially. If she was ever to get any peace from these endless questions she might have to make the journey.

Not such a bad choice, she concluded. It would certainly shake me out of my rut and at least I could settle the property issue before I returned home again.

Suddenly, with this tentative decision, Anna was galvanized into action. If the venture was to be brought into the realm of possibility there were so many things to be done.

Immediately, she started an action list on the back of the family tree paper.

- Work: (what will Andrew think?)
- Apartment: (must talk to Joseph).
- Samba: (the girls will be so excited).
- Travel arrangements: (where is my passport?)
- Accommodations in Scotland: (can I move into the farm right away?)
- Packing: (where did I put the cases?)
- Weather conditions in Scotland in winter: (I really need more information about the area where Helen's farmhouse stands).

"Lots to do!" Anna declared to the empty room. "I'd better get started!"

"Alina, just a quick message. I've decided to go to Scotland to find out more about this legacy. I'm off to work now but I will talk to you soon."

"Susan? Oh, hi Jake! How are you feeling? Yes, I heard you got a great report from the doctors recently. Good for you! Can you ask Susan to give me a call? I'll be home tonight after 9:00pm. Thanks and give those beautiful dogs a pat from me. See you soon."

"Maria, you'll get this when you get home tonight. I am going to

need some help packing for Scotland since I have no idea about what I'll need there. Don't you have a cousin in Glasgow? Any advice will be gratefully received."

"Bev, I won't keep you from your work. I am going to take a couple of months off to investigate the situation in Scotland. Can you check over my accounts and make sure that all possible bills can be paid directly through my bank here. I am thinking I should leave you with a power of attorney for this period. What do you think? I'll be at the Library until late tonight so you can send me an e mail there if you want."

By 8:00pm the Samba group had assembled in the Public Library downtown.

Anna was behind the circulation desk arranging books on the returns cart and when she turned around she was amazed to see them there. They were practically jumping up and down with excitement.

"We just couldn't wait to see you Anna!" they cried, in chorus. "The news about Scotland is just wonderful. What can we do to help?"

"Well, for one thing," replied Anna in an urgent whisper, "you can pipe down. My boss doesn't know about this yet, I was planning to talk to him tonight at closing time."

"Oops! We'll wait over here in the conference room if that's all right."

Signalling to a junior to take over the desk, Anna followed her friends into the conference room and closed the door firmly.

"Look ladies, I appreciate your enthusiasm but you really didn't need to come here tonight. I have already asked for your help in the voice messages I left for you earlier. Susan is the only one I didn't talk to and...."

"Oh, don't worry about that, Anna," Maria jumped in,

"we have agreed to take care of all your requests. I have talked to my cousin Tony's wife in Glasgow and made a list of packing requirements for Scotland. Bev and Susan will fast track the power of attorney and Alina is standing by with ideas for your apartment's sublet if you want."

"Really? You people are fantastic! You certainly don't let the grass grow under your feet, do you? Or is it that you can't wait to get rid of me?"

"You know better than that, Anna." soothed Alina, coming over to put her arms around her friend. "We are just so pleased you have made this decision. Does it mean you know now who the mysterious Helen is?"

"I wish I could say that's true, Alina. I have learned a bit more from Helen's lawyer but I can't really make a solid link from Helen to me that would justify the generosity of the legacy. That's one of the reasons why I need to go to Scotland. I am hoping to find missing pieces of the puzzle there."

"Well, you know we are with you one hundred per cent, Anna," said Susan in her decisive way as she rounded up the other three and headed for the door.

"I suggest we meet together at my place in a week and see what progress we have made. Send any suggestions to me and I'll set up an agenda."

"Good grief, Susan!" exclaimed Bev in mock alarm, "it sounds like an official board meeting instead of a Samba help committee."

"Time is of the essence, my dears," stated Susan with a chuckle. "Let's leave the woman in peace to break the news to her boss and don't forget to keep in touch with me about details."

Maria shook her head at Susan's manner and passed an envelope to Anna on her way out.

"This is the suggested clothing list. I'll put a few things aside for you at the store. Come down next week."

Anna could hear the chatter as her friends exited the

Library. They seemed more excited than she was herself, but the encounter made her realize that the die was cast now and she really did need to start the process of moving to another country and an unknown adventure.

A quiet knock interrupted Anna's sombre thoughts.

Andrew's head appeared around the door and with a concerned tone in his voice he asked if everything was all right.

Anna took a deep breath and started to fill him in on all that had been happening in her life in the last week or two. Andrew did not seem completely surprised. The request to change her hours to the evening shift had alerted him that something unusual was occurring but he was gracious enough to offer to keep her position open for two months.

"You know how much we value your work here, Anna. I don't want to lose you but I wouldn't dream of standing in your way. Let me know what you decide to do if you want to return."

"Oh, I fully intend to return, Andrew. I should be back in a couple of months, in time to train the summer Library Pages for you. Thank you for being so considerate. May I work for another week or two and sort out everything I can for my replacement?"

The remaining time before closing sped by as Anna and Andrew compiled a list of tasks to be completed. Anna had the distinct feeling that list-making would become increasingly important to her in the next few weeks.

Now that Andrew was aware of the situation, Anna's mental state shifted into high gear as the reality of her decision struck home. Her mind was so occupied with details that the winter weather made no impact on her at all on the way home to her apartment.

Despite another exciting day full of surprises, she could not sleep immediately and found herself in bed making notes at midnight. It was essential to complete some research before her work at the Library came to an end, so she had to arrive early on Friday and also produce a schedule of work over the next two months for whoever filled her position.

She fell asleep, finally, with the bedside lamp shining on pen and papers scattered over the bed covers.

Chapter Nine

On the last day, Anna was in a fever of excitement and frantically dashing from place to place making the final arrangements before she met the ground transportation bus to Toronto airport.

Alina was by her side, attempting to create a calming influence, but Anna's fear that she was making a huge mistake in pursuing this mad dream in a foreign land was causing her to be so distracted that she could not complete even a simple task without panicking.

Two substantial cases were open on the bed and a packing list supplied by Maria was almost checked off.

"I don't know, Alina, these new clothes are all too good to wear on something described as a farm house. I'll throw in some jeans and a sweatsuit, I think. What about this lined raincoat Maria made me buy? Do you think it's warm enough for March?"

Fearing that her friend's second-guessing might lead to a last-minute re-packing episode, Alina agreed with everything Anna said and deftly closed and locked one of the cases.

A quick glance at her watch confirmed they should be on their way downtown to the bus terminal in case they were delayed by rush hour traffic.

At least the weather was on their side for once, she thought. It was a good day for the beginning of March. 'In like a lamb' as they said, but Alina guessed they would pay for this later in the month. Anna would be well established in Scotland by then, of course.

A shudder went through Alina at the thought of her friend alone, a stranger in a strange land. She wished she could accompany Anna on this trip but spring craft fairs and her contract obligations made it impossible, and perhaps it was more important for Anna to judge the situation for herself and stand on her own two feet. Alina's mother had always insisted that the A Plus duo were unable to think independently. This opportunity should prove her mother wrong, once and for all.

"I'll take this case down to the car, Anna. Take a last look around and meet me at the entrance in a couple of minutes. I'll send Joseph up to lock up for you and give you a hand with the other case."

The two-hour bus trip to Toronto sped by for Anna. She had begged the women of Samba not to see her off as she suspected an emotional farewell would totally unnerve her.

A final hug from Alina was bad enough, but settling herself in a seat with carry-on bag at her feet and purse on her lap occupied the first few minutes and allowed Anna to compose herself.

In fact, she was worn out with decisions and organization. Never having left home for such a long period, she had no idea how much effort it would take to get to the actual point of departure. Yet, she was unable to relax. There was no incentive to sit back in comfort and watch the scenery roll by. The Ontario farmland's wintery bare fields punctuated by clumps of stark trees held no fascination. The cars and trucks streaming by on the multi-laned 401 highway flashed past so quickly that there was no chance to make even brief visual contact with the occupants and wonder where they might be heading.

Anna managed a weak smile as she imagined the surprise of her fellow bus travellers if they knew where she was going, and why she was taking this journey.

Looking around she saw that the few passengers were reading or sleeping. The driver's radio was turned down so only a murmur of music could be heard over the hum of the engine. No distractions there, then.

Longing for the oblivion of sleep, Anna surmised that she might achieve that state if her mind was more settled about the arrangements she had made. This thought forced her to check inside her purse in a panic. No, the passport and airline ticket were secured in a wallet with the international money orders and a reservation for one night in a Glasgow hotel. The train ticket for Oban and the directions to George McLennan's office were zipped inside a compartment for the next stage of the journey.

Her exploring fingers encountered a smooth, metal surface. This was the parting gift from her buddies; a cell phone that would allow her to keep in touch with the Samba group from Scotland.

Bev's son James had cheerfully provided several lessons for Anna on how to access the address book he had loaded with all the relevant numbers, but when his flying fingers attempted to demonstrate texting features, Anna had called a halt. Phoning transatlantic with a phone charger to remember, was enough for now. James had added his cell phone numbers to the address book and insisted on supplying technical backup when required. He was more than happy to help, in exchange for the privilege of driving Anna's car while she was away, thereby making his daily commute to college much easier.

James had pre-set the cell phone for connection to United Kingdom satellite service so it lay dormant in her hand until Anna could activate it in Scotland.

"Scotland," Anna whispered, as if trying the word out

would make the entire enterprise seem more real. There's a long way to go yet, she told herself.

Flying across Ontario, Quebec and the Maritime Provinces then out over the Atlantic Ocean in the darkness to arrive at Glasgow Airport by 9:00am. Such a short night in which to travel so far, she marvelled.

It was hard to grasp the distance, both literal and metaphorical, from the New World to the Old World.

Although Alina and Anna had often spent vacations together, they usually went south to Florida, Mexico, Cuba, or the Caribbean, favouring flights from London airport when-ever possible, rather than departing from Toronto and stealing valuable holiday time. This would be Anna's first flight from Pearson's new International Terminal 3.

She wished the bus would speed along and get there. Then she wished it would slow down and let her get used to the idea of all the changes she would soon encounter, but

Anna also knew she was caught in the inexorable grasp of events she, herself, had decided to put in motion and there was nothing to do now but wait.

In the hope that George's last letter would distract her from these conflicting thoughts, Anna scrabbled in her purse again. There was just enough daylight left to read the typed pages.

.............*so you can see it was a piece of great luck that I was able to find the record of the arrival of Aileen Anne Knox at the Quarrier's Homes. The entry in the year book stated that the child's mother had brought her to Bridge of Weir for fear that she might not be able to continue to care for her. It was the mother's intention to return for her only daughter as soon as her circumstances were improved, but Quarrier's lost touch with Aileen Knox after two years and the child was adopted by the time her mother's finances were secure.*

The adoption records were sealed by law in those days, to protect the new parents and we can only imagine the anguish your grand-mother must have suffered at the loss of her child.

Anna put the letter down and gazed unseeingly out of the window. No matter how many times she read this latter part, she could not prevent a wave of compassion flooding through her. She felt a common bond with this grandmother who she would never meet.

They shared a common sorrow in the loss of a child. Anna mourned the children she had not mothered, and her grandmother bore the greater loss in mourning the child she had given birth to and loved enough to save her life at the cost of losing the child forever.

Aileen Anne lived at the Quarrier's Village for two years. Long enough, perhaps, for a small child to forget her mother? Would that be a better or worse fate?

Anna's research had revealed that William Quarrier, a Victorian philanthropist, had established a self-contained community with forty cottages set up to provide a family atmosphere for orphaned or abandoned children. Despite the contrast with the more depressing institutional buildings of the time, Quarrier's made sure every child was disciplined, educated and given basic skills so he or she could be a productive member of society.

The discipline must have been strict, thought Anna. How would a six year old girl adjust to this rigid routine? After being an only child for all of her young life, how did Aileen Anne cope with dormitories and hordes of strange children clamouring for attention from a few, very busy adults?

Questions; always more questions, but Anna determined she would visit the present day Quarrier's Village, if only to see for herself this location which was now considered sufficiently unusual to have been preserved as a conservation site.

At last the first leg of the weary journey was over when the bus pulled up at the terminal doors. As it was an evening departure, the terminal was not overly busy and Anna could see the huge structure, as much like an aircraft hangar as anything else, stretching in one long horizontal from her left to the distant right. Most of the area was dedicated to airline passenger check-in desks and Anna's was near the entrance. Hauling her luggage, which seemed to be heavier than she remembered, she lined up with the other travellers and soon found herself with ticket and boarding pass in hand and only a carry-on bag to hoist over her shoulder, leaving her free to explore the airport.

Maria, Samba's most experienced international traveller, who regularly visited family in Italy, had impressed upon Anna a few cautions about air travel in the post 9-11 era.

First, she should not partake of food or alcohol on the aircraft. Maria's method for avoiding jet lag required the passenger to eat at normal hours and try to sleep on the plane instead of waiting endlessly for food service.

Second, know the restricted items that must not be in the luggage, checked or carried.

Third, make sure the carry-on bag is of the required size and can hold a purse also. These two should contain the essentials for the flight and changes for a day or two in case of lost or delayed luggage. Maria's recommendation was to wear several layers of clothing and Anna's heaviest shoes or boots, packing a pair of lighter shoes for comfort on the plane.

Anna had followed these suggestions faithfully, and she now set out to walk around the terminal facilities (another of Maria's requirements) to keep her circulation going and help pass the time until the required early arrival at the departure gates.

Bookstores and gift shops were discovered behind the check-in counters and several restaurant or fast-food areas with seating were provided, but Anna could not see anything she wanted to eat. Her stomach was clenched with a mixture of excitement and fear and moving around seemed to be a better option.

Maria had also warned that the distance from the terminal to the departure lounges was farther than Anna would expect and that she should keep her passport and boarding pass ready for inspection even after passing through the metal detectors. Anna congratulated herself on a shorter hairstyle that eliminated the indignity she usually endured because of the clips and hairpins her former style had required. She breezed through the metal portal and collected her coat and hand luggage without delay.

Maria's advice is right on target so far, she thought, as she walked down the long corridors to the lounges, passing coffee stalls and cheap jewellery displays.

She stopped long enough to buy a bottle of cold water for the flight, as the importance of hydration had been impressed upon her, but resisted donuts and chocolate snacks as she knew from previous experience the messy clothing that resulted when chocolate bars were opened in a warm and restricted space.

More waiting in the departure lounge then, finally, the boarding instructions, a blast of welcome cool night air coming up the covered linkway, and on to the plane and the window seat Maria had advised. With her carry-on bag under the seat in front, to allow her feet to be raised during the flight, Anna settled down with a glad sigh of relief.

There was nothing more to do now. The plane would take off shortly and the adventure would soon begin.

The last thing Anna could remember about the aircraft taxiing down the runway was the polite juggling for arm rest space with the man in the centre seat. The next thing she remembered was the jangling announcement of their imminent arrival in Glasgow and directions to raise the seat back into upright position ready for breakfast.

"I must have slept for the entire flight!" Anna exclaimed, blinking her blurry eyes.

"Lucky you," suggested a weary voice. "The movies were awful and the sound system was worse. I didn't get a wink of sleep."

The young man in the seat next to Anna was yawning and stretching as he complained.

Anna could only sympathise with him and claim exhaustion as her secret sleep weapon.

Quiet commiseration about travel in general, and businessman Steve's almost weekly commute from New York to London or Glasgow, via Toronto or Montreal, occupied the remaining time until landing.

Anna managed to spot islands in the sea through the grey clouds as they approached the runway. There were low hills shrouded in mist nearby, announcing to Anna that this was definitely not the flat plain of Toronto's airport.

Once inside the terminal, the contrast was gone, with the familiar carpeted corridors and long passages very similar to those in Pearson. The view through the large windows showed the usual bustling scene of a busy docking area with a light rain falling steadily from the overcast sky.

Anna followed the passengers ahead of her to the baggage reclaim hall. As they neared the end of the corridors, they passed displays of Scottish goods. Anna stopped to admire the gleaming whisky bottles and the tartan tins of shortbread and almost caused a collision as travellers rushing home had to divert around her.

Waiting for the luggage carousel to begin moving, Anna heard a selection of Scottish accents as passengers on cell phones announced their safe arrival to family and friends in the strident tones people everywhere tend to use in the belief that their conversation is inaudible to anyone else. Although some voices were harsh, the majority were not unlike her mother's and father's mid-Atlantic accents, similar to that of Steve, the businessman she had met on the plane.

One group of young women attracted attention by flopping down on the polished floor and chatting loudly to each other about their recent exploits in Toronto where it seemed they had taken part in a sports tournament of some kind. Short tartan skirts and black t-shirts emblazoned with sparkling mottoes and motifs did not help Anna determine which sport they played but their joking and chanting, much of which was unintelligible to Anna, certainly confirmed they were a team.

A loud grinding sound announced the imminent arrival of luggage and the waiting passengers edged closer so they could spot their belongings and beat the rush out of the airport.

Looking around her, Anna noticed that most people had acquired a luggage cart and she spotted the area to the side of the baggage hall where arriving travellers were lined up to pull the carts out of some kind of rack. She quickly got into the line and soon arrived at the carts only to discover that there was a charge of a one pound coin in order to release the cart. Anna had Scottish pound notes in her wallet, but no coins at all.

Seeing her situation, a woman behind her said, "Here, hen, ah've a spare pound. They machines are a damn nuisance. Trolleys used to be free, you know." With a deft twist of her wrists, the woman unhooked the trolley and handed it to Anna.

"You are very kind," stammered Anna in surprise, "please let me pay you for that."

"You're aw right dear. Welcome to Glasgow." And with a smile she gathered up a brood of children and two trolleys and marched away.

I can't imagine that happening in a busy Canadian airport, thought Anna, as she made her way back to the carousel.

Anna's two items were quickly identified in the mass of similar-looking luggage thanks to Maria's purchase of several brightly- woven straps cinching the centre of each case.

"I must thank Maria for her invaluable help," murmured Anna as she hefted the rain-wet cases on to a trolley and wheeled away to the exit.

Cabs were waiting just outside the doors and a man

wearing a yellow oilskin raincoat was keeping order in the line.

"Where are you heading miss?" he asked, as he signalled to the next cab, opened the rear door, and pushed cases into the front seat all in the same practiced motion before Anna could reply. "Oh, Jury Hotel in Glasgow centre," she stammered.

"That'll be the Jurys Inn, miss. Hope you enjoy your holiday." With this he deftly shut the cab door, turned to the next customers in line, and Anna's cab was whisked away to a traffic circle and spun out onto a motorway at great speed before she could fasten the seat belt.

"Ah am apologising for the weather, miss," said a friendly voice from the front seat. "Honest, it was quite nice yesterday. Are you here for a wee holiday, to see family, or is this a business trip maybe?"

Anna's gaze connected with the driver's smile in the rear view mirror and she was amazed to find herself replying to his enquiry in a way she would never have done in a Canadian cab where most drivers' conversation consisted of grunted monosyllables.

"I guess it's a combination of all three choices," she said with a grin.

"Oh, you'll be an American then, from your accent?"

"Canadian, actually," and Anna felt an unexpected rush of pride in the claim.

"Pardon me, miss. Ah had the same problem telling Americans from Canadians when ah was in Florida. It nearly got me in trouble a couple a times, ah can tell you."

"So you have been to the States?"

"Aye, right enough. Me and the wife have travelled all over. We're goin' to Australia for Christmas with some pals."

Anna could not think of a suitable response to this statement so she looked out of the cab and found they were racing along a six-lane highway.

Other than the fact they were on the wrong side of the

road, from Anna's perspective, it might have been a busy street in Toronto or Ottawa, with hotels, apartment buildings and offices on each side. An occasional glimpse could be seen between buildings of low, green hills in the distance, but nothing that announced 'Scotland'.

Well, what was I expecting, she chided herself, a pipe band in highland dress, perhaps?

Thinking ahead to the next day's train journey to Oban, she asked, "How far is the Queen Street station from my hotel?"

"No far at all. You could walk it easy without two cases. Here's ma card, miss."

The back of a muscular hand appeared in front of Anna and she took the card from its fingers rapidly, sensing the driver might need his two hands for the lane-changing diversions she had been observing all around them.

"Jist ask the hotel to give me a ring and I'll pick you up, no bother at all."

Anna thanked the cab driver, pocketed the card, and turned her attention to the road again.

Among the signs displayed above the lanes directing traffic to points east and west was the name Glasgow City Centre. She realised with relief that this cab ride would be considerably shorter than the boring two-hour trip from south-western Ontario to Toronto airport.

Checking her watch to see how long it had been since she arrived in Scotland, Anna hurried to advance the hands five hours for local time and when she looked up again she could see ahead of them busy streets thronged with pedestrians. Three lanes of cars facing in the same direction as Anna's cab were poised under a bridge or tunnel, waiting for the traffic lights to change, but it was clear they were going to turn left or right since the street ahead had no cars or buses.

"Oh, a pedestrians-only area," she exclaimed, "how convenient for shoppers."

"Aye, miss, and a damn nuisance it is for drivers. You'll be glad you're no driving in Glasgow. All they one-way streets are a nightmare, but your hotel's jist aroon this corner."

With that pronouncement, the lights changed to green and they turned to the right like a greyhound out of the blocks and in moments they were drawing up to the kerb outside the Jurys Inn.

Chapter Ten

Anna checked in with one of the smart young girls in navy suits and white shirts at the reception desk just inside the front doors of the hotel.

While she was waiting for the safe deposit locker to be opened (a suggestion of Susan's that her valuables would be safer under lock and key), she looked around the reception area and found that all of it was easily visible. To her left, a bright cafe or bar then two elevators, the reception desk, and to the right a restaurant busy with families and the clatter of plates and cups. The delicious smells of breakfast emerging from this location reminded Anna forcibly of how long it had been since she had eaten.

The remaining space in the foyer was occupied by comfortable, red plush seating areas now full of travellers with their luggage, waiting for transportation, or possibly for rooms to become vacant.

Anna gratefully accepted her room key and struggled to wrangle her cases into the narrow elevator without dropping her carry-on bag or envelope of travel papers. There did not seem to be any porters standing by to help but, in fact, Anna was glad to be able to manage by herself as she was anxious to divest herself of luggage without delay and be free to move around and explore.

When she reached the fifth floor, she was immediately impressed by the thick, patterned carpet that undoubtedly contributed to the hushed silence, contrasting with the crowd and noise of the reception area.

The room was clean and well supplied although smaller than those found in most Canadian hotels. Dumping her cases and bags, Anna was drawn to the window. As she divested herself of coat, scarf and some of the extra layers of clothes she had worn on the plane, she looked out to see her first real view of Glasgow.

At street level, buses commanded attention. Double–decker buses adorned with adverts for what looked like theatre shows or movies, followed each other in procession on the opposite side of the street from her hotel. Passengers streamed off at one of several bus stops only to be replaced by others who moved forward into the rain from sheltering doorways. There did not seem to be many private cars on the street although Anna was thrilled to see occasional chunky black cabs familiar from so many English movies.

The buildings were a strange combination of the old and the new. An ugly grey apartment building with a look of the fifties loomed above the street for eight storeys or so and a new-looking parking building with a huge banner proclaiming its purpose, occupied a corner above several small stores. Immediately in front of her, Anna could see the roofs of a more traditional structure in red sandstone with opportunistic small trees growing out of the gutters, advertising its age and condition. Further away the glint of a high glass pyramid announcing a new development of some kind.

"Quite a mixture of styles here," she declared to the view, "and not a speck of tartan to be seen."

Turning her head far to the right, Anna caught sight of another busy street running parallel to an area showing, through trees, the unexpected gleam of moving water.

From the little she knew of Glasgow, she deduced that this might be the famed River Clyde.

Immediately she had a purpose. Eat; then find access to the river.

Thankful that her hours of oblivion on the plane had granted her the energy to explore the city, Anna had a quick wash, changed her boots for shoes and donned her hooded raincoat again.

An efficient buffet service in the restaurant ensured she lost no time in helping herself to a substantial breakfast of cereal with fruit, scrambled eggs, bacon, beans and delicious sausages accompanied by toast and washed down with a surprisingly fine coffee dispensed piping hot from a metal urn.

Duly fortified, Anna ventured into the rain and raised the hood of her coat after passing through the collection of smokers huddling near the hotel's doors.

The 'No smoking allowed indoors' rule applies here, as well as at home, she realized.

Conscious of the fact that the Samba ladies were expecting regular reports from her, Anna looked for the name of the street where the Jurys Inn was located. Jamaica Street was discovered, eventually, on the side of a building, reminding Anna of Scotland's historic trading links to the rest of the world.

It was only a few steps to the corner where Jamaica Street crossed another busy street named, strangely, Broomielaw, and then became a solid-looking bridge with polished stone walls and wide sidewalks.

Anna negotiated the crosswalk carefully. She observed that the traffic did seem to move more rapidly than in Canadian cities and that she should remember to be cautious about this in future.

Her attention was focused on the river ahead but also on the massive stone piers immediately in front of her, which must once have supported another bridge. This appeared to have been supplanted by a higher railway bridge where a train now roared overhead.

In the midst of the noise coming at her from all directions, Anna longed to escape and see the river more closely. As if in answer to her request, she spied a walkway to her left leading away from the bridges. In only a few steps she found herself passing under the Jamaica Street's bridge with only about two feet to spare above her head. Emerging from this unexpected experience she descended a dozen steps and left much of the traffic noise behind.

For the first time in what seemed like months, Anna drew a deep breath and tried to catch up with her feelings after the disorienting turmoil of the last ten hours.

The river could now be clearly seen and its majestic size and depth contributed to Anna's new sense of contentment. Running swiftly and smoothly, contained on both sides between its walls of stone topped by iron railings, the Clyde seemed impervious to all the hustle and bustle of the large city it had given birth to. The grey skies overhead were reflected in its surface. No branches or debris floated by as Anna stood mesmerized. Only a cluster of white seagulls bobbed in the centre of the flow, preening their feathers and calling out with their echoing cries.

The walkway stretched ahead for what looked like kilometres. It was five metres wide in places and on the side nearest the city it was buttressed by gardens bearing large trees and bushes, some with the shiny leaves of evergreens.

At this point Anna was shocked to discover that she, normally observant by nature, had completely missed the fact that there was no snow to be seen anywhere. Indeed, there were signs of spring in the daffodils peeping out from the grassy banks between the trees where young leaves traced the branches.

"Of course, the temperature here is much milder than in Ontario in March," she declared, shaking her head in astonishment. "What was I thinking? I guess I wasn't thinking at all! Too much change coming at me too fast by far!"

A cyclist sped past Anna at this point and smiled as if a stranger talking to herself was not an uncommon occurrence in his day.

Anna walked on. Her attention was split between the far side of the river with its elegant stone buildings just far enough away to be tantalisingly indistinct, and the variety of old and new structures looming above her on her left beyond the tree bank.

Because the street level with its cars and pedestrians was obscured, Anna could see these buildings in the kind of detail that was usually hidden from passers-by above her.

The interesting variety of styles and architecture drew her eyes away from the river for a few minutes. Within two hundred yards she first saw a stately Customs House surmounted by a remarkable stone coat of arms with beauti-fully-carved lion and unicorn animals guarding either side.

Next to this building, stood a red stone structure of five storeys that was decorated at every level with different styles of tracery and many balustrades adorning windows of varying heights. The modern ceiling lights seen on the top floor gave the impression that this splendid edifice was now an office of some sort.

Anna had no time to wonder about this before the most amazing contrast came into view.

Two buildings that seemed to epitomize the difference between old and new stood together, each a splendid example of style but representing two entirely different eras.

A flight of wide stone steps ahead of her led Anna up to the street level so she could look more closely at the church opposite. She could just make out the signboard stating that this beautiful building facing the Clyde was Saint Andrew's Cathedral.

The stonework was lighter in tone than previous buildings Anna had seen. It seemed to draw the available light towards it so that the wet columns gleamed. The style might have been Gothic, she thought, but Anna realised she lacked the vocabulary to describe the soaring spires either side of the central tower or the curved doorway with its statues and embellishments. She did, however, recognise how impressive a sight it must have been when viewed from the river below. It must once have commanded the skyline.

The contrast was supplied by the attached, rectangular structure completely fronted in mirrored glass. At almost the same height as the cathedral, the two could not have been more different.

Could this be the equivalent of a church hall and offices, Anna wondered? What a bold statement blending traditional and twenty-first-century style, she thought, although she was not sure she approved.

Turning back to the riverside, Anna ran down the steps and continued to walk forward.

A watery sun was trying to filter through the cloudy sky as she reached another bridge over the Clyde. This one was a narrow suspension bridge for pedestrians. A girl with a baby buggy and a young man carrying a briefcase were the only occupants.

Anna quickly climbed to the bridge level and walked across the river admiring the view from this new perspective. She could see so many bridges from here and each one was different in style, materials and purpose. Obviously, Glasgow had needed many crossings over this broad river for convenience and commerce and it must have taken many years to provide them in this quantity.

When she reached the opposite bank, Anna was delighted to find a display board with information about Glasgow's bridges confirming her own deductions.

She read that she had just crossed the Portland Street Suspension Bridge, one of twenty-one bridges of eight types representing 150 years of engineering history. By checking the map provided, she discovered that the bridge carrying

Jamaica Street over the river was, named Glasgow Bridge, and the next one past the railway bridge was the King George V Bridge, built in 1928. Not very far from there was the newest addition, an S-shaped pedestrian bridge known as 'the squiggly bridge'.

"These Glasgow people are not afraid to mix the sublime and the ridiculous," laughed Anna. "I think I'm going to like it here!"

Now that she was across the river, the buildings that had seemed elegant before were now revealed in more detail. A solid line of three-storey houses with the formal, square shapes of Georgian-period architecture, fronted a cobbled street. Each building had matching stone steps and iron coach lamps. Brass plates mounted above the doorways announced that they were banks or offices.

Walking back to the Glasgow Bridge, along a sidewalk separated from grass lawns at the riverside by handsome black railings, Anna thought these Carlton Place offices must have been highly-sought-after residences at one point in time.

Crossing the river again, Anna could see her hotel ahead and she now had a much better view of the huge stone bridge piers she had noticed before. They rose to a height of about ten metres above the water level and were formed of rough-hewn, drum-shaped sections with a flat plinth above. Anna was reminded of pillars in Egyptian tombs except that these were the same width from top to bottom.

Carved deeply into the side of each, in Greek letters and in English, was the motto;

'All greatness stands firm in the storm.'

Anna stood, leaning on the bridge wall, contemplating these structures in the river, unaware of the buses, cars and transport vehicles rushing over the bridge behind her.

The nobility of the pillars struck her forcibly. Standing there, bereft of the bridge that they had once borne, they still commanded respect, and Anna thought of the engineers who made space for them, honouring their history despite the necessity of building the much more utilitarian railway bridge that almost blocked them from view.

In this contemplative mood, she suddenly thought of her father. As an engineer, he might well have known these many bridges although he had never spoken to his daughter about his work in Scotland. He had been a quiet man with an underlying strength and it must have been difficult for him to be demoted to mechanic while he regained his qualifications in Canada.

Not long after Anna had married Richard, her father moved to Calgary to live with Simon's family, and he had lived there until his death in his early seventies. Anna felt she had missed knowing her father as an adult and for the first time she felt a kinship with him.

If only he had shared his Scottish life with her, she thought sadly. Then, looking around her, Anna now realized she would not have been able to understand the loss of a country and a culture that, she could already observe, were able to blend the old and the new and yet remain true to their heritage.

"Lord above!" she exclaimed, "I am getting maudlin already and making pronouncements when I've hardly been here for five minutes. What would Susan think of me?"

The rain had stopped and a brisk breeze was pushing the clouds away to the east. Anna shook the raindrops off the hood of her coat, mentally adding this warmly-lined garment to the list of items for which Maria deserved her fervent gratitude. Turning up the collar she gave her attention to the Broomielaw crossing and with just one backward glance toward the Clyde, she made her way to her hotel.

What a morning, she thought, as she spotted a booth in the hotel bar where she could get a warming cup of tea. On the way, she stopped at a display stand and gathered a handful of tourist leaflets and brochures to examine while she relaxed.

Glancing at her watch, she was amazed to discover it was

barely afternoon. She felt as if she had been in Glasgow for a day at least and yet she was not as tired as she might have expected. Remembering other holidays, she knew that time slowed for the first few days and then speeded up once you were oriented.

This is not a holiday, Anna cautioned herself. I have an agenda here with important decisions to make.

Tea came with a tiny metal pot, a cup and saucer and a larger pot of hot water.

How civilized, thought Anna. I can enjoy a second hot cup without bothering the server.

She spread the leaflets and brochures on the table looking for a map of the city centre and found one that showed a sightseeing tour on a double-decker red bus, partly open on top.

She smiled, remembering rides on a similar bus in London Ontario, when she was small.

Stops along the route included more of the Merchant City, where she was now located, Glasgow Cathedral, the University, a number of museums and something called the People's Palace in Glasgow Green.

Now this would be an interesting tour for another visit, Anna decided, but I am not sure I have the time today.

A second leaflet unfolded to reveal a colourful border illustrating a wide variety of restaurants and theatre shows, with a map of the city centre in the middle.

The Clyde was on the southern edge of this map and Anna could easily find the location of her hotel. She spotted Queen Street station near George Square, and wondered if her feet would carry her that far. Much closer to her was something called Saint Enoch Shopping Centre which, if the map was to be believed, covered an entire city block.

"Now, a little retail therapy is exactly what I need", she announced, "and as it's on that pedestrian precinct I saw this morning, I can hardly get lost on the way there."

"That'll be Argyle Street, miss."

Anna looked up from the map and realised she had been talking out loud. The young waiter was clearing her tea things away and must have thought she had been asking for directions.

"You can't miss it. Just out the door here, and the second street on your right and you're there. Folk say you can buy anything at all in that place, though I wouldn't know. My wife doesn't let me near it!"

Chuckling at the ability of Glasgow people to strike up a conversation at any time, with any one, Anna gathered up her things and, leaving a nice tip on the table, ventured out once more.

Chapter Eleven

❦

"**H**ello there! Excuse me Mrs. Mason! This is the receptionist!" "Hello!"

Anna emerged from a deep sleep to hear a persistent voice and accompanying loud knocks on the door.

For a moment she could not figure out where she was, or why someone was hammering on her door. Then she saw the cases, and it all came flooding back.

Staggering out of bed on legs that had become more jelly than bone, she lurched to the door and managed to undo the locks while reassuring the person outside that she could, indeed, still hear.

"I apologize, Mrs. Mason, but I could not get a response to the wake-up call you left.

I've been ringing you on the phone for over an hour and I was afraid something had happened to you".

"Oh, no, I am perfectly fine, thank you," croaked Anna. "Sorry to worry you.

It's only jet lag, I think."

"Right then, I'll leave you in peace."

As soon as the door closed, Anna fell back into bed to calm her racing heart.

"What a horrible way to wake up," she moaned.

She was almost turning back to the oblivion of her soft pillows when it struck her that she had asked for a wake-up call for a reason. She was catching a train to Oban today at noon and there were things to do before then.

What time was it? The bedside clock said 10:00am. She must have slept for twelve hours!

She could scarcely remember the shopping centre and the meal she had eaten there, before falling into bed last night.

"It must be the tension of the last few weeks catching up with me. Oh, my God!"

Anna caught sight of herself in the mirror opposite the bed and groaned aloud.

"I need a shower, and a make-over, and a very large cup of coffee before I take one step out of here. I look like death warmed over."

Refreshed by the shower and the room service coffee that awaited her when she emerged, Anna felt almost human again. She brushed her hair into a loose style, and applied make-up to give some colour to her face then she repacked one case, checked her train ticket, looked under the bed for missed items and made her way down to the reception area to check out, before heading to the buffet to grab some break-fast. She almost, but not quite, forgot to retrieve her valuables from the locked safe. This scare brought her awake even more effectively than the coffee had done.

Reaching into her coat pocket she retrieved the business card the cab driver had given her. Was that just yesterday? Leaving it with the helpful reception girl, she grabbed a plateful of toast, scrambled egg, tomato, and another of those scrumptious sausages, with juice and more coffee to wash it all down.

"That's better! I feel more human now," she told herself, "I think I can tackle the rest of the journey."

In only a few minutes she was waiting at the hotel

entrance with her cases and bags, watching the clouds fly by above the city, revealing intermittent patches of blue sky.

It was years since Anna had made a journey by train and she was looking forward to the trip to Oban.

"Righty oh, lassie! Ye'll be off to the train station I suppose?"

The friendly greeting from Bob of Bob's Taxi Service, as his card had informed her, gave Anna a glow of pleasure. No one seemed to be a stranger for long here. This boded well for her mission to find out more about Helen Dunlop and Aileen Anne and to see what she could do with the McCaig Farm House property. She knew the task would not be easy without help.

Bob steered her into his cab and stowed the luggage into the trunk for the short trip.

On the way, Anna caught a glimpse of George Square with its red tarmac and white statues. It was crowded with people and the famous tour buses ready for the city sightseeing tour.

"Next time I'm here," she promised herself, "I'll make time to see a lot more of Glasgow."

With Bob's help, she found the right platform, the correct coach, and hefted her luggage to the space beneath the window seat and tucked under her feet. Bob swung the lighter bags onto an overhead rack. Anna could not believe Bob had escorted her into the station and onto the train, leaving his taxi parked outside in the busy street where Anna had seen 'N0 Waiting' signs.

"Bob, please don't get yourself a parking fine on my behalf," she pleaded.

"This personal service is far beyond anything I could have expected, but I am so grateful to you for taking such good care of a stranger."

"Ach, away with ye, miss. Happy to help. This is the Homecoming Year for Scotland and nothin' at all is too much trouble for visitors. Now, you huv a gran' time in Oban and watch out o' the windows on the way there. This West Highland Line is wan o' the most famous rail trips in the hale, wide world."

Bob's Glasgow dialect seemed to be getting stronger as he responded to Anna's emotional thanks, but there was no mistaking his sincerity.

Anna could not stop herself from giving this kind soul a big hug and slipping a ten pound note into his pocket, although she realised both actions were most uncharacteristic for her. As Bob made his way back to the platform, Anna could not help thinking how unlikely it was that she would ever make such physical contact with a North American cab driver. She would probably be arrested for assault if she had ever tried.

During the entire three-hour train journey, Anna was glued to the views out of the train windows. The sun followed the train, peeking out of clouds and illuminating scenes of splendor that were marred only by the fact that Anna had not thought to bring a map of the west coast of Scotland with her. Instead, she had to rely on the station names in an attempt to identify the breathtaking lochs and soaring mountains parading past her in an endless spectacle.

At the beginning of the journey, she was positive they were following the Clyde for about forty minutes and Anna feasted her eyes on new museums and housing developments that replaced the shipyards that once must have towered there. She saw her first castle on a huge rock between two stations named Dumbarton where the Clyde widened signifi-cantly. Then they were skirting a lake (I must remember to say 'loch', she warned herself), which might have been Shandon or Gareloch, as both stations were situated along its length.

A land-based stretch of track appeared, allowing Anna to focus on the hills which were becoming more and more like mountains, then the train sped alongside another loch fed by streams rushing down these mountains.

On the other side of the train line, a beautiful loch came into view and Anna knew from the conversation of a family near her in the coach, that it must be the famed Loch Lomond. She hummed the words and tune of the lament to herself. It was the lullaby her father used to sing to her when she was a child. Anna watched the loch, the islands and the greening slopes slide by, framed by the rocky, snow-topped mountain that seemed to be the highest peak she had yet seen.

When Loch Lomond disappeared from view, the train entered a valley where a waterfall tumbled down from the high hills and soon after this, they stopped at Crianlarich station.

A number of passengers disembarked at this point and it seemed as if the train would halt here for a while longer than usual.

Anna could not stand the lack of knowledge of her surroundings any longer so she ventured down the carriage until she spied a young couple with a map spread out on the table before them.

"Excuse me," she began hesitantly, "I am travelling without a map, if you can believe it, and I am driving myself crazy back there not knowing where I am, or what I am looking at. Would you mind if I have a glance at your map?"

"Not at all! Sit here and I'll show you what's ahead." The man shoved a backpack aside and swung the map around so that Anna could see where he was pointing.

His companion gave Anna a lovely smile and said, "Isn't it marvellous country? We've travelled from Australia to see this. My husband's father came from here and he has talked about it all endlessly, but we truly did not expect such a variety of beautiful scenery within such a small area. Can you imagine what it must be like in summer?"

Anna agreed at once and added that she had crossed Canada by train from Ontario and it had taken three days to get to British Columbia on the west coast before she saw anything like the views of the last hour or two.

"What mountain is that, for instance?" Anna gestured to the east where a high peak stood in solitary splendour above the hills.

"Must be Ben More, nearly four thousand feet," came the swift response from the tanned and fit-looking young man. "You've spotted the tallest mountain in this whole area."

"What should I be watching for next?" she asked eagerly, glad to have found tourists like herself, and glad to avoid embarrassment by displaying her ignorance to the local people.

Just then the train lurched forward. Anna made to get up and return to her assigned seat but she was stopped by an outstretched hand.

"I'm John Robertson and this is Maureen. Please stay and share the map. We'll be glad of the company."

"Anna Mason, and thank you for the invitation." Handshakes were exchanged all round and, for the first time since she had left home, Anna began to understand the lie of the land she had chosen to live in for the next two months.

John pointed out that they would very soon enter a valley called Strath Fillan, then past the station at Tyndrum they would finally turn west towards Oban, the terminus of this line.

"But, first," interrupted Maureen, tracing the route with her finger, "we travel twelve miles or so along the River Lochy, through Glen Lochy and at the very northernmost tip of Loch Awe...."

As she paused for breath, John jumped in as if they were of one voice and one mind thinking together. "... we'll see Kilchurn Castle!"

"This is obviously important to you both," implied Anna. No one could have missed the palpable excitement in the air between the two. Their eyes shone as they exchanged private glances and their hands touched across the map.

"My father's ancestors have some connection to the castle," explained John. "He often spoke about it in such romantic terms that we couldn't wait to see it for ourselves."

"It's a ruin now, we've been told," said Maureen, "but it was built in 1440 and from the top of the towers you could once look a long way down the length of Loch Awe, for protection from approaching clan warriors, I suppose."

"We'll be exploring this whole area," added John. "and that's one stop on the itinerary we can't miss. My father would kill me if I don't go there!"

The couple dissolved in laughter at the thought and Anna was hesitant about intruding on their special moment any longer.

"I'll just go back to my seat now, but thank you for the map tour," she said as she rose to go.

"Watch out for the Cruachan Power Station inside a mountain," insisted John, as she turned around.

"....and there's a bridge over Loch Etive at Connel," exclaimed Maureen. "When you see it, we won't be far from Oban."

Anna waved to them both and sank back down into her seat. The names of glens and bens and straths and lochs swirled around in her brain. It was a lot to take in all at once and she was not sure it was worthwhile to devote much energy to the task when other, more pressing, matters would require her attention very soon. Nonetheless, she watched in fascination as the miles to her destination rolled by.

Chapter Twelve

꧁꧂

George McLennan checked his watch for the fourth time in as many minutes.

Yes, almost three o'clock, the train should be arriving shortly. He stretched his neck to loosen the collar and tie that seemed to be restricting his breathing all of a sudden.

A sharp breeze that must have arrived straight from the cold Atlantic, bypassing the barrier of the Isle of Mull, swooped down upon him, ruffling the hair on his head with its icy blast.

The heavy, navy wool overcoat did not provide protection from this March weather.

Such a nice day earlier, he remembered. I wonder what she will think of the typically variable Scottish climate?

Lord save us! What have I got myself into, he thought, as he turned away from the wind.

I just hope Anna Mason hasn't come all this way for nothing. What on earth persuaded me to take on a project like this? The partners are certainly not happy with me.

The words of Alec Thomson rang in his ears again. They had been revolving around in his brain since the confrontation of a fortnight ago.

"We are not responsible for the vagaries of our clients,

George. You have stepped beyond the bounds of prudence in agreeing to act on behalf of Helen Dunlop in this matter.

If, at any point in the future," and here Thomson had paused in a most menacing way, "you should again be tempted to indulge in such foolhardy behaviour, I can assure you that a senior partnership in this firm will be entirely out of your reach, sir."

George felt the colour rise in his cheeks as he remembered the scene in Thomson's office.

Just like a scolding from the headmaster at school, he thought ruefully. I suppose I do deserve it, but who could have resisted that poor old soul with no one in the world to turn to at the end of her days? Her circumstances were so different from my own Gran up the road in Fort William, with two daughters and sons-in-law looking after her every need.

I just felt so guilty whenever I thought about her.

And of course, I have racked up a huge bill for research and phone calls. Ms. Mason had better be prepared to deal with all these personal and financial issues or I am in deep trouble, he concluded.

He could hear the train approaching now and he automatically straightened his shoulders to meet the coming challenge. There won't be so many holiday makers at this time of year, he reminded himself, so I should be able to spot her. She's bound to have luggage with her.

Scanning the scattered crowd descending onto the platform, he tried to guess which person might be Anna Mason. He nodded to, and greeted, local people who worked in Glasgow during the week, and dismissed the strangers carrying only briefcases with barely a glance.

The couple with the Aussie accents and the heavy rucksacks talking to a tall woman were not immediately likely candidates, but when the tourists moved away, smiling and waving as they marched down the platform, he could see that the woman had cases and bags at her feet.

So this was Anna Mason, at last. A cap of bronze hair

crowned a pleasant, older face with an intelligent, if puzzled, expression. She clutched the collar of a dark grey raincoat to her throat and shivered slightly as the wind whistled around her, but he could see a bright red suit peeking out beneath the hem and a pair of elegant black leather boots protecting her feet.

Jeanette will want a full report when I get home, he said to himself, mentally filing away the details for a later chat with his wife.

In a few strides, he crossed the platform, introduced himself, and watched relief wash across Anna Mason's face, erasing the wrinkle between her deep blue eyes.

Conversation about the weather and enquiries about the journey occupied the short distance to the car, and by the time he drove onto the street and past the Ferry Terminal, they were deep into a question and answer session about the town, its facilities, and how long it would take to get to the McCaig Farm House.

This latter enquiry was the one he had expected, and about which he had some trepidation. To delay the moment of response, he pulled into the North Pier and parked the car at the Columba Hotel, suggesting that Anna Mason might want to check in to the hotel overnight and leave her luggage there before venturing to the farm.

It was not difficult to see from her expression that this was not what she had expected, and a more detailed description of the condition of the house which had lain unoccupied for more than a year and a half, was required.

"I have had the chimneys swept recently," he offered, "and the place is supplied with bed linens, but, as you can appreciate, the property will need serious attention before you can stay there comfortably at this time of year."

She looked thoughtful for a moment, and then agreed with his assessment adding,

"I honestly had not thought beyond the point of actually getting here, George.

I can now see that was foolish of me. Thank you once again for taking care of the essentials."

She seemed somewhat crestfallen at this, so he suggested that there was still sufficient daylight for a quick visit to the farm, if she was not overly tired from the journey.

"That would be wonderful, George!" she responded enthusiastically. "I don't think I could sleep tonight if I had to postpone the visit after coming so far."

With that settled, George escorted Anna into the hotel and waited in the bar, downing a whisky to settle his nerves, then calling home while he had the chance.

"No, Jenny, everything's fine. She seems like a very nice person and she has agreed to my suggestions so far."

"There's not been the chance to talk about money yet, but I am sure everything will be fine."

"Now, don't you worry yourself, love, I have the letter safe in my overcoat pocket."

"Yes, I should be home for my dinner."

"Of course I will be careful on the roads. Yes, I have enough petrol for the trip."

"I'll tell you all about it later."

"Cheerio for now, love!"

Anna Mason appeared just as he was tucking the mobile phone back into his suit pocket.

She exclaimed immediately, in some distress, that she had completely forgotten to activate her own cell phone and what would her friends think of her for being out of touch for so long.

"Don't worry, Ms. Mason! I can sort that for you in no time at all. You haven't been away from home for all that long, you know. It just seems that way when you cross the Atlantic."

"You are probably right," she said with a sigh, "I have so

much to tell them already, but I guess it can wait an hour or two more."

"Then, if you are ready, we'll get on our way. The farm is about half an hour out of town and we'll be heading back towards the train station first of all, then onto Glencruiten Road and out past the golf course. Do you play, Anna?"

"I am afraid not, George, although many of my friends do. Wasn't the game invented here in Scotland? Wonderful exercise, they say, but it's an expensive hobby, I believe."

With this statement, Anna turned her head to watch the view from the car and silence descended. He wondered what she was thinking about.

He had plenty to think about himself, as they climbed the road out of town and left the speed limit behind.

What would she think of the farm house? It was certainly quite isolated.

Was she prepared for the more primitive conditions of country life after city living in Canada? How would she manage to get into town? Did she intend to hire a car and if so, would she require an automatic shift?

Would she decide to stay or leave? What would she think when she received the letter that was burning a hole, so to speak, in his coat pocket?

Anxious as he was to know the answers to these questions, he contented himself with attending to the road ahead and before long they turned on to the track that led to the farm.

"A bit bumpy here," he apologized, "but you will see the property as soon as we reach the crest of this hill."

Anna sat up and watched eagerly for her first glimpse of the McCaig Farm House.

The clouds had gathered since they left Oban and the light was fading, turning grass and track and hills into the same dull tones of grey, but she hardly noticed.

She felt like she had as a child on Christmas morning waiting endlessly for permission to gallop downstairs with

Simon to raid the parcels beneath the tree. How long was it since she had felt this kind of anticipation? And yet, there was an equally powerful feeling of apprehension fighting for space in her heart. The next few minutes would determine so much in her future. The suspense was almost unbearable. Her heel began a tattoo on the floor of the car and she stole a glance over at George to see if he had noticed her impatience.

His brown, curly hair was flopping into his eyes as the car shuddered over the holes in the road and he reached one long hand to push it back.

Such fine hands, thought Anna, deliberately distracting herself from the tension for a moment or two. I did not expect him to be so young. His phone voice and manner suggested a much more mature man but I am glad he is so obliging and approachable.

Susan said he was most professional as far as she could tell, and having dealt with lawyers all of her working life, she was the one who would know.

He seems somewhat nervous, however. I hope I am not requiring too much of him or being intimidating in any way. I have been accused of that crime in the past.

Before she could pursue that line of thought any further, George called out,

"There it is now!"

Surprise was her first emotion. The house was built of stone, with a second storey, unlike many of the single-storey countryside homes she had seen from the train or on this short trip out of Oban.

It had a steeply-pitched roof with a chimney on each end and two windows set into the roof. Most likely to be bedroom windows, she surmised.

There was a sort of tower projecting forward right in the middle of the house, dividing it into two equal parts and the main door could be seen on the side of this tower as they approached the gate in the fence.

"Oh, George, I didn't expect it to be so large. I haven't seen another house like this in the area."

"Yes, I suppose it is quite substantial. The house belonged to a large estate. This was the home of the estate manager and his family for a number of years until it was sold to Miss Dunlop."

"Can we take a quick look inside?"

"Certainly, I have the key in the glove box."

A large iron key was produced and Anna led the way up a gravel path to the door where George deftly inserted the key and turned the lock. The door swung open.

"After you, Ms. Mason."

Anna stepped into a square porch inside the tower-like structure she had seen. Light came from a window on her right and there were two doors leading into the house itself.

"On your left is the sitting room and the kitchen is to your right."

George's voice startled her. She would have been happy to stand for a few moments absorbing the feeling of entering this house for the first time, but his voice indicated that a brief tour was required.

She chose the kitchen and had to stand aside while George dealt with the unfamiliar metal hardware that opened the heavy door.

A set of three wooden stairs rose out of this room, turning at a sharp right angle to disappear upwards. The kitchen was square with a huge fireplace opposite the stairs, monopolizing the end wall. A window faced the front yard and another window, above a deep sink, looked out onto the back of the property.

The centre of the kitchen was occupied by a wooden table. An open shelf unit, near the sink, held dishes and cookware.

George had already climbed the stairs by the time Anna absorbed these few details and she heard his voice inviting her to follow him.

The upper staircase was enclosed and led to a short hallway from which two doors opened into other rooms.

George poked his head out of the left door and told her to "mind her head." This strange request became clear when Anna entered the bedroom to find the slope of the roof above, meant limited head room except in the centre of the room where a double bed was placed.

A small fireplace with a velvet chair by its side was near the foot of the bed.

"This is a dormer window," said George, moving into an oddly shaped little area that seemed to project forwards to the front of the house. It allowed Anna to stand almost upright but it contained only a tiny bench and the window.

"There are also two vellux-style windows," said George, but when he saw the blank expression on her face, he added, pointing upwards, "that's a roof window at the back. The house has plenty of light unlike most cottages around here."

Anna was conscious of the fact that there was only one more door in this upper level and she was fervently hoping that it would lead to a washroom of some description.

George crossed the hallway and announced, "This is the bathroom. As you can see there is a bath and sink and a lavatory but I am sure a shower could be added."

Anna had little time to take in the appearance of the antique Victorian plumbing before George added, "I realize this may not be what you were expecting Anna. A lot could be done with additional furnishings. It is sparsely furnished at the moment."

Turning to the wall behind the bath, he opened a door and Anna could see another, smaller bedroom with a single bed, and a similar fireplace positioned on the end wall.

George clicked a switch near the door and a dim light sprang into life from a bare bulb above the bed.

Thank God, there's electricity, thought Anna, I was beginning to think I had been transported into the nineteenth century.

"I won't ask you what you think at this point, Ms. Mason," said George. "I can see this is a lot to take in. If you don't mind, I would like to get back on the road before dark. We can return tomorrow, if you wish."

Nodding her head in agreement, because she did not trust herself to speak, Anna led the way back down the central stairs and took a quick look into the room George had described as 'sitting room'. This was the largest room in the house and equipped with a sofa and chairs, tables, lamps and other amenities. Two large windows showed that this room, like the main bedroom above, took up the depth of the house.

On the way back to the car, Anna turned around for another look and realised she had not seen the room above the porch entrance. In fact, she had not had time to absorb anything other than the most basic layout of the house, and, no doubt, she had missed much of what George had been adding as commentary in the brief guided tour.

She found herself unable to summon a conclusion and decided to say nothing.

George sensed her reluctance to talk and gave his attention to driving back to Oban.

She was most likely tired from the journey, he told himself. She needs time to think.

They reached the hotel in semi- darkness. Anna had fallen asleep on the way there, and was feeling dazed when George gently shook her shoulder to waken her.

"I am sorry to disturb you, Ms. Mason, but there are some things that need to be attended to before I can let you go tonight."

Anna blinked, cleared her throat, and turned to face him, surprised at his serious manner.

"First," he began, "I have made an appointment for you at my office for tomorrow afternoon." He handed Anna a business card with the time written on the back.

"I am certain you will have questions and concerns about this situation," he continued,

" I am sure this letter will answer some of those questions and, possibly, create more."

George's soft voice trembled nervously as he spoke. He withdrew a thick envelope from the inside pocket of his overcoat.

Anna received the envelope, still warm from his body heat, and saw that it was addressed to her, handwritten, but with no other information other than her name.

Before she could ask anything, George got out of the car and opened her door, saying,

"I can tell you nothing about the contents. It was given to me when Helen Dunlop made her will, with the instructions that it should be delivered into your hand if, and when, you ever arrived in Scotland and you saw the McCaig Farm House for yourself."

Chapter Thirteen

✿❀✿

Anna staggered up the carpeted stairs to her room on the second floor of the Columba Hotel and threw herself down on the bed in a state of exhaustion comprised of equal parts, fatigue, confusion, hunger and shock.

She simply did not know what to do first, but decided that food would be a necessity if she was ever to survive this day of surprises. Unable to face the thought of a meal in the hotel dining room she called reception and begged to have food delivered to her. Fortunately, the kitchen staff were agreeable to this break from tradition. No doubt they had been informed that she had travelled from Canada recently.

Waiting for the food, Anna unzipped her boots, massaged her aching feet, removed her outer clothes and wrapped a long robe around her which was retrieved from an outside pocket of her case, (Maria's advice again!). At this thought, she rummaged in her purse and found the cell phone which George had activated for her on the way to the farm house.

By sheer luck she accessed the address book on the first try and pressed Alina's number.

"Alina, it's me. I am so sorry for calling you this late."

"Thank God! We have been frantic with worry. Susan's here with me. We were just talking about you. What's been happening?"

"Alina, I don't know where to begin. Truly, I am feeling overwhelmed right now."

"Where are you, Anna?"

"I am in a hotel in Oban and I have just returned from visiting the farm house."

"Well, what did you think of it?"

"It's quite large but with only two bedrooms and the furnishings are so old!

You should see the fixtures in the washroom.....right out of a Victorian novel with a chain to pull to flush the toilet! It's miles in the country with no homes nearby as far as I could see. I only had a rushed look around, but it's positively primitive, Alina!"

"Oh dear! That doesn't sound good. What will you do?"

"I haven't a clue! I am supposed to be here for two months but I can't see how I can live there for that length of time. My plans might have to be changed."

"Of course! You must do whatever seems right for you."

"Let me speak to Susan for a minute, Alina."

"Hi Anna! Great to hear from you. How can I help?"

"Susan, I have just been handed an envelope with a letter from Helen Dunlop which I was to receive only if I came to see the farm house."

"Ah! That's interesting! What does it say?"

"That's the problem, Susan. I don't know if I can cope with any more today. I haven't even opened it yet."

"Well, I can understand why not. You do sound tired, Anna. Perhaps you should sleep on it and see what tomorrow brings. You can call me and we'll discuss the contents after you've had some rest. How does that sound to you?"

"It sounds like the best advice I've had in days, Susan. Trust you to put me back on track.

I am going to have a meal now and go right to sleep. I'll call you in the afternoon. That will be the morning for you, I think."

"Don't worry, Anna. It will all work out as it's supposed to. Take your time and take care of you."

"Thanks, Susan. Give Alina a hug for me and please tell the others what's been happening."

"I will. Talk to you tomorrow. We are all thinking of you. Bye for now!"

Anna woke with the morning light shining on her face and the cries of seagulls echoing through the room. She sat up, stretched, and threw off the covers to find she was still wearing the robe from the night before.

The open window looked out from the back of the hotel which was on a pier surrounded on three sides by sparkling blue water. An incongruous, red-roofed building blocked some of the view, but she could see an island not too far away and the misty outline of another, larger island in the distance. A few boats bobbed near the pier and a larger craft was approaching, escorted by the circle of seagulls that must have woken her.

Nothing else moved as far as she could see.

What time is it, she wondered? It took a minute to find her watch and confirm the time shown on the bedside clock/radio. It was just after 6:30am.

All at once, memory rushed back and she recalled the decisions that awaited her on this first full day in Oban.

What would she do with the farm house?

What was in the letter George had given her?

What facilities were available to her in this town?

Could she afford to stay on in this hotel indefinitely?

What would be required of her at George's office appointment?

How much more stress and uncertainty could she tolerate?

Her head throbbing with unanswered questions, Anna felt

her shoulders slump as she dropped down onto the bed in despair. This day was not beginning well.

A blast of cool, fresh air with the salt tang of the sea reached her nostrils from the window, and finally breathed new life into her brain.

"Hold on a minute!" she told herself, "This is supposed to be an adventure. Nothing this promising has happened to me in decades. Here I am in the middle of a mystery and I am already thinking negatively. Susan would say I am undermining myself before I even start!"

The mention of Susan's name reminded Anna of her promise to call later this afternoon.

The thought of reporting to the analytical Susan galvanized her into action.

Looking around the room she saw clearly the results of the distracted state of mind she had been in the night before. The supper tray with remnants of food still lay on the floor near the bed and clothing was scattered all over the room.

"Maria would be appalled at the way I have treated my new clothes," she lectured herself.

Collecting the discarded clothing and hanging it up in the large, dark-wood wardrobe whose style matched all the other old furniture in the high-ceilinged room, restored her sense of order. She was unsure whether or not to unpack her cases but decided to retrieve just a change of clothes for now and stow the cases out of the way. The food tray went outside the door in a moment.

A clearer floor space seemed to promote a clearer mind and Anna found it easier to see the next step.

The adjoining white-tiled washroom was spacious, if a trifle cold, and Anna found she had unpacked her toothbrush and shampoo at some point in the previous night, so she started the shower over the roll-topped bath and carefully stepped inside.

The warm water was soothing. By the time she emerged,

some of that negativity had washed away and her attitude, as well as the weather outside, seemed to have improved.

Dressed in her raincoat over a black skirt and sweater, Anna tiptoed downstairs determined to survey the town before she tackled any of the other demands on her mental list. She took Helen's letter and slipped it into her purse for later. She would start with the easier stuff first.

The hotel was either empty of travellers or full of late sleepers. There was no one to be seen, and only the distant sound of dishes being set on tables in the breakfast room proved there was a living soul around.

Once outside the heavy hotel entrance door with its stained glass panel of a seascape, the world came alive in sound and sight.

Anna was looking at a little sandy beach only a few metres from where she stood. Beyond that, across the water to her right was the hive of activity of the rail and ship terminal where she had arrived only a few hours before. This pier dwarfed the one on which her hotel stood and even at this early hour there were cranes unloading goods and fish, and train carriages were being shunted from line to line. She could see a queue of passengers forming beside one of the buildings near a waiting ship.

Turning her head to the left again she saw a row of stores across the street from the beach but before she could grasp any further details her eyes were drawn to the steep hillside above the seafront.

Atop ranks of stately, granite-grey homes interspersed with trees and shrubs, stood a structure that would not have looked out of place in Rome. Like a tiara on the skyline above the town, the tiers of arched shapes formed a coliseum-like image that had to be the most unexpected item in what looked to Anna to be a traditional, small Scottish town.

The laughter that exploded from her mouth at this thought, released the stress she had been carrying better than anything else could have done.

"I think I am going to enjoy this place!" she chuckled. "Someone here has a sense of humour, that's for sure!! I will climb that hill and find out about it as soon as I can."

Still smiling, Anna marched briskly forward to explore while the streets were quiet.

She breathed deeply and drew the crisp, clear air into her lungs. She could feel energy flowing into her and suddenly she saw positives rather than negatives around her.

A nearby Bank of Scotland reminded her to open an account and deposit the money orders that were locked in her suitcase. The store windows along the main street gave her ideas about soft furnishings to improve the farm house. Another store, strangely titled 'Ironmonger', held a wide range of useful electrical goods and supplies for the household.

A display of heavy sweaters in one window drew her attention. These were the famous Aran knitwear which looked appropriate for fishermen out at sea, but the window also contained a pair of knee-length, green, rubber boots that Anna considered might be more suitable for country living than the delicate footwear she currently possessed.

She had not found a grocery store, but she passed a newsagent with papers, magazines and supplies like milk and juice. That's like our corner stores in Canada, she guessed.

The main street along which she was walking turned out to be named George Street and this reminded her of her appointment at noon with George McLennan. She found the solicitors' office above a Chemist shop that looked like a drug store to Anna and made a mental note of how long it would take her to get there from the hotel.

George Street was now busy with traffic and she observed that it was a one-way street, suggesting that another street somewhere must lead in the opposite direction.

The decision on whether or not to drive in Scotland was already made. Anna had been alarmed at the speed of drivers in Glasgow but after her experience on the country roads last evening with George, she knew she would be too nervous to compete with these drivers even if she could afford the prices for hired cars. She would have to find another way to get around.

Almost without noticing it, Anna was beginning to plan how she would live in the McCaig Farm House. She stopped abruptly in the street and tried to figure out how she had managed such a complete change of opinion from the night before.

Could it be that sleep and a little exercise in the fresh air had effected such a transformation? Or was it possible that this quaint little town in this gorgeous setting between the mountains and the sea, had spun a web around her in some mystical way?

The appetizing smell of frying bacon assailed her nostrils from a nearby restaurant full of early customers. There is nothing like hunger to bring one back to reality, she thought, with a smile at the evident enjoyment of the customers seated inside.

Breakfast awaited at the hotel and it was going to be a busy day requiring serious caloric fortifying. One thing Anna knew for sure from her parents, was that Scottish breakfasts were substantial and not to be rushed.

Pushing aside one of the largest china plates she had ever seen, Anna settled back in her padded chair by the hotel window and poured a second, or was it a third, cup of steaming hot tea. The dining room was not full and procuring a table with a ground-level view of the pier had not been difficult. None of the tables near her was occupied.

"I think I am ready for this now," she murmured to herself, as she placed the envelope from Helen Dunlop on the tablecloth in front of her.

There was no point in delaying any further, so she slit the

envelope with a knife and saw two documents slide out. One of these was sealed and addressed to George McLennan.

The other was the letter from Helen.

Anna's fingers quivered as she unfolded the letter. The mystery of Helen Dunlop's connection to Anna Mason was about to be revealed.

Dear Anna,

This letter will come as a shock. I apologise for the secrecy that accompanies it.

I am your aunt, half-sister to your mother Marion Jarvis McLeod. My birth name is Aileen Anne Wilson and my adopted name you know.

My childhood was unhappy, resulting in an early marriage to Harold Fraser.

When my husband died, I had the financial resources to move away from Stirling leaving behind a life and its sad memories.

My years at the Farm House near Oban were the happiest I ever knew.

I sought you out in the hope that you, also, might relish the peace and serenity of its country setting.

There are no conditions. The property is yours to dispose of in whatever manner you may deem suitable to your circumstances.

I wish you, my only remaining female relative, joy and happiness.
Sincerely,
Helen Dunlop.
Postscript: Should you decide to stay in the McCaig Farm House, please visit The Osborne Residential Home. The manageress will expect you.

What a strange, sad letter, thought Anna. I don't know what I expected but this is a shock, indeed.

She read the letter again and found her tears blurring the careful writing.

So little information and so much left unsaid. The mystery

of Helen's life was solved, but only partially. More questions were raised than answered.

What had happened during that early marriage to make Helen leave her home and move to a remote farm house? Why had she left behind her married name of Fraser? How did she find out about my family in Canada? What must her life have been like?

Sitting in silence, contemplating the brief letter in her hands, Anna could distil only one concrete thing from Helen's letter. The house was where Helen had been happy and she wished Anna to know that same happiness. How could she ignore this request?

The negative feelings of the previous day dissolved in the more positive atmosphere created by Anna's early morning discoveries.

"I must give it a try!" she whispered to the letter. "I'll start planning today, Helen. Thank you for your generosity."

She bent forward and, in an act created by a sudden wave of emotion, she gently kissed the letter before placing it back in the envelope.

Chapter Fourteen

✦✦✦

George's office was one of a suite, guarded by a formidable-looking older lady at a desk replete with In trays and Out files and at least three telephones.

Anna was reminded of Susan's former job and knew how many responsibilities she had managed for her bosses. In an earlier conversation Anna had told Susan of Helen's brief letter and outlined her tentative plans for the day. Now it was time to tie up a few loose ends with George.

As she walked into his small office, lit by a window at the back of the building, looking out on a tiny concrete parking lot, she could see George's somewhat-battered Ford alongside a red sports car and a shiny, silver Subaru.

"How are you feeling this morning, Anna? Is it permissible to call you Anna? I had the feeling you were not too happy with me last night."

Anna turned from the window to see George entering the office with an anxious expression clouding his handsome young face.

"Forgive me, George," she rushed to apologize. "I had a lot to think about last night. We are certainly first-name friends, and I am more than grateful for all you have done to make it possible for me to be here today in this amazing country."

"Ah! So you like our wee town?"

"It is so beautiful, George. The hills and the sea are quite spectacular. I had no idea it was like this. Maps and Google do not do it justice, let me tell you."

"Can I take it, then, from your enthusiasm, that you are thinking of staying for a while?" To Anna, George sounded quite keen on an affirmative answer.

"Before I answer that question, George, I need to ask your help again to make some necessary arrangements."

"Of course, Anna, I am at your disposal."

"Now, that sounds more like the gentleman who wrote to me in Canada and to whom I spoke on the phone!" she exclaimed in delight.

Anna had wondered why George's speech when face to face was so different from the formal language of his legal correspondence.

George blushed slightly and the colour rose through his fair skin. "The blame must be laid at the feet of Mrs. Aitken, our secretary, I am afraid. She is most particular about a professional manner of speech and literacy and as I am the youngest member of the firm, I am obliged to follow her rules. I hope I did not mislead you in any way."

"Not at all, George! At the risk of embarrassing you further, I have to say that I am very fond of your lovely Scottish accent, although it may not be typical. I have noticed a wide range of accents in this area already."

"We are not as isolated here as we once were, Anna. You will find folk here from all over nowadays. I'm sure there are staff people in your hotel from Sweden, Germany and Poland as well as most parts of the Highlands."

"Well, I am happy I am not the only 'foreigner' around! But that reminds me, George, there are a number of accounts I need to settle right now."

Anna produced a sheaf of bills and handed over the

international money order she had brought for this purpose, made out to George, in person. He seemed relieved.

"Please check these totals, George. You have undertaken quite a lot of expense on my behalf. I have been to the bank this morning and deposited more money orders but I understand I can't make withdrawals on the account until five days have passed and my information can be verified."

"That is correct. Do you have sufficient funds for the time being, Anna?"

"Yes, I came supplied with a variety of financial sources, thanks to the good advice of friends."

A memory of sitting in Bev's kitchen flashed past Anna's mind, accompanied, unexpectedly, by a wave of nostalgia. What was a Samba minus an A for Anna, she thought briefly?

"What else can I do for you? You mentioned some additional help?"

"Yes. I hope you can supply some local information for me. I have made a number of purchases this morning and I need a hired car, a van or taxi, with storage room, to collect these things and take me out to the farm."

"I would be happy to help with that.........."

"No, no, George! I can't impose on your generosity any further. I am sure I have distracted you from your business quite long enough. If you can recommend someone reliable I will probably use them fairly frequently as I am not intending to hire, or buy, a car."

"I can do that right away, Anna. Can I presume from this that you will be staying for a time?"

"I am hoping to do so, George, and that brings me to a very important subject of interest to both of us. I mean, of course, Helen Dunlop's letter."

Anna could detect an immediate change in George's posture. Clearly, he was as eager to learn about Helen as she, herself, had been. In fact, George had initiated the entire search for Helen's connection to Anna.

"The envelope you gave me last night, contained two items," she continued, "a letter for each of us."

Anna reached across the desk and gave George his letter which he received with some surprise and then placed in a drawer, turning his attention to Anna once again.

"Helen's letter to me establishes the link to my family through my mother, as you may have guessed, George. It also mentions a marriage that Helen left behind her, in Stirling when her husband died. After that event, she bought the farm house."

"I never knew about that. She never mentioned a husband to me in any of our discussions." George's shock was evident at this unexpected news. Anna could almost see his lawyer's brain calculating the legal repercussions on Helen Dunlop's estate, of an undeclared family.

"I know nothing about this man, Harold Fraser, from Helen's letter, George, but, if I can presume upon your kindness again and ask you to use your sources to find out more about this marriage, I would be in your debt once again."

"Absolutely! As executor of Helen's will it is my duty to follow this lead Anna. I will be in touch as soon as I have any information."

"Right!" Standing and stretching her back, Anna remembered one more request.

"This is somewhat of an anti-climax, George, but I could not find a grocery store this morning. Where do people buy their food around here?"

"Oh, you would not have seen it from the seafront. We have a very large Tesco store hidden behind the main streets. Anything you need can be found there. My wife, Jeanette, won't shop anywhere else although we live outside Oban. Oh, I almost forgot. Jeanette would be very annoyed with me if I don't invite you to have a meal with us as soon as you are settled in."

"How kind of her, and of you, George. Please thank her for me."

After a moment's thought, George added, "May I suggest you make your way to Tesco and select your supplies and I will send a taxi to pick you up and take you to the farm after collecting your other purchases? You will need your receipts, of course."

"Excellent idea, George! I have already checked out of the hotel and my luggage is stored there for me."

"I'll just pop down and fetch the farm house key for you and point out the way to the store."

Anna found the Tesco grocery store without difficulty. The large parking lot was filled with cars at this hour of the morning and Anna followed the shoppers into a store that compared favourably in size to one of Loblaw's Super Stores in Canada.

Since her earlier shopping had taken place along George Street where the small shops were more similar to the older parts of Toronto, she was amazed to discover such a large modern convenience lurking behind the traditional facade of the town.

The next hour passed pleasantly as she filled a shopping cart with a variety of goods, some recognizably Canadian and others British in style. She tried to find a selection of food items to stock the farm house kitchen although she was unsure about cooking and refrigeration facilities there.

It was obvious to Anna that trips to the grocery store in Oban would be occasional rather than the simple daily task she did not need to give much thought to at home.

The cart soon filled with the basics plus a number of things Anna was pleased to see, as they jogged her memory regarding the inadequacies she had noted in the quick tour of the farm house. Matches and candles, a couple of soft pillows, a rain hat similar to a Nova Scotia sou'wester, a package of household rubber gloves for cleaning jobs and a selection of lamp shades were piled onto the cart. When she could no longer see over it, she knew it was time to struggle to the check-out.

She paid with the Visa card she had obtained especially for expenses in Scotland.

She considered that it was a wonder the card was not hot to the touch after the number of times she had used it already this morning. Bev would need to be warned about the size of this bill.

Anna calculated that the cost of the groceries, converted to dollars, was not much more than she would have been charged for a similar expedition in Canada. Tesco's was following a North American policy of charging for plastic grocery bags, so Anna took the opportunity to purchase some of their own huge, colourful, inexpensive bags, labelled 'Bag For Life' with a promise written on them that they would be replaced for free if they ever tore or wore through.

Although she was buying more plastic, Anna consoled herself with the thought that the bags could be taken back to Canada with her as a souvenir.

She made a mental note not to leave the farm without one of these bags in future as they might have a number of uses.

Emerging from Tesco's, Anna scanned the parking lot for a cab. Unlike Canada, taxis in Scotland often seemed to be private cars with a phone number painted on the side, making them harder to spot. She pushed the laden cart along the store forecourt and searched for a likely vehicle among the ranks of parked cars and trucks.

Near the exit doors she spotted a woman carrying a cardboard sign with 'Mason' printed on it. Thankful that George had been thinking ahead, Anna rolled over to the woman and noticed that although she was young, and small in stature, she looked strong and capable.

Introductions were soon made and Anna shook hands with Fiona Jameson ("Jist call me Fee, everyone does!"), confirming her observation that this was a powerful young lady, if her handshake was anything to go by.

"Right, Fee! As you can see, I have a big load here and more to come from places in the town. I hope you have a sizable vehicle?"

"No worries, there! Mr. McLennan told me what was needed. I have a People Mover waiting. Stay here and I'll drive up to you."

With that she was off with a swing of a brown pony-tail and a blue car coat over jeans, leaving Anna with a reassuring impression of confidence and strength.

That impression was confirmed in the first two hours of Anna's acquaintance with the formidable Fee. Not only did she do a fine job of packing Anna's groceries into the back seat of what turned out to be a type of sports utility vehicle, but she managed to find space for two cases and assorted bags from the hotel and still have sufficient cargo room for the variety of goods Anna had selected and paid for, earlier in the day.

In order to access the local stores on the one-way street, Fee had to drive from the Columba Hotel along a road that skirted the sea, giving Anna the chance to admire the view in more detail. Fee's services now included tour guide, and she happily informed Anna that they were on the Corran Esplanade, looking over the Sound of Kerrera, (not the open sea at all), towards the small Island of Kerrera where Anna could see a harbour and only one or two cottages on the shoreline.

The Esplanade passed shops, a hotel, a fine church and a row of elegant houses with boards advertising B&B facilities, then looped through a forested section to arrive at the north end of George Street.

It appeared that cars were permitted to steer from one side of this street to the other and park there at will, as long as they moved in one forward direction. Watching these manoeuvres, Anna was glad she had made the decision to leave the driving to someone else. After only a short period of time in Fiona's capable hands, she could not have been more delighted that George had selected Fee as the candidate.

On the way back to the McCaig Farm House, Anna was able to see the countryside in all its splendour and with Fee's local knowledge, she gathered valuable information.

It seemed there were no villages in the area. Fee declared they had faded away when the post offices were removed.

"You will find a crofter or two nearby for emergencies," Fee volunteered, "I'll be stopping at their cottages on the way back and I'll be telling them they have a new neighbour now."

Fervently hoping no emergencies would arise in this isolated place, Anna smiled in gratitude. She was glad to see Fee's driving was rather more sedate than George's frantic pace, but then she realized the weight of her purchases would undoubtedly cause the large automobile to move more slowly, especially when they reached the unpaved track, of about a kilometre in length, that led to the farm house.

By the time they arrived, rain had started. When Anna commented on the beautiful weather at the start of the day, Fee's response was; "The old folks say, 'Bright too early in the day means rain's on its way.' It's spring after all. We'll get plenty rain this month and through the next."

"Well, I won't mind," replied Anna. "In Canada we still have snow until May most years and rain does not have to be shovelled out of your way."

Anna took the heavy key out of her purse and managed, with some twisting and turning, to open the door so that cases and bags could be stowed in the porch. She found the gravel path from the front gate was difficult to walk on when carrying heavy loads.

It took a number of trips back and forth to unload the SUV and at least one of the pair of women was tired when the last of the grocery bags landed on the kitchen table.

Anna could see Fee's curious glances at the kitchen.

"Would you like to take a look around the house?" Anna asked. "I would love to offer you a cup of tea but I am not entirely sure how that could be done."

"I've never been in this house before," Fee confessed. "It used to be the old estate manager's place, is that not so? I didn't know the lady who lived here. She kept herself to herself, as they say. Mr. McLennan asked me to give you a hand in any way I could, so if you show me around a bit, maybe I can help you out."

"O, Fee! I was hoping you would say that. The truth is I'm a fish out of water here.

I have no idea how to run a house like this and I would really appreciate some tips."

Turning to the massive stone fireplace dominated by a black metal stove of some kind, Anna begged, "What on earth do I do with this beast for example?"

"Now, that's a good question," replied Fee with a skeptical look at the structure.

"I've heard my Granny talk about these but I've never ever seen one. As far as I know, this is your cooker and heat source, Ms. Mason, and likely it heats water for you too. Hang on a minute and I'll call my granny and ask her."

Flipping open a cell phone, Fee conducted a conversation which was completely unintelligible to Anna. Fee was, apparently, a Gaelic speaker. This young woman's talents had no end, it seemed.

"Granny says if you pull down a shelf at the centre front you'll see a space for a fire but she says don't start that until you have a goodly supply of firewood on hand. These old stoves use up a lot and have to be banked down overnight as well."

"Good God!" exclaimed Anna, in some distress, "What on earth have I let myself in for!"

"Ach! Don't worry yourself, Ms. Mason. The worst of the

winter's over and these walls are good and thick. We'll take a look around and see what's what."

With this reassurance that she was not entirely alone, Anna conducted Fee around the house and discovered, with two pairs of eyes at work, that there were many aspects to this house that she had missed on the first occasion.

There was a door on the back wall that led out of the kitchen and into a low room with stone floor and benches and no windows. It exited into the back garden but was empty of any clue as to its purpose.

Fee, however, took one look and stated with conviction, "That's your refrigerator!

This used to be a milk parlour where cream and butter were made and stored."

"Well, it's certainly cold enough," said Anna with a shiver, "Let's go back inside."

They took a quick look at the sitting room, which Fee declared to be, "a fine big room with a fire laid in the grate ready to be lit."

This reminded Anna that George had mentioned the chimneys had been swept recently.

Fee received this news with approval and said, "We just have to find some firewood and you'll be comfy tonight, for sure."

Anna was doubtful if 'comfy' was achievable at all, but she followed Fee upstairs and into the main bedroom.

"Another fireplace ready to be lit, and I'll bet there's a cedar closet in here with bedding and household linens."

Fee moved confidently to a door near the front window and opened it to display the top section of the tower entrance; a square room lined with fragrant cedar wood.

Anna attempted to follow her and was reminded, forcibly, that her greater height would have to be considered in any part, other than the centre, of this bedroom, because of the steep roof line.

Seeing the sheets and blankets folded neatly on the

shelves, Anna suddenly thought, with horror, that she had no method of washing and drying anything. The kitchen had no modern appliances.

Fee noticed the expression on Anna's face and enquired the reason. She immediately asked to see the bathroom and once inside, pointed to the ceiling above the bath where Anna could see what looked like a bundle of wooden sticks suspended from rope.

"That's how you'll have to dry clothes when the weather's bad," announced Fee.

"On better days you can dry things outdoors of course."

Somehow Anna did not find this information reassuring. She thought longingly of the heated basement laundry room in her London apartment building, maintained immaculately by Joseph.

One thing I know, she promised herself, if I survive this experience, I will never take modern conveniences for granted again.

Fee showed Anna where the rope for the drying rack was wound round a brass hook on the wall then she pulled the chain and flushed the toilet to check if it was working.

"That's good!" she declared. "The water's running clear. Sometimes the well water gets brown from the peat up on the hills."

Anna did not dare to ask about peat, or well water. She had enough worries for now.

A quick inspection of the smaller bedroom drew the response from Fee that it might be the best choice for the night as it was a small space and more easily heated.

"But, won't I need fuel before I can think about staying here?" asked Anna.

"I had a wee look out the back when we were in the bathroom," Fee replied. "There's a shed out there in the garden. I'll go and have a peek inside."

While Fee explored outside, Anna searched through her shopping bags for a purchase from the ironmongers, which had turned out to be a useful hardware store. She found the electric kettle and plugged it in, hoping the current was sufficient to boil water for tea.

By the time Fee arrived back with an armload of sticks she had kept dry under her coat, Anna had spread a feast out on the table, using the willow pattern dishes from the shelves in the kitchen. These had been thoroughly wiped with a clean dish towel she had rescued from the cedar closet.

"The shed's full of dry peat and wood," Fee announced, "and there's even a bag of coal! I found the key inside the larder. You'll be snug as a bug in a rug," she chuckled as she dropped her load on the stone hearth.

"Sit down and have something to eat before you go, Fee. I have bread and cheese, cookies and cakes and the tea's coming shortly."

"My! Oh, my! It's a party!" Fee responded with delight. "First, I'll just away up the stairs and start the fire in the small bedroom. It'll be nicely warmed up by the time you go to bed."

"You're a treasure Fiona!" called out Anna with heartfelt sincerity. For the first time since arriving in Oban, she felt it could be possible to live in this house, at least long enough to determine what she would do with it eventually.

Anna and Fee devoured sandwiches and cake and found out more about each other in the process. Fee revealed that her taxi services were to be charged to George McLennan and he would pass the bill to Anna at the end of the month. Anna agreed with this, provided Fee billed her for the hours spent, rather than the mileage alone. Another ride into Oban was arranged for two days hence, giving Anna a chance to settle in and inspect her property.

"You have been invaluable, Fee," said Anna, as the two went to the front door to say goodbye. "See you soon!"

Watching the big black car disappear down the lane, Anna felt the silence descend on her.

This was real country, she thought. No one around, and no

sounds other than wind in the stand of fir trees near the farm house.

It's time to check in with Canada she decided. They won't believe how much I have accomplished today, but I won't tell them everything ....not just yet anyway.

By the time she had spoken briefly to Alina and been told to re-charge her cell phone by Bev, (on James' prompting), the fatigue of a very eventful day was beginning to have its effects on Anna's energy level.

She summoned up the strength to take firewood upstairs and drape sheets over the end of the bed so they could be aired out a bit. She boiled the kettle again and used the hot water to wash dishes in the deep sink Fee had described as "a Belfast sink, an old style that's very popular again", then she placed the milk cartons, cheese and butter and other perishables into her storage pantry, or larder, in the adjacent cold room.

Unpacking other purchases, she took up soft pillows and a new blanket for the bed.

After she had hauled her luggage upstairs, (was it possible the cases were getting heavier each time she moved them?) she arranged toiletries in the chilly bathroom then realized it would be more practical to wash in the kitchen for now, so she could use the kettle for hot water.

This decision necessitated another trip down the stairs where she found her new towels and the candles in candle-holders which would sit on the bedside table when she went to bed. The timely purchase of a torch would serve as illumination on the staircase for now. The bare electric light bulbs were giving harsh, dim light only. Anna considered candle light would be more fitting in this house and certainly more flattering to her surroundings.

On the final trip upstairs with doors locked and secured, Anna could feel the strain in her knees from the unaccustomed climbing. I had better plan ahead to reduce these hikes from one floor to another or my legs will not cope for much longer, she predicted.

The bedroom was gently lit by candlelight and by the glow from the fire. A pleasant scent suffused the air from both sources as Anna slid thankfully between the warmed sheets, rested her head on the soft pillows and pulled the blanket over her.

In seconds she was fast asleep.

Chapter Fifteen

✿❀✿

Anna was momentarily disoriented when she awoke in a strange bed, in a strange room, but she soon shook off the feeling when she remembered how the same confusion of the day before in the Oban hotel had been strictly temporary.

Thinking of how much she had accomplished in that one day, Anna was proud of herself.

What a productive day! George's office, Helen's letter, shopping in Oban, meeting Fee, exploring the house and settling in to some degree at least....it was all very positive and exciting.

"And what will this day bring, Helen?"

Speaking her name out loud brought Anna to the realization that she was finally here, in Scotland, in Helen Dunlop's house, as Helen had wished. Although there was little to tell Anna about Helen's character or personality in these surroundings, she knew that her aunt had been a determined woman with a purposeful plan she had put carefully in place with George's help. How Helen had known about Anna and about her circumstances as a single woman, was a mystery still.

"Well, Helen! Here I am, right where you wanted me to

be. I am making no promises about how long I will stay, but I do promise to enjoy this adventure as much as I possibly can. Oh! and thank you, Aunt Helen!"

Anna surprised herself with this declaration. She was not superstitious, and yet, it was as if any shadows had fled from the farm house now that she had acknowledged her debt to the former owner.

Throwing off the bedcovers, Anna went to the window to look out on the day.

The morning light was slanting across the front yard and from the movement of the bushes by the fence, it seemed to be a windy day.

Anna thought Fee was right about the thickness of the walls as she could not yet hear the wind. The fire had burned to ash overnight leaving the room cool. Anna was glad of the slippers and flannel pyjamas she had purchased the day before.

Standing there in the funny little window that projected forward, Anna felt the relief of a day with no pressing agenda. For what seemed like the first time in months, she had nowhere special to be, and nothing urgent to do.

"Today, I shall explore my estate!" she declared out loud.

This thought brought laughter with it and Anna found that her more relaxed attitude gave her the courage to tackle the icy antique bathroom with more confidence and then skip downstairs to the kitchen which was much less intimidating in the morning light.

I won't tackle you yet, she decided as she looked at the monster stove, but I will check out all the cupboards in here as soon as I have made some instant coffee.

Retrieving a carton of cream from the adjoining cold room, she boiled water and spooned coffee crystals into the biggest cup she could find. As it cooled, she began to open any low, cupboard doors previously unexplored.

There was only a small amount of countertop on either side of the huge sink. On the left there was a draining board and on the right just about a half metre of a dark slate countertop matching the slate floors in both the kitchen and front porch.

Under the left side were two open shelves bare of contents, but the right side revealed treasures behind an unpainted wooden door. A small electric hot plate with two burners was stashed at the back. While this would be an outdoor camping item in Canada, Anna was delighted to find it here and promptly fetched a milk carton from her pantry,

(a shivery cold place this morning), and scrambled a couple of eggs. She also retrieved from the same cupboard a metal device that toasted bread, although it was not like any electric toaster Anna had ever seen before. The side grills flopped down flat and had to be fastened at the top once the bread was placed inside. The metal surfaces became very hot but the toasted bread popped out efficiently when it was done and Anna promptly scoffed two slices, dripping with butter and ginger marmalade.

"I must be getting used to these hearty Scottish breakfasts," she told herself, with some amusement. "I never eat this much in the mornings at home."

One problem became evident during the making of breakfast. The kitchen had only one electrical outlet. This obliged Anna to plan meal preparation with military precision.

The cell phone re-charger with its adaptor had to be unplugged first before the kettle could be plugged into the socket; then the hotplate could be used to cook eggs and keep coffee warm, and finally the toaster could take its turn.

The cell phone lying on the kitchen table reminded Anna of James' instructions to turn the phone on at noon each day so she could receive calls from Canada. In all the moving around she had been doing, Anna had neglected to do this. No doubt this would account for the panic calls she had received from Susan and Alina.

Switching on the phone, she waited to see if a service provider could reach her.

In a moment or two, Orange came online with a cheery signal followed by a series of 'pings' to announce missing messages. Anna was not at all sure how to retrieve these messages but she could predict they were from her friends in Canada, so she decided to call everyone as soon as it was a reasonable hour in Ontario and reassure them of her survival.

Meantime, there were things to do. Leaving the dishes soaking in the sink, (who will see them?), she ran upstairs and riffled through the railing in the cedar closet looking for suitable clothing for country explorations. She found the sweatsuit she had thrown into her case at the last minute and realized this was going to be the most useful clothing item she had brought with her.

In the entrance porch by the front door she donned a thick pair of socks and the green rubber boots the assistant in the ironmongers had declared, "The very thing to wear in any season, lass. The Queen herself wears them at Balmoral Castle."

"Impressive to be sharing footwear styles with the Queen," chuckled Anna.

Her lined raincoat and hood with the addition of the new sou'wester hat tied under her chin, should keep out all possible weather conditions.

The key that locked both front and back doors was large and heavy, so Anna hid it under a packet of pasta in the former milk parlour, now a useful pantry, and escaped, unfettered, into the garden through the pantry's side exit door.

Facing her was a high hedge matching a similar hedge on the left side of the garden. Obviously, both were designed to keep out the worst of wind and rain.

In front of this was a pole, firmly dug into the ground, with a rope attached to a hook near the top. Several yards away a matching pole challenged Anna's curiosity.

"Ah, I know what you are!" she declared, "You're a clothes line for fine weather."

Reassured by finding something she recognized, Anna

gazed around the garden and soon spotted the shed holding firewood and coal. A slate roof kept rain from this small wooden hut which had been built on a flat stone base. I must bring two of those grocery bags here, she noted. They'll make carrying fuel much easier.

Stone seemed to be in good supply in this garden. It was bounded by a stone wall of about a metre high on the north side, where the hill that commanded the view from every window at the back of the house reared up into the sky.

Large stones were dotted around the yard but appeared to be in their natural places rather than arranged by a gardener. The flatter stones formed a broken pathway across a tufted grass area towards the iron gate in the stone wall. Anna noticed part of this wall had fallen into the yard leaving a gap and showing her that the construction had been done without any bonding substance such as mortar. How will I fix that? she puzzled.

It was clear that this garden had been neglected since the departure of Helen Dunlop.

Stakes projected from overgrown beds near the sheltering hedges but whatever had been planted there once, was now unknowable.

Anna walked over to a tall tree that had been visible from the sitting room's rear window but she could not identify the species despite the green leaves sprouting from every branch. Searching the house for tree and plant books was becoming a necessity.

"Now where would Helen keep things like tools and spades and perhaps a wheelbarrow?" she wondered aloud.

Following the path down to the gate, Anna looked over towards the east side of the property that lay between the garden and the invisible stream or burn that George had said comprised the border of her land. A sizable, barn-like building stood facing her about twenty metres from the garden and another thirty metres to the east.

Anna opened the barred gate and found a track worn through the low grass leading toward the barn.

As soon as she left the shelter of the garden, the wind whistled around her, finding its way through her coat and under her hat with its chilly fingers.

"Wow!" she exclaimed, "I wasn't expecting that!" She tied the cords of her hood more firmly over both head and hat and breathed in the bracing air.

Anna decided to follow an impulse and see how far up the imposing hill she could climb.

Exploring the barn could be left for another day as she would first have to find the key to the padlock that secured the doors.

"I can't bear to go back indoors yet. This is too much fun!"

Near the barn, Anna found another track veering off from the first, and heading for the hill or mountain. Anna did not know the correct designation or name, and added this unknown item to the growing list of things she would soon have to find out about.

Striding out with energy and purpose, she climbed the first stretch easily, thanks to the stones that had been placed over the wet ground at the base of the slope. Someone must have climbed here before, she realised. I wonder if it was Helen?

Soon the boggy ground gave way to the shrubby, brown bushes that covered the lower parts of most of the hills Anna had seen in Scotland. Fee had told her this was bracken or gorse and it would transform into green and yellow before long.

The track was veering east and skirted large rocks from time to time. After about twenty minutes, Anna sat down on one of these to catch her breath.

The vista that met her eyes caused Anna to gasp in surprise. Already, the farm house below could be seen in its entirety from the line of fir trees on the west right over to the stream on the east. Anna was reminded of the aerial photograph George had sent to her.

The steep pitch of the farm house roof completely obscured the details of the building from here, but everything, including the fence at the roadside, was so much a part of the landscape of rough stone and woody tones interspersed with vibrant green boggy stretches and tufts of wild grasses, that Anna was struck by the natural way all of it blended together.

She could not wait to climb higher still, despite the caution in the back of her mind that her legs might not be up to the strain. "I'll rest later," she promised herself as she faced the sloping path once more.

Strangely, the wind was not so powerful at this height. Searching for a cause for this, Anna saw that a vertical outcrop of mossy rock projecting from the hillside to her right, was providing a welcome wind barrier.

By the time Anna reached the top of the hill she was using her hands to pull herself up by grasping rocks along the track and she was feeling the heat of exertion. Determination drove her up the last rough stretch with the thought of a rest at the summit and a view which must, surely, be worth the effort.

The first shock was the return of the wind. As she stood up, the blast cooled the sweat on her forehead and caused her to quickly refasten the coat she had loosened minutes earlier.

The second surprise was that she was not facing a hilltop with a slope descending rapidly on the opposite side from the farm house, but, instead, the land dipped down smoothly into a hollow where a pool of water reflected the blue sky, then reared up to new heights that could not have been seen from lower down.

In fact, Helen's Hill, as she now labelled it in her mind, was only the first in a range of hills that continued north into the distance.

From this elevation she could see far below to the tree clad lower slopes of this range and to the rugged landscape scattered here and there with the white dots of sheep. There were no dwellings within sight, although what might be the ruined walls of old cottages jutted out of their grassy graves in a few places.

Pulling her gaze back to the hollow below where she stood, Anna discovered the source of the stream on her property. The pool must have drained the rainfall from the surrounding heights and the overflow, which she could now see as well as hear, tumbled down the hillside to skirt the farm house and roll on until it met a lake, or loch, in the far distance.

Everywhere she turned there was a new vista. The sun was now high enough in the sky to illuminate the western reaches of the hilltop. Anna wondered what views might be awaiting her from that perspective, but she could not bear to leave the present aspect in case some glint of sun, or passing cloud cover, would reveal further unexpected splendours. Minutes went by unnoticed as she scanned the scene before her.

Finally, she sank down onto a grey giant of a rock. Resting her eyes for a moment, she noticed that the surface of the rock was patched with tiny lichens in golds and greens.

A tuft of sheep's fleece was caught in a narrow fissure where a miniature blue flower clung to life. Wonders abounded on every scale from large to small, she noted, in amazement.

From this angle she saw a human-made pile of stones below her, near the deep pool.

Remembering the custom of mountain climbers to add a stone to show others that they had reached the summit safely, she was impelled to add a stone of her own, but doubted she had the strength left to risk the further challenge.

"I will come back here again," she vowed to the wind and the sky.

Suddenly, and quite unexpectedly, Anna Mason was overwhelmed with the need to know more about Helen Dunlop.

Had she climbed up here and relished these views, adding a stone each time? Was this why she had chosen to live all alone, with private access to stunning views in her own back-yard? Was this the reason that had made her live in such a frugal way when a few dollars would have made her life more comfortable?

A strong gust of wind almost pushed Anna off her perch. She was beginning to feel the ache of over-exerted muscles. Dragging her eyes away from the view, she set off on the descent, grateful that she was not afflicted with a fear of heights.

By the time Anna had retrieved the key from its hiding place and collapsed onto a kitchen chair, her legs were shaking with exhaustion and she was feeling weak all over her body. And yet, she realized, her spirits had never soared so high in many, many years.

There was something about achieving the impossible that exhilarated her beyond the physical plane and she felt as if she had passed into a new, more positive phase of her life.

As soon as she had summoned the strength to feed herself, with an emphasis on sweet, energy-restoring treats, Anna used the cell phone.

"Hi, Alina! Yes, I have spent the first night at the farm and I just wish you could see it all, my dear, dear friend.

I know I said it was primitive, and that's true enough, but there's something about the simplicity of life here that's very appealing.

Yes, I am all alone but I have lots to do and more than lots to think about and I'm not too far from the town.

Listen! I have to tell someone! I just came back from climbing a mountain! Oh, it was just wonderful, Alina. The views were stun-ning. It's so beautiful around here you can hardly believe it.

I knew you would say that. I promise I will be careful and I will remember to take my cell phone and have the emergency numbers at the ready. Yes! I promise. Of course, it's an A Plus promise!

Don't worry! I haven't felt this good in years. It must be the air from the sea or something.

I'll talk to you soon and don't worry. Please call Simon for me and tell him I'll be in touch when I have more news about Helen.

I'm just going to check in with Bev and Susan and Maria if I can reach them. I know you'll all share the news.

Bye for now. I miss you already."

"Bev, it's me! Right, I have figured out how to use this thing, although I will need several more lessons from James before I will be a competent cell phone owner.

Did you get my message about the Visa bill? No, it will be a few more days yet until I can access my new bank account so I am relying on credit or cash for now.

I know I have spent quite a bit of money already but I am thinking ahead. If the house is to be sold, most of my purchases will add to the value, and in the meantime it is making life much more comfortable for me.

You can tell that from my voice? Absolutely! This is a fabulous adventure. I can't wait to show everything to all my Sambas. I will take lots of pictures.

Oh, I see! Long calls should be routed from Canada otherwise the cost is prohibitive.

Can you keep track of that Bev? I hope all this is not too much of an imposition. You must charge me for your time, remember.

Take care and thank James again.

Good! I'm glad my car is behaving for him.

Bye for now."

"Susan, it's Anna here. Yes, I am very well.

Bev says you should call me back right away on this number and it will be considerably cheaper for me. Keep a note of the cost at your end and I will pay for it.

Good! That works fine. Did you hear about Helen's letter? I know, I was astounded when George handed it to me! It was like a voice from beyond the grave and I just know there's lots more to the story. George is working on it for me.

Oh, he has been so helpful, Susan. I could not have managed without him. He thinks of everything.

What? He can't be more than thirty and he has a charming wife, I'm told. I am not here for romance, my friend. I am way too busy.

Well, the farm house is not quite what I expected. Do you remember the summer when we rented a cottage at the Lake, sight unseen, and it turned out to be a ramshackle wreck of a place?

Right! No, the walls and roof are intact here although the amenities leave much to be desired, but Susan, it's in the most amazing location you ever saw. I am exhausted, but enchanted also and learning every day.

Great idea! I will start a diary as soon as I get into Oban again and pick up more supplies.

Bye for now and love to all of you, two-legged and four."

You have reached Maria's Modes. Please leave a message after the beep, detailing how we can help you with your fashion needs. One of our associates will be happy to contact you as soon as possible. Press #3 for our store hours and location.

Maria, this is Anna calling from Scotland. Sorry I missed you today. This is a quick call to say I am surviving in style and will be shopping for outdoor all-weather clothing soon.

Can you imagine me climbing a mountain? Well, believe it! I did it today and it won't be the last time. Be good. Love to all the family.

Chapter Sixteen

❧

By noon the next day Anna had just about recovered from the mountain climb.

Her legs were still aching, and occasions to go upstairs were being strictly rationed, but she could stand upright for longer periods and as long as she rested her feet on a chair and cushion while seated, she was managing fairly well.

Fortunately, Fee was collecting Anna in the SUV at one o'clock and she had arranged to take Anna for lunch, so no strenuous movements were required until later in the afternoon.

Anna had longed for a hot bath to soothe her aching muscles on the previous night, but gave up the desire when she realised what would be required to fill the huge bath with water from a kettle. She compromised with a sponge bath and a foot soak then fell into bed in the larger bedroom this time, as the fire in the smaller room had not been re-set and she lacked the energy to fetch more fuel from the backyard.

Sipping a cup of tea, Anna made a mental list of all the things she needed to accomplish while in Oban. Painkiller was first on the list, then a visit to the local library was in order, after re-stocking her groceries and buying fresh vegetables.

She must investigate and see if she could buy suitable climbing boots and outdoor clothing. Maria's handsome over-coat had taken a beating on the way down Helen's Hill and the rubber boots with rigid soles were not the best solution for gripping wet, moss-covered rocks.

Another necessary item that had occurred to Anna, was a small radio. It had been ages since she had read a newspaper and knowledge of local events, as well as weather reports, would be most useful. The page of writing paper, found in a drawer in the sitting room, was rapidly filling with notes and Anna, gauging the possible costs of these items, wished she had access to her bank account. Why did it take five business days to check out her credit?

"Hallo there! Anybody home?" Fee's cheerful voice was a welcome interruption to Anna's thoughts.

"Come right in, Fee. I left the door open for you. I can't tell you how glad I am to see you."

"Oh, dear! That doesn't sound too good. Have things not been working out for you Ms. Mason?"

"No, no, that's not it at all. It's just that I am not used to so much silence, Fee.

And please call me Anna. I feel that we are friends already."

"Glad to, Ms. Anna, I mean Anna, and you look very smart in your red suit today, Ms. Mason." The laughter that ensued from this mixture of titles filled the kitchen with such pleasant sounds that Anna felt encouraged to impose on Fee's advice again.

She had been searching high and low for the key to the barn without success, and there was the problem of the stove and the hot water supply, and how she would get the break in the stone wall repaired.

Fee suggested that the key might be hidden behind a loose stone in the porch entrance. This was a favourite hiding place of old folks, according to her Granny. Sure enough, such a stone was found there and the key to the barn's padlock was revealed.

As for the stove, Fee announced that she had taken advice from her Granny on this topic and was prepared to start the monster up on their return to the farm.

"At least you'll be warm as toast tonight, Anna. There's some wild weather coming in, they say. You could also bake, if you've a mind to, or even take a bath after an hour or so to heat the boiler."

"That's music to my ears, Fee. I could wash a few things too, as well as myself."

"Good enough! We'll away to town then whenever you're ready."

Fee could not help noticing Anna's new, less-than-nimble walking style, so the first part of the drive to Oban was taken up by Anna's account of the climb up Helen's Hill.

After Fee had doled out praise and caution in equal measure, Anna asked the question that had been bothering her since their first meeting.

"Fee, I hope you don't mind my curiosity, but how does a young lady come to own a large automobile like this one, and why would you need it in this area?"

"Oh, I don't mind at all, Anna. In fact I am quite proud of my situation and glad to tell you about my plans."

As the countryside rolled past, Anna learned to her surprise how enterprising thinking could give a chance in life to a young person, even in the current global financial difficulties that must have impacted a small country like Scotland even more harshly than most.

The story that unfolded in Fee's unsentimental style revealed that she had been brought up by her grandmother after the drowning death of her father whose fishing boat capsized in a fierce storm when Fiona was only three years old.

Her mother, grieving the loss of her husband so desperately, fell ill shortly afterwards and died of, what was believed by all who knew her, to be a broken heart.

Fee and her Granny survived well together despite a lack of funds. This upbringing had supplied the girl with both a keen sense of the value of money, and an independent, self-motivating attitude toward earning it.

"You see," she continued, "I wanted my Granny to have a more comfortable old age since she had sacrificed so much to take care of me. As soon as I could, I left school and did a series of odd jobs while I looked around for something that was recession proof.

I learned from my Granny and her friends that most older people need transport at various times in their lives, so I borrowed money from a government Business Incentive program and bought this second-hand vehicle on hire purchase."

"Very impressive, Fiona!" exclaimed Anna, then added hesitantly, "May I ask how you have managed financially?"

"Well, I have a contract to do the school run for two families from north of Oban.

That pays well in term time, and I am on call at the local doctors' offices for patients that need to go to hospital for treatment as well as seniors' trips to the grocery store and so on.

I do deliveries for Oban shops also, and I share expenses with a partner who drives the taxi on overnight delivery jobs to Stirling, Glasgow or Edinburgh."

"Quite a thriving business, you have there, Fee," said Anna, with genuine admiration.

"Ach, it's good enough for the time being." Fiona shrugged her shoulders and Anna realized there was more to come.

"I discovered something about myself while driving all over the countryside. I want to qualify as a wildlife inspector for the Scottish Wildlife Federation."

"How did that come about?" Anna gasped. This young

woman was full of surprises.

"I've aye been interested in birds and animals. When you have little or no money for entertainment, watching what's around you is a good substitute. I even worked as a volunteer in the Scottish Sea Life Sanctuary, counting coastal seals, but the lonely moors and the forests attract me the most.

I often stop and walk between appointments. In only a few minutes you can be a part of the solitude. Nature is everywhere around you hereabouts. I take pictures of foxes and stoats and otters and sometimes I see the osprey catching fish in the lochs. I've sold a few photographs to tourists but I'm mainly interested in preserving the countryside and its wild nature for the future."

"From what little I have seen, Fee," responded Anna, "I can heartily agree with your ambitions, but what sort of training would you need for the wildlife work?"

"It's a two year college course in Inverness," said Fee with a lot less enthusiasm than she had shown when talking about her aspirations, "but I have to finish secondary school first. I am taking A level qualifications through the Open University. I work on my studies whenever I have the time."

Anna was stunned at the responsibilities this young woman was carrying on her slim shoulders. She felt impelled to offer her help, saying spontaneously, "I was a teacher before I retired, Fee. I don't know the Scottish curriculum, but if there's anything I can do to help you while I am here, I would feel it a privilege if you allowed me to do so."

"Ms. Mason, I mean Anna, that's uncommon kind of you, but I couldn't impose on you like that. You are here for a holiday not to work with a ...."

"Stop right there, young lady!" interrupted Anna, "I am sitting alone at night with no television and only my own thoughts for company. If you came by, I would consider it a favour. Let's have no more objections. It's a done deal. Bring your books any time you can and we'll see what can be accomplished together."

Fee opened her mouth to protest but recognising Anna's serious 'teacher voice', she decided to nod her head in grateful consent. She could not prevent a tear from sliding down her cheek, however, and although she wiped it away quickly, Anna noticed and was even more determined to help this girl whose path in life had been so difficult.

"Right then," she stated decisively, "that's settled. Now, back to business!

I think we are getting close to Oban. I have a lot of shopping to do there, but, for pity's sake, Fee, tell me what on earth the mini coliseum is doing on top of that hill!"

Laughter broke the sombre mood, and the tale of McCaig's Folly and the unknown connection to the farm house of the same name, occupied the rest of the way into town.

Anna insisted on treating Fee to lunch although it would be a fast one, as Fee had to collect children from the Rockfield Primary School at 3:30pm promptly.

Fee recommended the restaurants on the North Pier which Anna had seen when she looked out of the window from the Columba Hotel. Given the choice between pizza and seafood, Anna selected the latter as she could smell the delicious aroma of frying fish on the salt air. A winning combination, she thought, as her mouth began to water.

Fee translated the restaurant's name, *E-Eusk*, meaning simply, Fish, in Gaelic.

The fish and chips, a Scottish national dish in many opinions, was delicious, but the view from the plate glass windows of Kerrera island and the blue waters beyond, was fascinating to Anna. Fee insisted that she would have to make time to sail to Iona, the sacred isle of Christianity, and tour some of the beauty spots in the area before she went back to Canada.

"Stop in at the Tourist Information Centre on Tweedale Street," she suggested.

"They will give you plenty of ideas. If you wait there

when you have finished shopping, I can pick you up, as it's close to George Street."

Feeling revitalized after an excellent lunch, Anna waved goodbye to Fee and set off on her shopping expedition. Now that she had a better idea of the town's facilities she could find what she needed more quickly. This left time for a visit to the town's library which was near the Tourist Office in another Victorian house that had sacrificed its front garden to make parking spaces for patrons.

Anna was curious to see how a library in a Scottish town compared to the one she knew so well in Canada. She had read that Glasgow's Libraries and Museums were world famous, but she had not had time to investigate for herself. She approached today's opportunity with professional interest.

Oban's library was small but welcoming. The bulletin board announced a number of community services including, to Anna's surprise, programs for local school children which included scheduled visits during regular school hours.

"Now, that's a bright idea for saving costs and space in schools," she murmured.

"Can I help you at all?" Anna turned to see an elderly gentleman peering at her from behind a pair of glasses perched on the mid-point of his nose.

"Thank you, no. I am just looking around."

"You would be a visitor then?" he continued. "We don't get many tourists at this time of year."

"Yes," Anna replied, "I am staying at the McCaig Farm House."

"Good! Good! "His balding head was nodding so vigorously that Anna was afraid the books he held would fall to the ground together with his glasses.

"We can issue a temporary card for you if you wish to borrow anything," he offered eagerly.

"Well, I would be interested in something about the birds and animals in the surrounding country," Anna ventured tentatively. She felt a little sorry for the old fellow who did not seem to have many customers today. Any rooms Anna could see were empty of people.

Although she could have found items for herself, she allowed the gentleman, who introduced himself as Kenneth Macintosh, to take her on a tour of the book shelves pointing out various titles of highland flora and fauna.

Like most librarians, Kenneth was a mine of information, and Anna was soon deep into discussions about collections, staffing and funding problems, and the contrasts she noticed to library systems she knew in North America.

"Perhaps you would like to give a talk to our Library Board while you are here, Ms. Mason? I know they would be most interested in your observations, as an outsider."

Anna had no intention of becoming involved in the community. She had too many issues to decide without complicating her life any further. She declined the invitation as politely as she could and asked if she could leave her shopping bags for a few minutes while her temporary library card was being issued for the stack of books she had just chosen.

Kenneth was pleased to oblige, and Anna walked up the hill to Tweedale Street where she collected maps and leaflets about local attractions and found a number of items of Scottish Celtic jewellery that would make lovely gifts for her Samba friends.

Fee found her there. She was intently studying the large wall map trying to find the name of Helen's Hill. This was proving to be impossible, as Anna did not know the area well enough to identify one small section of high ground in terrain that included many ranges of mountains.

Fee was happy to stop and load up Anna's purchases at the library. To Anna's surprise Kenneth and Fee broke into an animated conversation in Gaelic as soon as they saw each other. Fee explained, in English, that Kenneth was a friend of her Granny and wanted to know how his old friend was managing with her rheumatics.

I suppose everyone knows everyone in a small town these days, Anna guessed, as Kenneth escorted them to the taxi and waved as they drove away.

"If you don't mind, Anna," said Fee, I would like to take a detour before we return to the farm house."

Anna was intrigued and readily agreed. Fee took a side street and the car climbed steadily upward. Anna was enjoying the view over Oban from the rear windows and did not at first notice they had reached McCaig's Folly. She turned to Fee to ask if they were going inside when the sound of bagpipes rose into the air. All conversation stopped while Anna absorbed the spine-tingling tunes and drum beats that emerged from the arches above their heads.

When the last, melancholy notes had died into the open air, Anna exhaled deeply and waited for Fee to explain what had just happened.

"While I was in town this afternoon, I heard that the Oban Pipe Band was holding a practice session. They compete at Highland Games all summer and meet here regularly to march around the tower and use these best-possible acoustics."

When she could catch her breath again, Anna declared, "Fiona Jameson that was an unforgettable experience. I now know I truly am in Scotland."

Fee seemed pleased that her surprise had been so success-ful. She smiled often on the way back to the farm house. Anna, seated by her side, was silently wondering how her own parents had been able to leave this land and its customs behind with never a backward glance, and had neglected to pass on anything of their heritage to their two children.

The attack on the kitchen fireplace began with Fee's instruc-tions on how to lay a fire.

Anna, who had never camped outside and whose experience of fires was limited to gas appliances such as barbecues, followed the steps carefully. If she wanted to be warm and clean in this house, she knew she would have to feed this monster stove on a regular basis with its desired food.

Fee had assembled a large supply of fuel from the garden shed. First she placed rolled newspaper in the fire basket in the centre of the stove. Anna helped to prepare these by rolling, then twisting, sheets of paper into a tight knot. On top of these Fee laid a layer of dry sticks criss-crossed over the paper twists. Only one or two larger sticks were carefully balanced on top with a few small pieces of coal.

Anna asked if this would be enough for the evening ahead. Fee laughed and replied that this was only the first stage in the process and they would have to stand by until the fire got properly started.

Chastened by the thought of her ignorance, Anna watched carefully as Fee made sure all doors in the kitchen were closed to draughts. Next, she picked up a long-handled pair of tongs from a set of fire implements at the side of the hearth stone and reached into the chimney until the metal tongs connected with a hook. Explaining as she pulled on this hook that it caused a plate to open in the chimney above, allowing smoke to escape, Fee cautioned that this step was vital if Anna did not want to be choked with smoke inside the kitchen. Fee then knelt down and applied a lit match to the bottom layer of paper.

Anna could not help thinking of the ceremonial nature of this performance and how humans down through the ages had worshipped fire as the giver of life.

She could now understand the importance of fire in a way she had never before experienced. Despite her sweater and new wool suit, the chill of evening in the farm house was inching its way through her clothing. There was a perceptible drop in temperature as soon as the sun dipped below the horizon in these parts.

As she watched with bated breath, yellow flames began to lick at the paper twists and soon there was enough flame to ignite the sticks above and, finally, the larger pieces of wood.

Fee explained that coal was the main heat source in a long-lasting fire but the secret was to get the wood and paper to catch fire before they collapsed and the whole process had to be repeated from the beginning.

Handing the tongs to Anna, Fee supervised as Anna carefully placed more coal on the young fire.

"Take it slowly now," warned Fee, "too much, too soon will snuff out the flame. At the end of the evening, when the fire is good and hot, you need to put a layer of coal, or peat, over the top and this will keep it burning at a low level until morning, if you are lucky."

This did not sound too hopeful to Anna. She could envisage spending a lot of time nursing fires in the coming weeks. Well, she concluded, it's all part of the learning experience although I can now fully appreciate the benefits of central heating.

Fee set out for town as soon as the fire was burning brightly and the warmth was radiating around the kitchen.

When Anna opened the front door to bid her farewell, Fee looked up at the darkening sky towards the west and the distant sea coast.

"There's a storm out on the Atlantic tonight by the looks of it. We got that fire going just in time. Keep everything closed up tight and you'll be fine."

As Fee moved off down the gravel path, Anna could see how the rising wind bowed the branches of the fir trees to the west and caught at Fee's coat and hair. With a shiver she closed the door on the world and gave thanks that the thick walls and north-south orientation of the farm house would undoubtedly save her from the worst of a storm from the sea.

Chapter Seventeen

I n the end, Anna decided to spend the night by the
kitchen fire.

She had gone upstairs earlier to change clothes and
light candles, but the roar of the wind combined with a scatter
of hail clattering on the roof made her nervous. It was more
comforting and quieter in the kitchen so she gathered up
nightclothes and bedding and made herself comfortable in a
soft chair and footstool she dragged in from the sitting room.

The fresh supplies from the Oban stores provided an
excellent supper and with a large pot of tea, and a small dram
of whisky, (a Dalwhinnie single malt, recommended by the
bewhiskered Scotsman in the Wines and Spirits establish-
ment), she settled down to read for a while and then write the
first entry in her new journal.

She awakened with a start as the journal and books
tumbled to the floor from her lap.

Her first thought was for the fire. Yes, it was still alight but
getting lower in the grate.

Throwing aside the blankets that covered her legs, Anna
rose to bank down the fire with a layer of coal as instructed.

She noticed at once that the wind noise had reached a
ferocious pitch. Rain battered the window frames to the

front and rear of the house and torn branches sped past, tumbling over and over in the storm. Grateful that no car was outside which might be damaged, Anna lit fresh candles and wrapping a blanket around her shoulders, looked through her shopping bags for the small radio she had bought.

Once the coal had been carefully placed on the fire, she sat down with the radio on the table and fiddled with the controls until she heard a human voice through the crackling of interference.

.... *in Ross and Cromarty. Gale force winds are expected with flooding likely in some low lying areas. Temperatures will drop overnight and frost or snow will fall over high ground. Motorists are warned that roads in Glencoe as well as over the moors will be hazardous. More road and shipping reports will be available at midnight.*
And now, back to our regular programming.

Anna listened for a few moments to a discussion on medical matters pertaining to the prevention of a swine flu epidemic, but found she could not concentrate on the topic with
such noisy distractions outside her windows.

Looking around for something to occupy her mind, she spotted the whisky bottle and decided to enjoy another 'tot' with the required 'drop of water to bring out the hints of heather and peat', that she had been informed about.

Sitting by the fireside with glass in hand, she wondered what her mother and father would think. With no prior knowledge or incentives about Scotland from her parents, the thought that she would ever find herself in a situation like this, could never have crossed their minds.

Life is full of the unexpected, she mused, and this drink really warms you right down to the toes. Dad used to like a whisky on occasions. What would he say if he could see me now? As her eyelids closed, Anna relaxed inside her cozy kitchen and all disturbances drifted away.

An entirely different situation met Anna's eyes when she awoke six hours later.

All was silent again, but a strange white light was flowing into the kitchen, reminding her of mornings in the depth of Ontario's winters.

"Am I getting confused about the seasons? Isn't it spring here?"

As soon as she stretched and pulled away her blankets, Anna noticed how cold the room was now. The fear of an extinguished fire reawakened.

Stumbling over to the fireplace stove, she peered into the bottom of the grate praying that a tiny flame might have survived the night. There was a reddish glow far down in a bed of grey ashes and she immediately grabbed a page of newspaper and rolled it into a long taper. When the paper lit, Anna sighed with relief and with her left hand she pulled small sticks toward her from the hearth and gently poked them into the ashes.

Fifteen minutes later, with the fire saved and heat beginning to fan into the kitchen, she turned to the windows to see what the source of the odd light could be.

AS she drew close to the single-paned glass, with frost marking the edges, she could already feel chilly air entering the room. When she looked out to the front, the entire landscape had disappeared under a coat of snow.

"Snow!" she exclaimed, in surprise, "Now this is more like home!"

Rushing to the rear window, she leaned over the sink to find a similar view. The snow was piled against the stone wall on the edge of the yard and also on the tops of the hedges. She wondered if the top of Helen's Hill was also rounded in snow but did not dare to open any doors to go outside and see. More cold air entering the farm house was not a welcome thought.

As she gazed out in delight at the transformation, a movement caught her attention.

One of the mounds of snow was moving! Now there were two, and three!

The white mounds actually jumped over the broken part of the wall and Anna realised they must be sheep who had taken shelter from the storm.

This thought led her to deduce that fences must have blown down in the night. The next logical conclusion was that the limited electric power might also be interrupted.

Anna plugged in the kettle and waited to see if the familiar noises of water coming to the boil would occur. After a minute, she had to admit nothing was happening. Checking the light switch confirmed she was now without electricity for the foreseeable future.

The battery-powered radio provided information that a wide area had been hit by a severe spring storm. Crews would be sent to outlying areas as soon as access roads could be cleared of snow drifts, but residents were being warned to stay indoors until the situation improved. She left the radio on low for any news updates.

As soon as Anna knew she had no electricity, she craved a hot drink of coffee in the worst way.

She surveyed the monster stove as the only remaining source of heat. Didn't Fee say her Granny remembered all the household cooking and baking being done on there?

Anna found a saucepan and poured water into it. She doubted that she could balance the pan over the fire without risking a collapse that might extinguish the flames, but she tested the metal surfaces on either side of the fire basket and found one of them was quite hot. If she put more coal on the fire, she figured, the heat would likely transfer over to the metal and eventually boil water for coffee.

With this experiment underway, she tried to calculate how long her remaining wood and coal would last, but found herself unable to judge. An expedition to the shed was going to be a priority as soon as a hot drink had been consumed.

What else could be cooked with hot water? Eggs could be boiled, of course.

Her mother used to make porridge on winter mornings when Anna and Simon were children and although they had preferred sweet, cold cereals, Anna could now understand the value of a plateful of steaming oats on a day like this.

Another item for my next shopping list, she noted, as she ventured out to the pantry for eggs, cheese, butter and bread.

It took some time, but breakfast was achieved and Anna was remarkably pleased with her resourcefulness. She had even managed to make toast by holding the bread to the fire using a long fork she had found in the cutlery drawer.

While washing up the dishes, she learned there was hot water on tap for the first time.

A quick bath was in order, she decided, even if the bathroom was freezing cold.

Anna washed speedily while the water was still warm and as soon as she rubbed herself dry she dumped some dirty clothes into the bath water and let them soak. Dressed in layers of her warmest clothing she rubbed the dirty items with soap and rinsed them with clean, cold water, hanging them to drip over the bath on the wooden pulley, after wringing as much water out of them as she could manage.

"There's nothing like hard physical work to warm a person up," she announced to the air, "but how did women survive without washing machines for so long?"

Back downstairs, she checked the fire again and switched on her cell phone in case Fee or George was trying to get in contact. It took a few minutes, during which Anna began to be concerned about being cut off from everyone, but a signal did arrive and it appeared no messages had been missed so far.

Yesterday's shopping expedition had resulted in the purchase of a water-and-wind-resistant blue jacket with its own warm, zip-out lining. The same hiking supply store had fitted Anna for waterproof, leather, climbing boots, guaranteed to assure safe footing no matter the conditions. Gauntlet-style gloves to match the jacket's black and red trim, completed the outfit. The total cost of these items surprised Anna. By the time she had converted the price to Canadian dollars she was in shock, but, if she intended to climb Helen's Hill again, she had better be equipped for the task. Safety was more important than savings at this point.

Slipping the cell phone into a nifty pocket designed for the purpose, Anna zipped and fastened, laced and studded her way into the new attire. She also pocketed the house key in case the exterior pantry door should jam shut while she was out, and as a last thought, she included the slim torch also.

With three of Tesco's 'Bags For Life' hanging from her arm, she stepped into the snow and immediately discovered the value of good footwear. Her feet hit the ice hidden beneath the covering of snow and she would have fallen hard had it not been for the superior gripping quality of her new climbing boots.

Alarmed by the vision of lying in the snow with a broken leg, waiting for someone to come along and help her, Anna proceeded very carefully across the yard and forced open the shed door scattering ice behind her. As Fee had said, there was a good supply of firewood, papers and coal inside. Leaving aside the brown, brick-like material which must be peat, and which Anna had no clue about, she filled all three bags and retraced her steps back to the house.

"Mission accomplished!" she declared after the supplies had been deposited to the side of the hearth stone. "Now what?"

Since it had taken quite a bit of time to attire herself for the great outdoors, Anna thought she might as well venture a little further and explore the barn.

The heavy barn key joined its house partner in one of the jacket's deep pockets and she set out toward the iron gate in the stone wall. The gate's hinges protested in the cold but it opened enough to let Anna pass through.

The snow was not very deep compared to Canada's winters and Anna reached the barn doors without difficulty. The padlock required some dexterity but it finally released, and Anna opened the double doors wide to let some daylight into the dark interior.

As soon as she stepped inside the barn she was forced to drop to her knees and raise her arms to protect her head. A pale, silent shape was swooping down upon her with claws outstretched, heading for her eyes.

Anna screamed.

When she dared open her eyes again she could hear or see nothing. The corners of the stone structure were dark right up to the roof beams. As her eyes grew accustomed to the dim light, she searched for a winged shape. Something much bigger than a bat and with wings much wider than a pigeon was in this space, she knew, and she did not want to be surprised by it again.

Staying near the doors for a quick exit, she used her torch to shine some light into each of the corners at floor level. There was a scrambling kind of sound from the far left corner where a pile of sacks lay, but nothing could be seen.

Fearing rats, Anna took a step backwards and shone the narrow beam upwards. Immediately, two huge eyes were illuminated. Anna stifled another scream and waited to see what would happen. When the eyes blinked in the torch light, she guessed she might be looking at an owl.

Calming her racing heart with deep breaths, she directed the light to the side of the place where she had seen the eyes gleaming. In the indirect light, she could make out the shapes of not one, but two or three owls with heart-shaped white faces, perched on a wide roof truss and gazing down at her with solemn concern.

Obviously they had not entered the barn through the

doors, she decided, once her thinking mind took over from her panic. There must be a hole somewhere in the roof.

A barn should be a perfect place to hunt for mice and rats in the winter and although this thought was not entirely pleasant, Anna needed to see what was stored in the barn, other than wildlife.

Her torch light revealed a number of useful items scattered around on the stone floor.

Gardening equipment and household tools were there, as she had suspected, but she could see also a brass log carrier, a ladder, broken chairs, a pair of rubber boots with a walking stick standing inside near a collection of heavy winter coats, (these must have been Helen's she thought), and three wooden crates with unknown contents.

As she moved forward to check if these crates were sealed, Anna heard again a very faint scrabbling sound. Determined to find out if rodents had invaded this space, she directed the torch beam toward the sound and was astounded to see the striped back and bushy tail of a cat disappearing into a hole in the floor near the back wall.

Why would a cat be here, in a barn, in the cold, with no homes around for miles?

It must be competing for food with the owls above and might well be in danger of becoming a meal itself. Anna's affection for cats and dogs made her want to save this little animal and bring it into the house, but she could guess that it was scared of people and must be approached very carefully if she did not want to chase it away to an even more dangerous survival situation. She decided to return with food for the cat as soon as she could.

After locking up the barn doors, Anna made her way back to the farm house with the aid of the walking stick she had found. On closer inspection, the stick was revealed to be a collapsible hiking pole, similar to the very expensive ones she had noticed in the store where she bought her jacket. The height had been adjusted. Anna imagined that Helen must also have been a tall woman who had probably used the pole on climbs.

"You are not making it easy for me Helen," she murmured, as she gripped the shaped handle, "but I am gradually finding out more about you and I won't stop till I know you better."

The kitchen fire needed only a few more pieces of coal to make the water boil again. Anna enjoyed a cup of tea with one of the delicious chocolate biscuits from the packets she had stored in the pantry, then sat back to consider her options for the coming night.

The chair and footstool had not been the most comfortable of beds, so she went upstairs to see what the bedrooms felt like.

The larger double room was freezing cold so that decision was made quickly. Fearing that she would have to spend another night in the kitchen, Anna went through the bathroom door and discovered to her delight that the adjoining small bedroom was quite cozy owing to the heat radiating from the wall where the kitchen chimney rose up to the roof. Fiona was right about this, she remembered.

Anna thought this small room would suffice. She could later set a small fire in the fireplace if necessary, now that she knew how to do it.

Returning to the bathroom she watched the wet clothes dripping into the bath and worried that it might take days to dry her underwear. She inspected her raincoat which she had sponged to remove mud and grass stains after her first mountaineering adventure.

"All of these will have to go down to the kitchen fire," she decided.

Lacking a device on which to hang the clothing, she draped things over dry towels from the closet, arranged over four kitchen chairs. This tactic effectively screened all heat from the fire but it would be worth it to get clothes dried more quickly.

She was just considering if it might be time for another hot drink when a loud knocking sound abruptly ended the silence.

At first she couldn't think where the noise was coming from, but after a repeat fusillade of knocking she realised it must be coming from the front door.

Who on earth could it be on a day like this?

A stranger stood on the doorstep stamping his feet to shake off the snow. A border collie waited by his side gazing up patiently at the man's frowning face.

"Can we come inside?" he asked without preamble. "The dog's feet will be affected if he's out any longer."

Anna was too surprised to say anything at all. She opened the door wide and let the pair into the porch.

"I'd be obliged to you if you have an old sack to wipe the ice off Prince's pads.

He can bide here for now. He won't be a bother to you."

The stranger's abrupt manner evoked a similar response in Anna.

"Not at all!" she declared, "bring the dog inside. There's a fire in the kitchen and towels for his feet. You can come too."

"I'll not be disturbing you, miss. I just wanted to see if you were managing all right.

Young Fiona told me you were here and asked me to keep an eye on you."

"Oh, I see!" relief softened Anna's tone and she repeated her invitation, asking,

"How did you get here? Have you come far? I don't see a car out there."

"No, there's nae use driving in this weather. Ma cottage is about a mile from here around the shoulder of the hills. I was out with Prince here to find sheep that have broken through the fencing. We've penned a half dozen in your garden if you

188

dinna mind. They are cropping what grass they can reach for now."

"Yes, I saw some sheep there earlier. I'm afraid there is a break in the wall."

"Dinna fret yoursel'. I've thrown a few boulders into the gap for now. I'll come along and mend it for you when the weather clears a bit."

"Thank you. That's very kind of you. Can I offer you a cup of tea?"

"Ah should be gettin' back to the hills. There's new lambs in danger from the cold winds, but..." Here he seemed to hesitate, and Anna quickly put the pan of water on the stove before he could change his mind.

"........Prince could do with a wee rest, I suppose. Leave him be in the entrance there, though. He'll be no use to me if he gets ower warm."

Anna took a towel out for Prince to lie on and a bowl of water in case he needed a drink. She received a lick on her hand for thanks.

The farmer, or shepherd, perched on the edge of the kitchen table and looked around the room taking in details like the radio and the evidence of breakfast dishes.

"Ah see you've a good fire going. Fiona was a bit worried since you're just a city lassie."

Anna lifted her chin with pride and assured him she was managing very well, for a city woman, thank you very much.

It occurred to her that this man might be a source of useful information so she asked a question while she poured hot water into a mug.

"Did you know Helen Dunlop at all?"

"Aye, I saw her around here. She liked to walk the moors and climb the hills."

"Did she drive a car? It's quite a distance into Oban from here."

"Nah, nah, she wis'na one for travelling very far. She had a bicycle she used sometimes."

"Oh, really! I must look around for that."

Silence returned as Anna watched the rugged-looking man with reddened skin sip his tea noisily.

"Well, I'd better be on my way. Thanks for the tea."

"No, thank *you*. It's good to know someone is nearby, but I'm afraid I don't know your name."

"It's Alan Matthews. Goodbye now." Tipping his cap in farewell, he was out the door with Prince at his heels before Anna could say anything more.

Strong, silent type obviously, she concluded, as she stood by the sink watching him steer the sheep back through the gate in the wall.

She was just about to open a can of soup when the cell phone's musical tones came faintly into the room over the sounds of the crackling fire.

"Now where did I put the darn thing?" she cried, running around the kitchen and lifting laundry, towels and anything that could obscure the small gadget. As she neared the porch, the sound grew louder and she realised the cell phone was still in the pocket of her new coat, which she had hung on a hook when she came indoors.

On about the fifth ring, she fumbled the phone out of its pocket and opened it quickly saying, "Hi, it's me!" before she had time to think of a more appropriate response.

"Anna? Are you all right? You sound out of breath."

"Oh, George, it's great to hear your voice. No, I am fine. I couldn't track down the phone for a minute. It's been a strange day so far."

"That's partly the reason for my call. How did you deal with the storm last night?

Jeanette has been nagging me all morning to find out how you were surviving out there all by yourself."

"Honestly, George, I don't feel all alone. I've just had a visitor in fact."

"Really? Who was that? The roads are impassable in places."

"Now, don't sound so doubtful, George! I'm not making it up. A farmer called Alan Matthews called in to see how I was doing. He says he lives near here."

"Well, I am glad to hear it. Jeanette would strangle me if I let anything happen to you before she even met you."

Anna had to laugh at the thought. She was anxious to meet this woman who could make the seriously-conscientious George McLennan shake in his shoes.

"When are you coming into town again, Anna? I have some information for you about Helen and I thought we could have dinner afterwards at my home."

"I do have to get to the bank soon, George, and I would love to meet Jeanette but when do you think the weather will improve?"

"These spring storms don't usually last long, Anna. The weather report says there's a south wind coming, so the roads should be clear by tomorrow."

"Excellent news! I look forward to meeting you in your office. I'll call Fee and let her know. By the way, George, I owe you a debt of gratitude for connecting me with Fiona. She's a treasure!"

"Oh, I am glad she's working out for you, Anna. Keep warm and I'll see you tomorrow in the afternoon."

Chapter Eighteen

Fiona was impressed when she arrived at the McCaig Farm House to collect Anna.

The fire was carefully banked down, so as to last for a number of hours and Anna seemed full of enthusiasm for the new things she had learned about housekeeping, Scottish style.

She had not yet climbed the hill in her new outdoor gear but Fiona could see she was well prepared for another expedition.

The events that happened in the barn came up for discussion and Fiona was able to advise Anna about owls and other barn occupants.

"You say the milk and bread you left out were not touched today?"

"Yes, Fee, I thought that was strange. I couldn't find any sign of the cat, so I looked outside at the back of the barn and I found paw prints in the snow. I think there's a gap under the bottom layer of stones and when I checked closely, I found a few strands of long hair."

Fiona decided to go out and look for herself while Anna happily dried her hair, put on some make-up and dressed for town.

Fiona managed to retrieve some of the strands of hair and confirmed that they belonged to a cat, but she began to suspect that this was no ordinary stray animal. The paw prints were very large and the brown and black outer hairs were long and attached to a few, very soft, inner hairs.

Fiona could detect striations in the hairs that indicated this was, indeed, a striped cat. It could be a feral cat, of course, but Fiona's instincts told her it might be an actual wildcat.

If she were correct, Anna would need to be warned. Scottish wildcats were a rare and ferocious breed, much larger than normal felines and strict carnivores. Although it was unusual for such an animal to take shelter indoors, at this time of year a female might be pregnant and seeking a temporary safe haven. Fiona's studies had informed her that kittens could be born as early as April.

When she returned to the farm house, Fiona told Anna of her discoveries.

"This is exciting," Anna replied. "I would love to get a glimpse of this special creature."

"That would not be wise," Fiona declared. "If there are kittens, the mother will defend them fiercely. There are cases known where wildcats died for their own, or their kittens', freedom."

After a moment's thought she added, "I think you should remove anything you need from the barn and then leave it closed up for now. I will take these samples to the vet and also ask Alan Matthews if he has lost any lambs lately."

"You mean a wildcat could kill a lamb?" Anna's horror was clear from her voice and her shocked expression.

Reluctantly Fiona stated that it could happen, but the predator would take only parts of the lamb to her den and revisit the kill if she was undisturbed.

"I guess you are right, Fee. I'd better stay well away."

Fiona noticed how smartly Anna was dressed for their outing.

Her red suit and black sweater with long boots and a hooded overcoat were definitely city wear and her rich browny-red hair shone in the sunlight. She seemed happy to be leaving the farm, but Fiona could see Anna's pride in the way she had adjusted to the challenges of country living.

As they bumped down the farm track, Fiona noticed the snow melting away in the bright sunshine. In only a few hours there would be little sign of the storm's effects.

The electricity supply had now been re-connected and phone lines were operative.

In Oban, everything was back to normal after the hiatus. Fiona's school run had taken place on time this morning and she had two doctor's appointment pick-ups after she dropped Anna off at the bank. The run up to Dunbeg to collect Anna from George and Jeanette's place would be her last job of the day and she could take a back road to the farm house from there and still get home to see Granny settled for the night.

The long days left little time for studying and she worried that her dreams of qualifying for the Wildlife Federation career would be on hold for far too long.

Anna's offer of help with school work was the first sign of hope she had seen in years and she determined she would take full advantage of this opportunity starting tonight, if the dinner party did not go on too long. She checked over her shoulder to see if her book bag was still on the back seat of the big car. The language of the Shakespeare plays was the hardest part of her English studies. She hoped Anna could cope with that, even though she was Canadian.

By the time Anna reached George's office, the sun was dipping behind the bulk of the Island of Mull and clouds were forming in the west.

It's quite strange, she thought, not to be able to predict the weather from the cloud patterns and the light, as I could do so easily in Ontario. The one thing I have learned is that weather changes quickly in this part of the world. It must be something to do with the amount of water surrounding a fairly small land mass.

George was waiting for her with a summary of his research about Helen's marriage on his computer screen. He had used contacts in Stirling to trace the dates and relevant information about Harold Fraser.

"I am afraid it is another sad chapter in Helen's life, Anna," George began, with a look of sympathy directed at Anna sitting across from his desk.

"Just tell me the story, George. I am more and more involved in my aunt's affairs already and curious to learn all I can about her."

"Certainly, Anna," he agreed, and clearing his throat he began.

"It seems that Helen's adoption by the Dunlops went smoothly to begin with.

For several years she must have been the beloved child they had never expected to have. Then the unexpected happened. Mrs. Dunlop became pregnant and gave birth to twin girls, followed a year later by the birth of a much-longed-for son.

When Helen was about twelve years old, she attempted to run away from home for the first time. We can only assume that she was unhappy with the family situation.

In any case, she left home permanently by the time she was eighteen, and shortly after that she married an older widower, named Harold Fraser.

They lived in Stirling where Harold owned a construction company. There are no records pertaining to the next twenty-five years of Helen's life until the accident."

"What accident? Was Helen injured in some way?" interrupted Anna.

"No, it was her husband's accident. While working on a

new housing estate on the borders of Stirling, Harold had a heart attack. He was driving a JCB, a type of large digging equipment, when his heart gave out. The newspapers reported the extensive damage caused when the heavy machinery backed into a partially-constructed house. Two workers were killed and another was seriously injured."

"How awful! That was tragic. How did Helen cope after that terrible time?"

"I can't tell you, Anna. There's nothing to indicate how she felt other than a grainy newspaper photograph of her with her head lowered, leaving the coroner's inquest into the accident."

George consulted a new page on his computer and resumed the account.

"The next indication of Helen's activities comes when she signed the purchase papers for the McCaig Farm House a few years later.

"Wait a minute, George!" Anna's mind had clicked in again after trying to imagine what kind of person could survive this series of unhappy life events.

"She was known as Helen Dunlop at this point. Why did she change her name from Fraser?"

"I really don't know what she was thinking Anna. She never even mentioned being married when she came to me to set up her will. We can only presume there were no children from the marriage and she intended to leave that entire part of her life behind her when her husband died."

"It sounds like she spent her life running away from things and people," Anna commented sadly. "I wonder what made her finally seek out her original family?"

"I doubt we'll ever know all the answers now, Anna. Although my firm did not oversee the land purchase for Helen, I did discover from a real estate company in Oban that it was a cash purchase, meaning there's no mortgage remaining on the property and you are free to sell it if you wish."

"I think it really means she had plenty money after her husband died, George," Anna laughed. "As far as the farm goes, I still have no idea what I will do with it, but having now survived a vicious storm I find I am more inclined to consider the McCaig property as a possible home."

"That is good news, Anna! Now if you will be patient for a few minutes, I will ask the secretary if she has any messages for me, and then we can be on our way."

While she waited for George, Anna tried to understand what had made her declare she was thinking of the farm house as a home. She had never really come to that conclusion yet, and could not fathom why it had popped out suddenly in her conversation.

Perhaps, my brain knows something I don't yet know consciously, she thought, but it is way too soon to be making this kind of decision.

Jeanette met them at the door of a small, modern house in a housing development near Dunbeg, a town a few miles north of Oban. Anna was surprised that the ultra-conservative George would be living in a new house rather than a traditional old Victorian, but she was not surprised by the appearance of the charming Jeanette.

As soon as she opened her mouth to welcome Anna inside, it was as if they had known each other for years. Jeanette was English, with a Canadian father, and Anna knew she had met someone who could interpret Scottish mannerisms and speech for her with ease.

The meal was a delicious beef stew with vegetables including mashed potatoes that reminded Anna of home, and the conversation over the table just flew as Jeanette had so many questions for Anna. It was evident that the whole mystery of Helen Dunlop and Anna Mason was equally as fascinating to Jeanette as it was to her dinner guest.

"Now, dear," interjected George, in an attempt to turn the

discussion on to other topics, "you know that is privileged information and you should not be letting on that I have discussed it with you."

"Oh, George!" she soothed, patting his hand and smiling widely, "Anna knows I wouldn't breathe a word of this outside our home, but I can't resist a chance to hear what she thinks about it all."

Anna was delighted to share her feelings about her situation and after a fragrant apple pie, with a choice of cream or custard, had been served, George excused himself and retired to his study to finish some work.

"Now we can really get down to the gossip," Jeanette giggled, "George is a darling man but a little stuffy at times. I put it down to the influence of those old codgers he works with."

She invited Anna into the tiny kitchen and they chatted on while Jeanette made coffee and cleared up the dinner dishes.

Anna relaxed at the space-saving, fold-down table and watched as Jeanette moved around the kitchen. When she reached up to stow dishes on a high shelf Anna noticed a tummy bump on her slender frame.

"I realize this is what the Scots call a 'cheeky question'," she said, "but are you pregnant Jeanette?"

"Didn't George tell you?" Jeanette dried her hands and sat down on the nearest chair.

Her face glowed with happiness and the neatly trimmed side wings of her dark hair swung forward as she nodded her head.

"Yes, five and a half months now. We tried for years and I gave up my job as soon as we passed the three month stage. That's why we are still renting here and saving for a better house when the baby comes."

Anna was delighted to be included in this special news although she decided not to mention her knowledge to George, imagining the colour of his face as it flamed in embarrassment.

George emerged from his study in time to drink coffee and greet Fee's arrival.

"Won't you both stay for some more tea or coffee?" Jeanette pleaded, but Anna was anxious to get back to the farm house and inspect the all-important fire. They parted with a warm hug and an exchange of phone information.

Before Fee had driven onto the main road, Anna was planning to ask Alina to make one of her lovely crocheted baby outfits for Jeanette and George's new arrival.

It had been such a successful evening that Anna did not want it to end. She asked Fee if she had time to talk about her study plans before she headed for home. Fee replied that she had been thinking about Anna's offer to help and she was easily persuaded to stay for an hour in the farm house kitchen where the fire had dried Anna's clothes and still retained enough heat for any amounts of hot water.

Two things had to be settled before they began. Anna handed over cash for Fiona's services to date and discouraged her from counting the amount so that she couldn't refuse the bonus Anna had added for Fee's invaluable help.

"I will allow George to handle future accounts, Fiona," she warned, "but this is a first instalment, to ensure your continued availability. I have quickly discovered I can't manage without your assistance in this location."

The other item was a quick lesson from Fee on the use of peat as a method for banking the fire at night, so that Anna could leave it without worrying it might be extinguished by morning.

After those two essentials were dealt with, they got down to work. Anna was not surprised to learn that Fee's current difficulty was in understanding the antique English language expressions in Shakespeare's plays.

Undoubtedly, her early education in Gaelic added to her confusion, but Anna bypassed all the problems by employing a technique that usually worked well with second-language learners.

First, Anna read aloud a soliloquy passage from As *You Like It using* all the dramatic emphasis at her command. Fee was instructed to close her eyes and listen to the meaning.

Next, Fee had to tell Anna what the character had said, in her own words.

To Fee's amazement, the nuances of the speech had come through to her in spite of the barrier of the language, and she could interpret the emotions involved.

Once that barrier had been breached, Anna knew the major stumbling block was gone. What remained was the necessity of reading the text aloud with as much drama and passion as the writer, himself, had intended. In other words the plays should be performed as in a theatre reading, rather than read in silence as a lone student would do.

The hour sped by as Anna and Fee took different parts in the text then exchanged the same parts. Fee learned from Anna's initial interpretation and found the entire task easier as they progressed.

"Oh, I can really grasp the meaning now," Fee said with relief. "I think I can take the exam later this spring after all and that will be one more step toward my goal. Thank you so much Anna." Fee's eyes were moist as she closed up her book and pulled on her coat and beret.

"I'll away home now, but I promise to work on the plays and show you my progress the next time I come for you."

"Please don't mention it, Fee. You have been such a help to me. I'll call you when I need a ride and you can always bring along your studies."

Anna checked on the fire one last time, locked the doors and made her way upstairs.

The bedroom was warm enough tonight and the candles she lit gave the room a soft glow.

She washed her face in warm water, which could only be obtained by filling the sink from both taps first, as there was no mixer tap and the hot water alone was too hot for skin comfort.

"I won't complain about hot water," she announced, "but I do wonder why this washroom has no mirror. I hope I can find one or two mirrors in the crates in the barn tomorrow."

Thinking that she might also manage another climb up Helen's Hill, Anna tucked herself up in bed, but soon found sleep to be elusive. Her mind was full of future plans, and she also needed time to absorb the latest information about Helen's troubled life. There must have been some reason why she left Stirling. It seemed more and more clear to Anna that Helen's story lacked the personal detail that would make the woman herself more understandable. Bare facts were not enough to explain why she did such unexpected things. Anna's mind refused to let the mystery go and after a half hour of struggling to sleep, she accepted it was a hopeless task.

Re-lighting the candle on her bedside table, she drew her journal towards her and wrote about the day focusing her comments on Helen, Jeanette and Fiona.

Feeling somewhat more settled in her mind, she was about to attempt sleep once more when she suddenly recognized the uneasy emotion that was keeping her awake, despite her fatigue. She was missing her Samba pals.

A quick check on the time confirmed that it was only just after six o'clock in Canada.

Anna reached Alina on the third ring and the sound of the beloved voice dispelled all the unease that had been disturbing her mind. They chatted for about ten minutes while Alina brought her friend up to date with all the happenings in Canada, including recent political events. Anna was delighted to get this news as she had been unable to find one thing about her homeland when she read the local and national Scottish papers.

In turn, Anna related the latest about the Helen saga, the storm, the barn inhabitants, George's wife and Fiona's ambitions.

"Anna, I am astounded at how quickly you have found a place in this new community.

This is not like you at all yet you sound so happy and excited and I am thrilled that things are going so well for you." Alina paused, as she considered the next question.

I have to ask though; will you stay there or will you sell the house? Everyone wants to know."

"I can't give you an answer yet, Alina. I am back and forward on that question.

It seems like every day I have a different opinion depending on what has been happening to me. One thing is clear, my dear. I can't leave until I know more about Helen Dunlop."

"I don't blame you for that, Anna. I am just as curious about her as you must be.

She must have been a very unusual woman. Perhaps when you get to the bottom of the mystery you will know what to do."

"I hope you are right about that, Alina."

"Oh, one more thing, Anna. As we agreed, I will pass on your information to the Sambas, but you should know that Susan has taken Jacob to Florida for the month."

"What happened?"

"Jake's condition took a turn for the worse recently and Susan decided to visit Jake's sister and give Jake a chance to relax in the heat for a change. The weather here has been miserable lately."

"Please give them my love. Who is looking after the dogs?"

"They are in Florida too. They took the van and closed up the house."

"Mmm, Florida sounds appealing right now after the storm here, but I am told the sun will shine tomorrow."

"You sound like the intro to a musical number, Anna!"

"I'm too sleepy to sing, Alina. I'll say goodnight now. Please remember to make me an outfit for George and Jeanette's baby."

"I will do that for sure. Sleep tight Anna. I miss you."

"Miss you too."

With her mind emptied of worries, Anna slid easily into sleep. She left one candle glowing in the dark as a reminder of the importance of the link with her friends, no matter how great the distance between them.

Her last, sleepy thought was, perhaps absence does make the heart grow fonder.

Chapter Nineteen

✿❀✿

The view from the summit of Helen's Hill was nothing short of spectacular.

The climb had been much easier with the assistance of good boots and the hiking pole, so Anna had enough energy left to venture down to the pool (Fee had called it a tarn), and place two stones on the cairn there.

The hollow was sheltered from the wind which was blowing from the south today, but there was still a covering of snow around the pool. Anna could see the prints of birds at the water's edge so she sat quietly on a nearby rock and waited, happy to breathe in the sparkling, cold air and enjoy the peace of the countryside.

Before long, a parade of birds passed by on their way to drink. Anna could not identify the species although one little bird with a black cap could have been a chickadee.

Several song birds arrived and entertained her with tuneful trills and chirps similar to the calls of the finch bird family in Canada. They were colourful little fellows with pink chests and backs, grey heads and two bright white wing bars. Anna was annoyed at her inability to name them until she thought of Fee's expertise and decided to try to take a photograph with her cell phone's camera. This required some stealthy movements and a concentrated study of the phone's icons. She chose the one that looked most like a camera and pointed the phone toward the birds, pressing the button in the hopes she had captured the image she wanted.

She managed to do this without alarming the birds, then suddenly they flew away on the wind when a tiny little bird with a red breast and a beady black eye arrived in their midst. The sight was so incongruous that Anna laughed out loud and the sound scared off the tiny one also.

Making a mental note to bring one of her library books with her on the next expedition, she climbed back to the ridge and began to move west along the crest. She was looking for the cottage where Alan Matthews must live.

After scrambling around for ten minutes, she caught sight of a coil of smoke far below and guessed the shepherd's house must be beneath her, hidden by the mountain's bulk.

She was turning back to her point of descent when, looking up from her feet for a moment, Anna saw the gleam of the sea in the distance.

She stood still with the wind in her face and gazed at the sight. Something about seeing things from this height was fascinating. It was almost like being a Greek God in Parnassus watching the world below.

She could track cars on the road to Oban and see sheep move on the slopes below her.

A huge hawk-like bird rose up from the trees to the west and soared beneath her on the wind's arms. Best of all was the blue glint of the sea. Anna could just spot a ship on the far horizon beyond the coastal islands.

I must go there, she promised herself. Maps had shown her there were Inner and Outer Hebridean isles within reach of Oban. Although she had enjoyed summers in Canada at Lake Huron and Georgian Bay, nothing she knew had ever compared to the easily-accessible, rich and varied scenery in this part of Britain.

Binoculars next time, she promised herself. This is too good to miss.

The trek down to the farm house was accomplished with ease now that she could depend on the hiking pole for support when the trail was steep or slippery.

Anna unlocked her back door and sighed in contentment. Not only was she coping with an environment so different from what she had known in Ontario, but she sensed she was also gaining physical and mental strength, both from the outdoor exercise and the challenges of daily life indoors

"This is a win/win situation, Anna!" she congratulated herself. "Now, if I could just decide what to do with the rest of my life.........."

Thinking this might be too big a task for such a good day, she made a sandwich instead and with a full teapot balanced on a tray, she ventured outside to see if the bench below the south-facing sitting room window was capturing the sunshine.

This involved opening two doors and backing through them carefully and she was just about to set the tray down outside, when a car horn blared in the lane behind her and almost caused her to drop the whole thing.

Turning around angrily, Anna saw at her front gate, a white van with a huge fish painted on the side. She marched down the gravel path to remonstrate with the individual who had the nerve to despoil the peace of the afternoon with unnecessary noise pollution, when the driver's window rolled down and a smiling face surmounted by a white hat popped out.

"There you are, my dearie. I heard you was living here for a whilie. Would you be after wanting any fresh fish for your tea now? I can tell you they was caught this morning and haven't stopped flopping around yet."

As Anna stood still in amazement, an energetic young

man jumped out of the van and opened up the rear doors to reveal a display of fish on metal trays that slid out. Before Anna could reply, he was offering her a whole fish, complete with head and tail attached. The stranger continued to talk rapidly. "That nice lady, Helen, was particular fond of this salmon, you know, but I can fillet a cod or sole for ye, in the twinkling of an eye and you'll no find anything better anywheres at all."

Once she had recovered from the surprise of finding home delivery this far from town, Anna took advantage of the opportunity to buy fresh fish and by the time she had fetched money from the house, the voluble man had prepared a few slices of haddock for her and presented them, wrapped in clean white paper.

Thanking her for her custom, he departed back down the lane and the van soon disappeared from view.

When Anna placed the fish on a cool pantry countertop she was already planning how to fry the fish for her supper. She cut off a small portion from one slice and left it on a plate. She was going to open the barn doors today to remove anything useful from the crates inside. Following Fiona's advice meant she would not be inside the barn again for some time, and Anna could not resist leaving a forbidden treat for the cat.

No one will know, she told herself, as she returned to the tea tray outside.

The tea was cold by now so she looked around for somewhere to pour it out in the garden. Just behind the bench where she was seated, right against the wall of the house, she spotted snowdrops and primroses raising their faces to the sun.

"You shall have a nourishing drink," she informed them and watched as they absorbed the cold tea.

This place is a continual surprise to me, she thought. I wonder what else will spring up from this garden in a few months, and, more importantly, who will be here to see?

Anna opened the barn doors very slowly. She was prepared to duck down if anything seemed to be moving toward her, but the barn owls must have been sleeping.

She grabbed a tool from a box and quickly prised open the lid of the nearest of the three wooden crates.

Carefully packed inside were a number of useful household items.

She extracted two round mirrors, a folding frame that she recognised as a wooden rack for hanging washing in front of the fire to dry, and a heavy, black, flat pan with an iron handle spanning its width that she was sure could be suspended on a hook over the fire to cook food speedily. Just the thing for frying my fish tonight, she observed with a grin.

Near the bottom she found an old-fashioned, wind-up clock in a separate box.

The second crate held mostly books which Anna decided to leave for now. Her busy days did not seem to allow much time for reading at the moment.

The last crate was farther into the barn and beyond the reach of daylight. As she did not have the torch with her, Anna decided to leave this crate for another day and concentrate on moving the things she had selected to the area outside the barn doors.

Until now, she had been deliberately quiet in her actions so as not to alarm any wild animals in the vicinity. She was aware of the warnings Fiona had given about the ferocity of the Scottish wildcat and although she was willing to take the risk of leaving a fish treat, she was not willing to risk an encounter with a large animal defending its territory.

In the silence, she suddenly heard the unmistakable mew of a tiny kitten.

Afraid she might be imagining things, Anna stopped still and listened intently.

She was about to turn and leave the barn when the pitiful

sound came again. Anna's mind raced as she tried to fit this with the picture she had been given of an adult feline taking shelter in an abandoned barn during bad weather.

Could Fiona have been wrong? Could a stray cat be what Anna had seen vanishing under a stone on the barn floor, and not a wildcat? Could a litter of kittens be hiding here? What if the litter had been abandoned?

Without any evidence to support this idea, Anna jumped to the conclusion that she must intervene to save the kitten. But how?

To give herself time to think, she lifted the selected items from the floor of the barn and placed them outside, then closed one half of the barn doors.

It occurred to her that she should first check at the back of the barn where the cat hairs had been found in case there were more signs of recent entry.

Immediately, on rounding the corner of the barn, she saw a tiny body and a trail of bloody paw prints leading away from the hole she had seen before.

The dead kitten was lying in the mud just outside the hole at ground level.

Anna drew in breath sharply with shock. She stood with her hand at her mouth trying to figure out what had happened. The bloody prints were much larger than a kitten could make. Were those belonging to the mother cat or was the kitten a victim of some other animal?

It did not occur to Anna that this dead kitten could not have made the sounds she had just heard, until the mewing sound came again. This time the sound was from inside the barn.

At once she was galvanized into action. Throwing all caution to the winds she ran back

inside the barn to the toolbox. Grabbing a trowel, she raced to the rear of the barn again and gently moved the dead kitten aside. Trying to be as quiet as possible while still glancing over her shoulder to inspect the hillside in case her mission of mercy could be interrupted, she dug the frozen earth away until she had widened the hole.

Down on her knees, she peered into the cavity between the cold stones and slowly reached her gloved hand into the space. She could feel nothing, but a tiny scrabbling sound indicated that there was a live animal there. Praying that it was not a rat or an adult wildcat, Anna tried again. Her arm at its full extent, she wriggled her fingers.

Still nothing. Then she remembered the hole had an exit inside the barn.

Rushing around to the front again, she slowly tiptoed inside and toward the rear corner where she had first seen a cat disappear. The slow pace allowed her eyes to adjust to the dark, and with the additional help of her ears, straining to hear the smallest sound, she knew she would spot any movement.

She waited with her heart racing, and finally saw the small face of a young cat emerge from the ground. Identity confirmed, she thought, but how do I catch it?

Turning her head, she saw one of Helen's old coats hanging on a hook to her left.

If she could reach out without alarming the kitten, she might be able to throw the coat over the little creature and trap it inside the folds.

With utmost caution, Anna lifted the coat and held it in front of her. The little face had withdrawn again but Anna knew the kitten was there and she waited patiently, hoping it would not choose to escape to the outside.

Minutes went by. Anna scarcely breathed as she shuffled forward, inch by inch.

The kitten would have to come right out of its lair if her plan had a chance of working, but how could she entice it to come out?

In her coat pocket was a piece of raw fish wrapped in plastic. Anna had no illusion about fish being a suitable meal for a new kitten but at least, she thought, it might be an interesting smell to be investigated. She pulled out the packet, opened it, and tossed the fish as close to the hole as she could.

It took several more endless minutes but finally the kitten moved far enough into the open, with its nose twitching, for Anna to drop the coat over it and scoop the coat and its squirming contents up into her arms.

She managed to run back to the garden without tripping over anything inside, or outside, the barn. She jumped through the gap in the stone wall and raced for the house.

Backing through the unlocked outer pantry door and then into the kitchen the same way, she dropped into a chair and while she caught her breath, contemplated her next move.

The interior of a house would be a foreign environment to this creature, but Anna could hardly hold it in her lap forever. She really wanted a closer look at her captive yet she did not dare to unfold the coat. At the very least, this was a wild animal and its behaviour would be unpredictable.

Saner second thoughts were crowding out the impulsive actions of a few minutes before.

Anna began to understand that she had a responsibility to this creature now that she had removed it from its home. The bundle in her lap was silent and not moving. Had she killed the kitten? Looking around frantically she saw the floor level cupboard at the base of the shelf unit housing the kitchen china. If she placed the coat with the kitten in front of the deep, empty cupboard and opened up the door, perhaps the kitten would feel safer inside a dark place for a while. If it was still alive, that is.

Afraid to wait any longer, Anna moved over to the cupboard and nudged it open with the toe of her shoe. Then she bent down and gently opened up Helen's coat to let the little prisoner go free.

Retreating back to her chair, Anna waited anxiously to see what would happen.

In the end, she missed it. After what seemed like an hour, she quietly removed the coat from the floor and gently shook it. Nothing fell out. Anna backed away and kneeled down so she could peer inside the cupboard without getting too close. If there was no kitten in there, she decided, the whole operation had failed and the creature had escaped inside the barn.

In the dim light from the window it was not easy to see anything at all. Anna strained her eyes. Was that a little round ball in the back of the cupboard or just a shadow? She could not make up her mind which it might be until a rumble of thunder rolled by the farm house and a face emerged for just a second and Anna saw, with relief, white rims around a pair of frightened blue eyes.

She tiptoed over and closed the cupboard door, leaving a narrow opening for air.

Just then, heavy rain began to patter on the roof of the house. Anna remembered the household items she had left outside the barn and raced outdoors again, closing the kitchen door firmly behind her.

In the few minutes it took to collect the items, relay them back to the house and lock up the barn, Anna was drenched.

The cold drops running down her face, brought clarity to her thinking.

If the kitten was to survive, she must feed it soon. It was reasonable to assume that the mother cat was injured and had left the lair. There was no way to tell how long ago she had last fed the kitten so Anna had to act quickly.

Looking around at the pantry's contents she took a carton of cream, poured a little into a pan and diluted it with milk. While the mixture warmed up on the stove, she found a kitchen towel and cut off the corner. If the kitten would not drink from a saucer, she would have to soak the cloth and put it into the kitten's mouth herself.

Anna slid the saucer carefully into the cupboard and waited on the chair again. It might take a long time for the kitten to overcome its fear and approach the warm milk, or it might be too weak to lap the liquid.

Anna realised she was out of her depth in this situation. She suddenly thought of Fee's help and latched on to that lifeline.

Without taking her eyes off the cupboard door, she reached the cell phone on the kitchen table and called Fee's number.

"Fiona's Taxi Services," said the familiar voice, "We're here to help you."

"Thank God, Fee!"

"Anna, is that you? What on earth is the matter? You sound frantic."

"Oh, Fee, I think I've got myself into a mess. I rescued a kitten from the barn and now I don't know what to do with it."

"A kitten? You don't mean the wildcat had a litter in there?"

"Yes, it could be, I suppose. One kitten is already dead, I'm afraid."

"Have you touched the live one, Anna?"

"No. The poor little thing is in a cupboard in my kitchen here and I am trying to feed it."

"Right! Stay there. I am on my way. I just dropped off the school children at home.

I'll take the short cut and be with you in fifteen minutes."

"Thank you, Fee. Thank you."

The relief that poured out of Anna as soon as she had unloaded the problem on Fee, was

huge. She began to realise the toll the stress of the last hour had taken on her nerves.

Her hands, and her legs, were shaking.

My mother would make tea to soothe nerves, she remembered, and sweet tea is probably a good idea at this point. Afraid that any strange noise would further frighten the kitten, Anna decided to boil water on the hot plate of the stove rather than in the kettle. She did what was required as quickly and quietly as possible while keeping an eye on the cupboard.

By the time Fiona arrived, she was feeling a little calmer.

Fee looked concerned when she listened to the tale Anna had to tell. She insisted on going out to the barn to inspect the dead kitten and examine the paw prints, and then she returned to report her findings to Anna.

"I'm afraid this is a wildcat kitten, Anna, and not a stray. Judging from the size of the dead kitten, the female may have given birth prematurely and that means this live one is in danger if we can't feed it."

"What do you think happened to the mother?"

"I don't know for certain, but there is enough blood left to indicate she was badly injured. I am no expert, but I think she was on three legs from the prints. I followed them up to the burn then the rain washed the rest of them away."

"Will she come back?" asked Anna fearfully.

"I doubt it. The bigger issue is that as wildcats are the rarest mammal in Britain, we may already have broken a number of regulations about their protection."

Anna jumped up as this information sunk in. She stated firmly, "You have no responsibility here, Fee. I am the one who took action and I don't regret it if this animal can be saved."

"I admit I have to agree with you, Anna. First, let me make some calls and then we'll see what can be done with the kitten."

Fiona went through to the sitting room to make her calls while Anna kept watch on the cupboard again. In a few minutes Fee returned and announced that part of the problem was solved. Alan Matthews had found a dead, wildcat female in a thicket of bushes when he was out with the sheep. Prince alerted him to its presence and he saw the injury.

One foot was entirely chewed off causing huge blood loss. Alan was now checking all the high cover in the area looking for a suspected illegal steel trap which probably caught the wildcat by the foot.

"Oh, Fee! That's horrible news!"

"Unfortunately, that's not all the bad news, Anna. I got the information about Alan Matthews' discovery from the local vet, Callum Moir. He is not happy about the situation we have here and demands the kittens, both the dead and alive, are brought to his surgery without delay."

"Can he do that, Fee?" Anna was incensed that this man could dictate to her on her own property.

"I don't think he can forcibly remove them from you, but I fear he does have the authority to investigate and report to the Wildlife Service."

Anna stood up and walked to the window while she thought about the predicament she now found herself in. She had taken action to do what she thought was the compassionate thing and now she was at odds with the authorities and, even worse, she might have inadvertently involved Fee in an incident which could affect her future.

"Fee, I want you to leave right away and keep out of this situation. I will figure out what to do. I don't want you to be implicated in my decisions."

Fee looked around in surprise at this announcement. In a split second she assessed the reason for Anna's request and rejected it equally speedily.

"No you don't, Anna! I am not leaving you here without transportation. We are in this together and we will take the fall-out together whatever it may be."

Anna had to admit she was relieved to hear Fee's fervent support. Secretly, she determined that Fee would be protected from the effects of her defence of Anna's actions, but she was delighted to have an ally with the kind of knowledge that would make all the difference to the outcome for this kitten.

"I am so glad to have you on my side, Fee. Now, what do we do to help this animal?"

Since the saucer of cream had not been touched, Fiona

removed it and added sugar, warm water and more cream, pouring the mixture into a cup. She asked Anna for a towel which she then heated by the fire for a minute saying, "Anna you probably saved this kitten already by bringing it into the warmth of the kitchen. It would likely have frozen to death by now without the mother's body heat."

Fiona approved of Anna's earlier idea to feed the kitten using a cloth 'nipple', but first she had to get hold of the kitten. With the warmed towel in her hands, she slowly moved into the cupboard. The kitten had no way out with Fiona covering the entrance, so she was able to scoop it up in the folds of the towel and take it to a chair near the fire.

Anna stood by with the cream-soaked cloth as Fee slowly unwrapped the towel to reveal the tiny head. Anna saw thick fluffy fur; brown with darker markings, and very long white whiskers. The kitten's nose twitched at the scent of the cream mixture and it let out one plaintive mew as Fiona placed the cloth in its mouth. Anna could hear the strong sucking sounds and saw the kitten's eyelids close in ecstasy.

The cup was almost empty when the kitten gave a sigh and fell asleep. Fiona whispered to Anna as she opened up the towel to inspect the animal.

"The eyes were a cloudy blue colour so it is a newborn, but it is much larger than a normal kitten would be. Its body is longer and the paws show how big it will be when full grown. I think it is a male. The long, dark-ringed, bushy tail indicates it is a wildcat although I have never actually seen one before, other than pictures in books."

"An excellent report, Fee," responded Anna in admiration. "Can I touch the kitten?"

"I think we should avoid handling him, Anna. We don't know what is to happen to the wee thing and it's safer to have no human contact."

"Good thinking, Fee. Can we put him in this china bowl for now and put him back into the cupboard where he will feel secure?"

Fiona nodded, lowered her bundle into the bowl and slid it back into the cupboard, closing the door almost shut so no light or sound could wake the kitten.

The two women smiled at each other in satisfaction. They knew they had accomplished a good deed no matter what the repercussions of the deed might be. The kitten would live.

"He will need feeding again in a couple of hours," Fiona stated. "You won't get much sleep tonight I'm afraid, Anna. I will take the other kitten's body to Dr. Moir and ask him what supplements we can add to the milky mixture to make sure this wee fellow thrives."

"Don't worry about me, Fee, I'll be fine now I know what to do for .... What will we call him?"

"Well, I think the proper name for the species is *felis sylvestris grampia,* but we really shouldn't name him or even think of him as a pet. He's an animal of the wild and that's where he belongs."

"I'm sure you are right Fee, but excuse me for saying it, he's so cute! Let's name him Sylvester. We won't tell anyone else."

"Oh, Anna! You are a wonder!" The two women laughed as quietly as they could, till the tears ran down their faces and the tension of the last hours disappeared.

Anna would not let Fiona drive back to town until she had sampled some of the fish, quick-fried over the fire in the large pan. Fee called it an iron skillet and said her Granny still swore by hers for making oatcakes.

The fish was the best Anna had ever eaten. Perhaps it was her hunger after so much rushing around, or perhaps it was because she had rarely eaten such fresh seafood.

A shake of salt and the butter-coated meal was perfect on its own with the addition of parsley, which Fee found out in the garden while Anna was cooking.

"Now, remember, Fee," said Anna as she bade farewell to

Fee at the gate, "I insist that you tell the vet I accept all responsibility for what has happened here today. He must call me if he has any questions. You are not to be blamed in any way at all, and I swear I won't let you go unless you promise."

"I promise," said Fee solemnly. "I'll be back sometime tomorrow to see the kitten."

"You mean Sylvester!" reminded Anna, and the ringing sound of their laughter followed Fiona all the way back to Oban.

Chapter Twenty

❦

The dawn light fell on Anna, dozing in the chair by the fireside. She had not been to bed at all, since duties of feeding Sylvester and feeding the fire had occupied so much time that it didn't seem to be worthwhile to climb the stairs.

The kitten was still weak but latched on to the cloth nipple quite readily. Anna was careful not to touch the little body and kept the towel wrapped around it while feeding him Claws, and fangs, of formidable length were already in evidence.

Anna had raided the linen closet for older towels and now had a layer of these in the cupboard to absorb cat urine. She knew enough about cats to realise this output was a good omen for the kitten's survival.

She was just beginning to stretch her aching back and think about breakfast for herself, and Sylvester, when the cell phone beside her made her jump. She caught it on the second ring and before she could answer heard a male voice demanding, "Is this Anna Mason?"

"Yes," she offered hesitantly.

"Do you have any idea what trouble you have caused?" The angry words reminded Anna of her initial contact with

Alan Matthews, but this voice was even more belligerent, despite a lilting highland quality.

"Excuse me," she replied, gathering her wits about her, "to whom am I speaking, and why are you using that tone of voice with me?"

"This is Callum Moir speaking, Ms. Mason, I represent the Argyll and Bute Regional Veterinary Services."

Anna noticed at once that her strategy of attack, rather than surrender, had forced this bully to back down from confrontation. She was aware of the likely topic of concern from this gentleman, but her approach had allowed her some time to prepare a reasonable defence.

"And what do you want with me?" she asked, applying more delaying tactics.

"Fiona Jameson delivered a dead wildcat to me last evening. I understand you are in possession of a live wildcat from the same litter?"

Anna realized she would have to proceed with caution from this point on.

"Yes, but I must insist that Miss Jameson acted on my instructions. I called on her because I have no car here and she was kind enough to assist me. Surely you agree that she did the right thing in reporting to you?"

"Well, of course," came the reluctant reply. "but what on earth persuaded you to remove a wildcat from its environment? Have you any idea how dangerous they can be?"

"Dr. Moir, is that the correct title?" Anna now employed a more conciliatory tone.

"You have to understand that I am a visitor from Canada. I have no knowledge of Scottish flora and fauna. I merely discovered a poor abandoned animal *on my property* and attempted to rescue it. Would you have preferred that I left it to die, perhaps?"

Anna could hear some muffled humming and hawing in the background as this declaration sunk in.

"I can see your point, Ms. Mason, but the regulations for

the preservation of wildlife in this country, have stringent requirements prohibiting human intervention."

"Isn't it unfortunate that I was unaware of these regulations, Dr. Moir? I suppose it's too late now, to turn back the clock."

"Indeed it is. The animal is doomed to a totally unsuitable life, even if it survives. There are no wildcats in captivity. You would have been wise to let it die."

Anna was appalled to hear this statement but she concealed her distaste and thought quickly, searching for a solution to the situation.

She continued in a placatory voice. "I am sure I have heard of adult animals of another species becoming foster mothers for abandoned litters. Would it not be possible to attempt this? If successful, it could be in the nature of an experiment and of great interest to those in the profession, don't you think?"

Anna could practically hear the brain cells clicking over the phone as the vet calculated the future benefits of such an experiment, but he was not going to back down so easily.

"It's never been done before," he insisted, "and would not be likely to succeed now that you have contaminated the creature with human scent."

"I can assure you, sir, that on Fiona's advice, I have refrained from any physical contact with the kitten, and I will continue to do so."

Another long pause occurred while the vet considered the situation.

"The girl has given you good advice then. I'll away and think about this and see what can be done. Fiona will bring you a supplement to add to the milk. We'll leave it at that for now."

"Goodbye, then," said Anna.

"Aye, goodbye to you," came the reluctant reply.

Anna put down the phone and jumped up and down in

delight. She had fought hard for a chance at life for this little kitten and it seemed she had succeeded.

I turned a tiger into a pussycat, she told herself. Wait till Fee hears about this!

As if he agreed with her summation, the kitten in question began to mew for milk.

Fee arrived just after noon. Anna had lost track of the number of feeds by then and fatigue was beginning to make her very drowsy. Fee recognized that it was time for her to take over, and let Anna sleep for a while, but first she sat down to listen to Anna's account of the phone call with the vet.

"I don't know how you managed it, Anna," she said. "He's known as a very prickly character who doesn't suffer fools gladly, yet today he called me and congratulated me on handling the situation here with good sense."

"Oh, that's exactly the effect I wanted, Fee." Anna sighed in relief.

"I think you have had an effect on Dr. Moir that you didn't expect," suggested Fee.

"He asked me all kinds of questions about you and told me he would visit you personally and collect the kitten when he finds a foster cat to wean it."

"I don't care, Fee. I'm not afraid of him. He can't do anything to harm me. It was your reputation I was concerned about and that's safe now."

"Well, he is a very busy man and the only house calls he's made, that I've ever heard about, were for very sick animals. He really doesn't care much about people."

"Never mind about him, Fee. Take a look at Sylvester. I think he's put on weight already."

Fiona agreed, and mixed up a new batch of food for him while Anna went upstairs for a nap. She looked around in the kitchen and pantry and found a basket with a hooped handle as a new bed for Sylvester. She placed this in front of the cupboard so Sylvester could hide in his dark place if he felt threatened. She also washed out the soiled towels and hung them to dry on the folding rack in front of the fire. She had brought a linen cloth to be cut into pieces for feeding the kitten and when that was done, she set about making a meal for Anna.

Her Granny had been informed of the events of the previous day and she had contributed fresh-baked bread and vegetable soup together with a key piece of advice.

The kitten should be washed with a damp cloth every day to simulate the licking of his mother's tongue. This would not only clean his coat but also stimulate his bowels and bladder.

When all had been done to her satisfaction, Fiona took out her books and studied her literature text by the fireside. She did not need to collect the children from school until 3:30pm so she decided to let Anna sleep in peace.

At 3:00pm Fiona tiptoed up the stairs and found Anna fast asleep on top of the single bed with her clothes still on. As she watched the regular rhythm of her breathing, she couldn't help thinking about the positive influence this woman from another land had brought into her life. In such a short time, Anna had found a place in this isolated community and formed ties to a surprising number of people. Fiona wondered if Canadians were more outgoing than the average Scot. Most people she knew, were quite reserved and kept to themselves.

Fiona touched Anna lightly on her arm and whispered her name.

The first attempt to wake her did not succeed so she tried again. "Anna, I have to leave soon. Are you awake?"

Anna struggled through a fog of sleep toward consciousness and finally opened her eyes to see Fee's anxious face above her.

"I've just fed Sylvester and made some food for you, so you can take your time getting up. I'll be off now but I'll be back tomorrow. Call me if you need anything."

"Thanks, Fee," Anna managed to croak out the words as Fee disappeared with a wave of her hand and the smile that always brought her solemn face to life.

Anna had a wash and brushed her hair. Now that she had a mirror propped against the sink, she could see that her bronze-coloured hair was beginning to show grey roots.

The new shorter style and hair colour was such an improvement that she was not about to relinquish it, and finding a local hairdresser would be a new reason to go into Oban, once Sylvester could be left alone for a few hours.

She brushed her hair over the parting, hiding the grey, and noticed that her complexion was much brighter than usual. "Must be the fresh air," she murmured, "I certainly have not spent any time on my skin lately."

The meal Fiona had left was quickly heated up and Anna enjoyed every bite while watching Sylvester curled up in his new basket bed.

Now that he was more visible, Anna noticed how beautiful he was. Of course Nature had arranged that all kittens were irresistible, probably to ensure their survival, but this little fellow was particularly attractive. His soft brown fur was already long and thick with the bars of darker brown showing through. His tail was longer than that of a domestic kitten and curled around his body as far as the nose. Perfect camouflage, thought Anna, as she tried to visualize the life this cat would have had in the wild.

She cautioned herself not to get too attached to him. He would be leaving her care forever if Callum Moir took her suggestion and found a cat to mother the kitten. Anna could not resist a little smile of satisfaction as she remembered the way she had smoothed the ruffled feathers of the irate vet.

The tick of Helen's clock that now resided on a shelf of the dresser above Sylvester's basket, brought Anna back to the present. I still have time to call Canada today, she calculated.

Her first call was to Simon. He was interested to hear the

latest discoveries about Helen's life and asked how Anna was coping with being in such an isolated situation.

"The way you describe it, Sis, it sounds like the place is devoid of human comforts.

I mean, no central heating!" Anna could hear the shiver in Simon's voice that accompanied this thought. She felt compelled to defend Helen's house against his attack.

"Honestly, Simon, it's not as bad as you might think. There's something to be said for an open fire although it does cause quite a bit of work, especially when you have to clean the accumulated ash out of the grate."

"Ha! You just proved my point, Anna! I can't imagine you settling in such a grim spot."

"What you are missing in this picture, Simon, is the amazing scenery around here. The farm house is in a beautiful location and I've even climbed a huge mountain right in my backyard."

"Really! A mountain like in the Rockies? That doesn't sound like my sister."

"Well, no, but my mountain would be about eight times higher than the ski hill back home in London, Ontario."

"Ah, that's more likely. Still, good for you Anna! I'll tell the grandkids. I'll admit you are probably enjoying better weather than we are," he said reluctantly. *"We are still thigh-deep in snow in Alberta with no thaw in sight for six weeks or so."*

"I don't miss the cold, Simon, but the weather here is quite changeable. It's never boring. One day can have three seasons in it, or so it seems to me."

"So, when are you coming home, Anna?"

"I haven't made any final decisions, Simon."

"Well, think about it carefully. It's a big deal to change your whole life at your age. Friends and family are important to everyone."

Anna ended the call with Simon after sending greetings to all Simon's family.

Her brother had given her plenty to think about. Time was going by and she was no nearer a decision than she had been when she arrived in Scotland. She felt as if the entire period had been an enormous learning curve. The Anna who had reluctantly left Ontario was not the same Anna who was sitting comfortably in a farm house in Scotland.

The contrast was hard to encompass, but she recognized the change in herself and, more to the point, she liked the change.

The next phone call found Alina working at home.

"How are you getting on, Anna? Everyone asks about you. I mean to phone more often but by the time I get my work done, it's usually too late to call you."

"Don't worry about that, Alina. I've also been busy lately. You wouldn't believe what's been happening!"

"More news about Helen?" Alina's eager voice reminded Anna of her vow to get to the bottom of the Helen Dunlop Mystery.

"No, I haven't made any progress on that front, although I have found some of her personal things in the barn here."

"Is there a diary, or some letters?"

"Not so far. I am really getting to know her by living her life here."

"But it must be so different for you, Anna. Don't you miss all the comforts of your familiar life in Canada with 24-hour shopping and everything so convenient? Don't you miss your job at the library?"

Anna recognized the real question Alina was hinting at, and she took a moment to frame her answer.

"My dear friend, I miss you every day, of course, and, in many ways this is not like my real life at home, more like an adventure holiday with challenges at every turn. A holiday always comes to an end sooner or later."

"Does that mean you have made a decision about the farm house?"

"I wish I could say yes, Alina, but I am not ready yet. I think I

will know when the time is right. Now, enough about me! How are the girls and what have you been up to?"

"Bev is busy. James is doing very well at high school and is running a computer club. Maria is in the States buying clothes for the summer season, and I am up late every night completing orders for knitwear. Twin sets are back in style and my hand-knits are doing very well. Susan calls from Florida and tells me Jake is better recently. Everyone sends their love. Oh, I almost forgot.......Joseph said to tell you he is keeping an eye on your apartment and the sub-let tenant is quiet and clean, but he misses the Samba nights!"

Anna dissolved in laughter on hearing this, and had a flash of nostalgia for that simple life with good friends and no major decisions to make.

"Alina, you do me good! It's lovely to talk to you but I have to go and feed a kitten in a minute, so I must say goodbye."

"You have a cat, Anna?"

"Well, in a manner of speaking, I do. It's a long story, Alina, and not yet concluded. I'll fill you in when I see you."

"That sounds promising! Take care please, my dear."

When Sylvester was settled for another two-hour nap, Anna thought about preparations for the coming night. She needed more firewood, coal and peat and she wanted to look into the third crate in the barn, now that the area was no longer out of bounds.

The sun was sinking through clouds in the west and she knew darkness would fall soon.

The torch was still in her coat pocket so, as soon as supplies for the fire had been moved inside the house, Anna made her way to the barn.

She hoped the owls were off hunting as she opened the doors and approached the crate.

Alina's comment about Helen's possible diary or letters came to mind when she saw the piles of books stacked inside. She could not carry all of them so she used the torch and picked out those that might be of interest. Most of the books were classics, such as Sir Walter Scott's Ivanhoe or historical novels about Mary Queen of Scots, but nothing that looked like a diary was visible. She pulled out a slender telephone book and one or two cook books and was pleased to discover illustrated guides to local plants, birds and animals. No photograph albums or souvenirs of holidays were in evidence.

It is almost as if Helen's life started when she bought this farm house, Anna thought.

She propped the torch on top of the crate while she gathered the books together and when she looked up from the floor again, she saw something metal shining in the torch light against the opposite wall of the barn.

Of course, she remembered, Helen rode a bicycle. Alan Matthews had mentioned it. Anna promptly took possession of the cycle and loaded the books into the handy basket on the front of the handlebars, wheeling it back to the house through the gate and propping it against the kitchen window where it would get some protection from the inevitable rain.

She hoped there was a bicycle pump strapped to the leather bag behind the saddle. If so, freedom was at hand. Although she would never attempt to ride into Oban, at least she could ride around the farm area and explore some of the terrain she had seen from the top of Helen's Hill. The lack of a car was beginning to be a nuisance, but then, she would never have met Fiona if she had been able to drive herself.

The second night of cat-sitting passed more quickly. Anna adjusted to the need to sleep between feeds when the kitten did, but when she could not fall asleep fast enough, she gave up and thumbed through the books she had rescued from the barn.

By breakfast time she had identified the colourful chaffinches she had seen on Helen's Hill and discovered they were very common birds in Britain; confirmed that the bold bird with the red breast was, indeed, a tiny version of the North American robin, and read about the rowan tree in her back garden, a species that claimed to protect the household from witches. She had also found a number of recipes that might vary her bland diet somewhat, and consequently, she had compiled a lengthy shopping list.

The Scottish equivalent of the Yellow Pages had provided some of the most interesting reading of the earlier part of the night. Anna learned that Tesco would deliver goods to customers who lived outside the Oban area and the grocery list could be established through their internet web site. The same document listed a variety of useful services available in the wider region. There were also adverts seeking people who would be willing to do knitting and fabric 'piece work'. This sounded like the kind of thing Alina did at home and Anna made a note to ask Fiona exactly what was required.

Anna found a coal delivery company that would provide 'chopped sticks for kindling, and dry logs', and even an architect located in Inverness, who specialized in 'modern, custom renovations for traditional homes'.

With all this mental stimulation, Anna was wide awake and full of ideas when Fiona arrived with a bag containing a series of baby bottles in graduated sizes.

"Excellent idea!" exclaimed Anna. "Now we can feed Sylvester in a quarter of the time! He's a hungry little guy."

"Have you heard anything more from the vet?" Fiona enquired.

"Nothing at all. I suppose it could take some time to track down a suitable nursing female cat."

"Well, if anyone can do it, Callum Moir would be the very person. A few years back he found new homes for a whole collection of animals when a nearby Rare Breeds Farm Park closed down. There was everything from goats to llamas left homeless and he scoured the country until he had a place for every one of them."

"I see what you mean about his reputation as an animal lover, Fee. That was quite a task he set for himself."

Turning to the phone book on the kitchen table, Anna quizzed Fee about the services she was interested in.

"I can see this phone book is a couple of years out of date, but it is a fund of useful information, Fee. I have learned so much about this area and it is amazing how much goes on in a small place like Oban. Have you ever been to the Peace and War Museum, for example? They have a Royal Air Force flying boat model there and the history of McCaig's Tower."

"I was there years ago on a school trip but not since then. It's along the Corran Esplanade and you could easily find it on your next visit."

"I'll do that, if I ever get a chance to leave the house. About that, Fee............I see I can have groceries delivered to the farm house. I'll go to the library in Oban and return my books and use their internet to place an order for the food basics, then I can spend more time getting to know the town better."

"Surely! Was there anything else you wanted to know about?"

"Well, I saw this advert for people to do 'piece work'. Would you know what might be involved, Fee?"

"Ah, there's a tradition in the Scottish Highlands of women working from home while they looked after their families. In the old days they would card and spin wool from their sheep, weave the tweeds and knit the Fairisle patterns that are famous all over the world."

"Oh, Fee, I think my mother had a sweater with that pattern. Was it a band of intricate coloured designs around the shoulders of a sweater?"

"Yes, that's right. No one today has the time now to do such detailed work. It's all mass-produced in China these days."

"Well, then, why would someone be advertising locally for workers, Fee?"

"I think there is still some demand for very expensive hand work. Americans usually buy it nowadays. I can ask about the company. Did you want to buy something Anna?"

"Not for me. I'm thinking of a friend who makes beautiful knitwear designs and I'm wondering if there might be a market here for her crafts."

"I'll ask around for you."

Before Anna could thank Fee, they both stopped in amazement and watched as Sylvester climbed to the edge of his basket and flopped over the edge onto the floor.

"Would you look at that?" said Anna. "His eyes are not even focused yet and he's off to explore."

"It must be feeding time," laughed Fiona. "I'll try out one of the new bottles."

The conversation was at an end for a time, as Anna set about catching and feeding the kitten.

Later in the evening, when Anna was sitting thinking by the fireside, she began to acknowledge that something had happened in the last day and night, fundamentally altering her mindset.

The Canadian phone calls had forced her to seriously consider the decision she had been postponing. Then, something as simple as a phone book had opened up possibilities for her. For the first time, she found herself thinking of a future life here in Scotland.

She could not yet see the details of that life but an image was beginning to form.

It could just be an illusion caused by lack of sleep, she thought to herself, or possibly cabin fever. Time will tell, of course, but my time here is flying by.

Chapter Twenty-One

✤✤✤

E aster came and went in the middle of April. There were no chocolate eggs for Anna but an even better treat was on its way. Winter had vanished after a two-week period of daily downpours that soaked the ground, filled streams and lochs to overflowing, and drenched Anna every time she ventured outdoors.

Helen's Hill was off limits, for the time being, so Anna concentrated her attention on the interior of Helen's farm house. Anna realised she was no architect, but she had lived in a number of homes over the years and knew what she liked and needed in a residence.

Sylvester's feedings were now further apart and interspersed with periods of activity in which the rapidly-growing cat had to be confined to the kitchen to save the soft furnishings of the house from his claws. While he slept during the day, Anna roamed through the rooms and imagined what might be done to transform the space.

The south-facing front aspect was the obvious place to start. To capture the elusive sunlight, she envisioned removing the kitchen wall and replacing it with a pair of French doors or a patio window leading out to a new, glass-paned room, with a raised roof in the conservatory style often advertised in Scottish newspapers.

The monster stove would go, of course, in favour of a more modern, fuel-efficient appliance, and the kitchen would be remodelled, with an island to provide more counter space, a direct link to the pantry, and a separate exit to the back garden.

By reducing the size of the porch entrance, Anna thought she could create a small downstairs washroom.

The upstairs was a difficult problem because of the sloped roof, so Anna thought more sleeping space could be devised by dividing the large sitting room into an office/workroom and a family room with two convertible couches.

Most of this fantasy planning was done in rough sketches to occupy the evening hours while Fiona was studying in the single bedroom upstairs. With her exams fast approaching and the schools on Easter Break for two weeks, Anna had invited Fiona to spend the night, while she did intensive revision for her A levels.

Without interruptions or distractions the studying was going well. Fiona would ask Anna to grade the trial exam papers she was completing, and they discussed these while watching Sylvester's antics or sharing a meal by the fireside.

Fiona saw Anna's drawings for the farm house renovations and they laughed as they added more imaginary improvements like elevators, laundry rooms and hot tubs, and played guessing games about the exorbitant costs of such fripperies.

When Fiona was driving during the day, Anna imagined how the interior of the house could be made more comfortable with drapes, rugs and bright paintwork. She had already replaced the electric light bulbs with a higher wattage and added shades to soften the look.

The better lighting had revealed dirty walls over the fireplaces and spaces here and there where paintings must once have been displayed. She wondered if these paintings belonged to an occupant prior to Helen, or, if not, where the paintings had gone.

When the rain finally stopped, it was as if the world woke from a winter slumber and a new season emerged, like a child, bright and eager for the longer days ahead.

Anna's day began with the dawn chorus. A blackbird serenaded her daily from the rowan tree and her first task, on waking in the larger bedroom, was to go to the window overlooking the garden and reward him with pieces of bread. Wood pigeons and collared doves cooed seductively from the hedges and invited Anna to step outside as soon as possible.

She did this with a coffee in hand, after taking one in to Fiona, and then she could wander in the garden until the morning light flooded the land and dried up any lingering wisps of mist.

Plants were springing up through the earth at an alarming rate. Anna made good use of Helen's nature books to identify the species and find out what she could do to encourage their growth.

A clump of bluebells appeared under the rowan tree and the underlining in Helen's book informed Anna that she should appreciate their fragile beauty as they would fade once the tree was in full leaf. Violets covered the shady ground under the east-side hedge and its partner on the opposite side had a fringe of blue forget-me-nots.

Near the stone wall, a bush that had looked like a tangle of dead sticks, was identified, after a considerable search of the sources, to be a camellia with large pink flowers.

As this plant would be a summer exotic in North America, Anna was amazed to see it and risked cutting a few blooms for a vase in the house.

The low tufts of grass would never make a lawn, by Canadian standards, but they were the perfect cover for wild flowers. Yellow celandines and white anemones, which normally appear in woodland, popped up here and there, and tiny wild daffodils arrived in clumps.

A kitchen garden still survived near the pantry exit. Anna used the herbs in cooking the recipes she had chosen from Helen's cook books. Fiona helped with this task, and between them they devised a variety of meals that could be made on their limited facilities.

"I have never eaten so well in all my life," remarked Anna after they had enjoyed a particularly good lamb stew that had been simmering all afternoon on the warm stove top. "And I don't think I have spent so much time out of doors for years. The climb I did today and the bike ride yesterday, gave me so much energy, I feel fitter than I have in ages. I might even need to have some clothes taken in before long."

Fiona agreed that Anna looked well. Secretly, she was dreading the announcement that Anna would be returning to Canada soon. They had spent more hours in each other's company since Fiona had been studying in the evenings, and Anna had become a valuable ally who sometimes had more faith in Fiona's career ambitions than did Fiona herself. Before Anna's arrival, there were times when, after she traded over the car in the evening to her partner, and facing the prospect of opening books and studying for three hours, she could hardly summon the courage or the energy to begin.

When Anna left for home in Canada, everything would change. But for now, Fiona determined to make full use of the opportunities Anna had so generously provided.

Anna was washing dishes and listening to music on the radio when her cell phone began to ring. Thinking it might be Canada calling, she picked it up with wet hands and sang out a cheery, "Hi there!"

A hesitant voice replied, "Is that Ms. Mason of the McCaig Farm?"

"Yes, it is she." Anna modulated her voice to a more sober

tone as she deduced the caller could be the formidable Callum Moir.

"Fine, then, I am calling to inform you I have found a foster cat for the wildcat."

"Oh, that's excellent news! Where will Syl...the kitten be going?" Anna swallowed and coughed, to conceal the fact she had almost revealed her forbidden personal connection to the little orphan. She was sure the vet would not condone such a lapse in behaviour.

"Excuse me for a moment. I must turn down the radio." Anna took a moment to think.

Dr. Moir continued without acknowledging her apology.

"I will collect the wildcat tomorrow if it is convenient. It is to be weaned in a litter with a hybrid mother."

"Just a minute, Dr. Moir, what is a hybrid mother?"

"That would be a cat which is the progeny of a wildcat father and a standard cat mother."

The vet's impatient tone of voice indicated that only a moron would not know this fact.

"I did not realize such a thing was possible," responded Anna. "This would presumably give the kitten a better chance to survive."

"Well, that remains to be seen. Hybrids are unusual to start with. I will be seeking an approved zoo or an animal sanctuary to house the animal eventually. When its natural characteristics emerge, it will be unsuitable for a human household."

"I must thank you, sir, for taking all this trouble. I appreciate that this situation has added to your workload, and I do apologize for acting impulsively."

"You cannot be blamed for ignorance of the breed, Ms. Mason. I am sure many Scots would not have recognized what they were dealing with in similar circumstances."

The more placatory manner surprised Anna. Perhaps she had misjudged the man. If Fiona was correct in her estimation, he was overworked and protective of animals, even if his attitude to the human race was less than sympathetic.

"How is the wildcat kitten surviving in your care, these days?" enquired the vet.

"I have never heard of such a creature, who clearly belongs in the wild, living for long under these circumstances."

Anna restrained herself from insisting that without the care she and Fiona had provided the wild creature would not have survived at all.

"He is fine, as far as I can tell. I am sure you will see for yourself tomorrow," she replied, in as polite a tone of voice as she could manage between her clenched teeth.

"I have surgery until 6:00pm. I will be by after that."

"Can I, perhaps, offer you some supper, or will you be rushing home for a meal?" Anna had the sudden thought that she could possibly arrange a more relaxed meeting between the vet and Fiona, which might lead to future benefits for the girl.

"No need, no need at all. I won't be troubling you for that."

"It's no trouble, I assure you. I'll be expecting you between six and seven."

Anna said a quick goodbye before the vet could refuse again. She was delighted to have the chance to meet Callum Moir face to face, and demonstrate how well she had coped with these unusual circumstances, with Fiona's help of course.

The vet's mud-spattered Jeep arrived at the farmhouse gate just after 7:00pm. Fiona had been keeping watch out of the bedroom window, with study notes in hand, while Anna made the final preparations to the meal.

The fish van had appeared earlier in the day and a fine salmon had been purchased.

The salmon steaks were now simmering in herbs and lemon juice in a large, covered willow-pattern serving dish. A rhubarb crumble, contributed to the feast by Fiona's Granny, waited in the warming oven.

The kitchen table was set with the matching blue and white tableware, and a vase of flowers from the garden scented the warm air.

A white wine had arrived with sundry groceries from Tesco's delivery truck, earlier in the day, and Helen's crystal glasses were found and washed. Anna admired their sparkle in the soft candlelight.

Sylvester had been warned to remain on his best behaviour and showed his disdain for these instructions by retreating into his safe haven in the cupboard for a nap.

Anna and Fiona had shed a tear or two when they figured this would be their last night with the kitten, but they knew he would soon need the kind of space and care they could no longer provide.

Callum Moir marched up the gravel path with a small animal cage in his hand.

Anna opened the door to welcome him and watched as he carefully removed his tweed cap and hung up his waterproof jacket, then sat on the bench to extract his leather-shod feet from a pair of hefty rubber overboots. He was taller than Anna, which put his height at around six feet, and his lean frame in a brown corduroy jacket and pants, showed the kind of sinewy strength that Anna thought must be a prerequisite for a country vet with a practice that included both farm and domestic animals.

When he stood up and ran a hand through his dark hair, Anna silently admired the silver wings at each temple and thought the shaggy eyebrows and hawk-like nose perfectly suited his craggy disposition.

Polite conversation was not his forte, however, as his first statement demonstrated.

"I'll just collect the animal and be out of your way."

Anna suppressed a nasty comment and replied in her sweetest voice, "Please stay for a bite to eat. We are just about to start and perhaps you can tell us more about wildcats?"

She saw him hesitate for a moment, and sniff the inviting aroma of cooking. Fiona had revealed to Anna that the doctor lived alone with a housekeeper to prepare his meals before she returned home each day.

"Well, if you are sure it's no trouble. Will your husband be joining us?"

Anna smiled as she pictured the unlikely event of her urbane ex-husband appearing in this rural setting.

"No, I am not married. Fiona Jameson is staying with me for a week or two.

She is studying for A levels and planning to train for the Scottish Wildlife Service."

Dr. Moir's eyebrows rose at this news. "I see. That explains the girl's interest in animals. I think I have seen some of her nature photographs in the local shops."

"I am sure you have. She is a very talented and hard-working young lady."

Anna relaxed somewhat, now that the evening was going according to plan.

She motioned to the vet to sit at the table and called Fiona down from the bedroom.

When she placed the salmon dish on the table, she noticed the vet's puzzled expression.

"Have you got the wildcat animal in a cage somewhere, or is it outside?"

"Not at all! He is about three feet from you right now."

As if on cue, Sylvester poked his nose out of the cupboard and padded forward on his furry feet to investigate the new arrival in his domain.

Callum Moir was thoroughly surprised at this. He bent

down to take a closer look and was met with a low growl and bared fangs as the kitten reacted to the stranger's smell.

Neither Anna nor Fiona had ever seen this aggression from Sylvester. Fiona exchanged a glance with Anna then moved to sit beside her and see what would happen next.

"Well, a remarkably healthy specimen I would say. I have never been this close to one; I imagine few people have had this opportunity. It is about three times the size of a domestic kitten and that tail is quite extraordinary."

The tail in question was waving back and forth in what could only be interpreted as a warning gesture, but Sylvester apparently decided against attack and returned to his den without further incident.

The meal proceeded to the accompaniment of animated conversation as Fiona and Anna related their methods of feeding and cleaning the kitten and the vet recounted all he had tried in the attempt to find a suitable home for a wildcat.

Anna noticed how often the vet's eyes strayed to the cupboard in the hopes that Sylvester would emerge again. Sylvester had already sampled the raw salmon and declined to join the party.

The vet seemed impressed with their success in keeping the kitten alive and became much more sociable as the evening progressed. Anna plied him with wine and asked his opinion about Fiona's prospects, while Fiona, in turn, praised Anna's courage in taking on the farm house as well as helping her with her studies.

It was evident that such convivial events were rare in the busy vet's life. Fee had checked out the local gossip and found out there had once been a Mrs. Moir but she had left for the brighter lights of Edinburgh some years ago after complaining that her husband 'worked all the hours God sent'.

Anna felt pleased that using a softer approach, she had managed to make an ally of this difficult man. She hoped he could be of tremendous help to Fiona.

After coffee and biscuits had been served, Fiona bundled up Sylvester for the last time and placed him in the vet's portable cage, padded with the towels that had his own scent. She also included several bottles of the milk mixture that had assured his survival.

Dr. Moir thanked Anna for her hospitality and requested the chance to return the favour soon. He promised to keep both Anna and Fiona apprised of the wildcat's progress and tipping his cap, headed down the path to his Jeep.

Anna and Fiona stood in the doorway with their arms around each other and watched the car with the kitten disappear down the track.

Sylvester had become an important part of their lives in the last weeks and they would not forget him. Anna did not know it, but Fiona had been photographing the kitten and had a series of excellent pictures to develop and enlarge for Anna.

"Right! Off to bed for both of us," proclaimed Anna. "I'll clean up in the morning. It will give me something to do with all my extra time."

Fiona nodded through a yawn and expressed the hope Anna would enjoy her first night of unbroken sleep.

Anna got ready for bed in the big bedroom and settled herself in the double bed after lighting the fire. The flickering glow from the flames made her feel sleepy almost at once but her mind was so full of recent events that she could not seem to drift off to sleep.

The conversation over the dinner table kept re-playing in her memory. Had she imagined Callum Moir's invitation to a future meal together? Would she agree to a dinner date with this unusual man? It had been so long since she had been willing to risk the disappointment of a date with the usual lonely, male candidate seeking a substitute housekeeper, that she now preferred to refuse all invitations.

Still, she thought, it could be important for Fee if I keep in touch with the vet. We'll see what develops, she decided.

With that item settled, Anna closed her eyes again, and once again, sleep eluded her.

The unsolved mystery of Helen Dunlop presented itself. Anna had been so involved in other things lately that it had been some time since she had given much thought to Helen.

I promised myself I would get to the bottom of the story, she acknowledged, *and yet, I still have more questions than answers.*

Why did Helen choose to live here and keep the Dunlop name, when she was not very happy during the early part of her life? How had Helen found out she had a niece in Canada when she never contacted Anna's mother or father? Why all the secrecy of the letters George had been instructed to keep for Anna?

What will I do, go or stay?

This last question was the one that would not go away. Anna gave in and sat up in bed to consider her options.

I have to be realistic about this. Simon was right. It's a major change if I attempt a new life in a new country far from family and friends. In any case, how could I afford to do it? I have no source of income here and I would need a car, not to mention improvements to the farm house.

I haven't experienced a winter here.

Andrew expects me back at the Library soon.

I really miss Alina and Maria and Bev and Susan.

But...............I love it here in this crazy, old-fashioned house, in this beautiful country.

I can't wait to get back to Oban again and sit by the sea watching the tide wash in and out. I need to explore the islands and walk by the lochs in all weathers. I want to see Fiona get the life she deserves and watch Jeanette's baby grow up and find out how Alan Matthews manages his sheep, and volunteer at the little town library and make my garden and have two cats and a dog and keep chickens and..................

Anna was astonished at all the pent-up feelings and plans that poured out of her.

It must be fatigue, she thought, or the result of her sleep pattern being disturbed for so long, but, strangely, she had never felt so alive. Alive with possibilities for the future, perhaps, but how could she choose between two such different futures?

Anna got out of bed and pulled on her dressing gown and slippers. If not for the risk of waking Fiona, she would have gone downstairs and had a tot of that soothing whisky to calm her nerves. Her stomach was in turmoil and a throbbing behind her eyes warned of an incipient headache.

She looked out the window, searching for answers. Cold air flowed from the glass panes and she stepped back just in time to see the silent, white shape of an owl float through the night and fly toward the barn.

Did Helen wake in the night and see the owls too?

The cold outside stilled her mind, and in the clarity she remembered the postscript at the end of Helen's letter. After a minute's searching, she found the letter in the drawer of the bedside table and lit a candle so she could read it again.

Should you decide to stay in the McCaig Farm House, please visit

The Osborne Residential Home. The manageress will expect you.

Well, Helen, you have been leading me along blindly in this adventure and it's time I called your bluff. I need more information about you before I can make such an important decision and I am going to find it.

First stop; The Osborne Home.

Suddenly, Anna was overwhelmed with exhaustion. She blew out the candle and dropped into bed with robe and slippers on and a sly grin on her face.

Chapter Twenty-Two

❧

F iona had heard Anna moving around in the night so she tiptoed out of the house in the morning to collect the school children without waking her. Now that the kitten was gone there was no need for Anna to rise early to feed him.

Fiona would return to her Granny's house tonight and resume her usual schedule.

The two weeks with Anna had helped her Shakespeare and Literature studies tremendously, but she had to concentrate now on the Science and Math topics.

The dreaded exams were only a few weeks away in Glasgow. She knew she had to pass them.

Anna woke late. The fire had turned to grey ash and the room was chilly. She stood up and discovered immediately that her head was throbbing and every muscle in her body was aching. Shuffling to the washroom was an effort, relieved by the fact that hot water remained in the pipes, indicating that either she or Fee had banked down the kitchen fire successfully the night before.

Anna could not think of what to wear and since she

seemed to have slept in her dressing gown, she decided to warm up downstairs in the kitchen before tackling anything else.

On the way down, she managed to trip and landed heavily on the last step, jolting her head so badly that she had to stop and rest till the room stopped swinging around her.

"What is wrong with me?" she croaked.

Her throat felt raw and scratchy. Swallowing saliva, she thought a hot drink would sort out these effects of her broken sleep, but as soon as she reached the table, the rancid smell of left-over salmon turned her stomach and she was sick in the sink.

There was no denying it now. Something was far wrong with her. She longed to struggle back to bed and lie down flat until the nausea and headache diminished enough to allow her to think more clearly. She threw coal on to the fire but could not summon the energy to do more.

A slow crawl upstairs was as much as she could manage, and she chose to go into Fee's bedroom which was warmer because of the kitchen chimney, and closer to the washroom in case she had to be sick again.

I'll be fine once I get some sleep, she told herself, as she piled all the bed clothes on top of her and closed her aching eyes.

The next thing Anna knew, it was dark in the room. Must be a storm coming, she thought, but there was no sound of rain or wind.

Sleep had restored some energy to her limbs so she attempted to get up and find aspirin to quiet her aching head.

It soon became obvious that her stomach was empty and the nausea was still a problem. A few sips of cold water in the washroom were all she wanted. Outside the window it was night, not a threatening storm. Have I slept a whole day? Is this the same night when I looked for Helen's letter? I must feed Sylvester........... no, I must feed the fire.

The mental confusion shocked Anna into focus. She looked in the washroom mirror and did an inventory of her condition. I am flushed and I have a fever. My head and stomach ache and my chest feels tight. I have a bad cold or, heavens!.................... I could have swine flu!

This prospect sent a wave of adrenalin surging through Anna. She realized she was alone in a cold house with no help.

Fee was not due to return for a day or two. The cell phone was in the kitchen and she could not remember if she had charged it before bed last night.

In any case, Fee must not come into contact with her. The British newspapers had listed the most vulnerable sections of society and Fee was in one of the categories.

I am not supposed to be affected by swine flu, she told herself. I am too old to be susceptible and I have hardly left the house for weeks. But there was no denying she was ill.

Her first instinct was to call Alina, or one of her Samba pals for help. She knew, If she could only say to Alina the two words 'Black Bear', she would know what to do immediately. But that was impossible. The distance between them suddenly became real. There would be no help from the usual sources, but she needed someone.

"I'll call George. He'll know what to do. But I have to get downstairs for the phone."

Summoning all her strength, Anna went slowly down the stairs holding on to the wall.

The kitchen fire was out and the dirty dishes were still on the table from last night's meal.

It seemed to Anna that weeks had passed since that pleasant event. She glanced up at the clock and was rewarded with a sharp pain behind her eyes. Ten o'clock at night.

Praying that the phone would work, she picked it up from the countertop and switched it on. The battery power was low. She had only one chance to get help. She called George at home.

"George, can you send someone to the farm house. I need help."

"Anna, is that you? You sound awful. Are you ill?"

"Yes, George, I have a horrible cold, or worse, so you must not come here. You can't risk infecting Jeanette. Fiona can't come either. Can you send someone older to me tonight? I don't want to go to a hospital or wait until I can see a doctor. The phone is running out of power. Please hurry."

"Of course, Anna! I'll.....do....................soon......."

At this point the sound faded and Anna's burst of energy went with it. She collapsed into a chair and placed her head on the table. Tears trickled onto her folded hands but she lacked the strength to wipe them away.

It was impossible to know how much time had passed since the phone call.

Anna had drifted in and out of a feverish dream state. She was standing in the wind, in the centre of McCaig's Folly. Darkness surrounded her but the stars, glittering through the arches above her, were brilliant in a cloudless night. She was planning how the building would benefit the people of Oban by providing work for the town's unemployed men. This would be a fine way to use the riches she had earned in business. But, wait.............she was not Anna Mason, it was McCaig himself who stood on the hilltop.

Anna was on a much higher place planning another project; a scheme to bring someone from a distant country to live in Scotland. Anna could feel the keen mind checking over the complex steps in this scheme and wondering if it would succeed. Long silver hair blew across her face and she held a walking stick that was moulded to the shape of her hand from long use. Once again Anna understood she was not the woman on the hill.

It was Helen Dunlop who stood there.

The shock made Anna step away and she fell backwards off the hill, screaming through the icy air to her death.

Before she hit the ground, she opened her eyes and gasped in fear. She was shaking from head to foot in terror and someone was in her kitchen.

"Here she is. Thank God. This place is like ice. The poor thing will freeze to death.

Put the kettle on Alan and get a fire going. I'll help the lassie up the stairs and get her into bed, then I'll come down to see what else we can do."

Alan Matthews nodded and followed his mother's instructions as quickly as possible.

George McLennan's phone call had prompted the two of them into instant action.

A neighbour needed help and despite the lateness of the hour, Allan knew his elderly mother would follow the High-land traditions she lived by, and do whatever she could to help out.

They had driven to the farm house at top speed, fearing what they might find. George had sounded very worried about Anna Mason on the phone.

Everyone in Britain had been warned about the symptoms of swine flu. The newspapers and the television were full of stories about those who had contracted the disease, and words like 'pandemic' were being bandied about in what Alan's mother considered to be a foolhardy manner.

Now that he might be facing contamination himself, and had seen the current dire state of the handsome, confident woman he had met in this very kitchen not long ago, Allan was anxious to leave as soon as he could. If anything happened to him, the burden on his mother would mean the loss of their family farm.

He was making a start on washing the dishes when his mother returned.

"Good, Alan. The place is warming up already. I'll make tea for all of us. We'll need to keep Anna warm. She spoke for a wee bit. She is worried about Fiona and Dr. Moir.

She says they were here last night for a meal and she wants to know if they are ill also."

"I can call them, mother, but it will have to wait until the morning. It's too late to be disturbing people. What do you think is wrong with her? Is it swine flu?"

"Dinna fash, Alan. I don't ken what is the matter with the lassie yet, but she is strong.

We'll know more in the morn."

Alan finished the dishes while his mother rummaged around in the pantry. She returned holding aloft an earthenware bottle in triumph. "I was sure there would be one of these beauties in a house this old. When I was a girl no one went to bed without a jug like this wrapped in cloth at their feet." She filled the sturdy bottle with boiling water and screwed the rubber and metal stopper firmly in place.

"I'll away up and put this in her bed. You make sure there's enough wood and coal for the night and then get yourself to home, Alan. You'll be up before the dawn with the cows and the sheep to see to. I'll bide here with the lass and make porridge for her breakfast."

Alan Matthews knew Anna would be in safe hands with his mother in charge. She had always been the most capable woman he had ever known. Bringing up a family of six in a cottage was nothing to her. She had ruled the roost and kept farm and family up to scratch, never faltering until his father's death five years before. Even then, she was back feeding chickens and hand-rearing orphan lambs before the year was out. She always said, "There's nae use complaining about life. We'll all be a lang time dead."

Anna tried opening her eyes but there seemed to be a heavy weight on her lids.

She managed to raise them a fraction and saw a white-haired woman in the room, holding a cup in her hand.

"Mom, is that you?" Anna knew vaguely that her mother had been dead many years, but she was still disoriented enough to think her mother had come to her aid in her illness as she had done so often in Anna's childhood.

"No, lass, it's Alan Matthews' mother from the croft nearby. We came last night when you were so ill."

Anna tried to process this information but her head was full of wool or something and her thinking was not clear.

"Alan's mother, you say. Do I know your name?"

"It's Kirsty Matthews, my dear," answered a gentle voice.

"Kirsty? That's an interesting name."

"Well now, it's a name from the islands. My people came from Skye."

Kirsty placed her hand on Anna's forehead to check her temperature.

"That's enough talking for now, dearie. I'll help you sit up a for bit and drink this hot tea. Then we'll see how you are."

Anna was happy to let herself be cared for. Truthfully, she thought she didn't have the strength to resist this cheerful, round woman wearing a flowered apron over a dark sweater and skirt.

When the tea had been sipped and no further sickness resulted, Anna was encouraged to attempt a bowl of porridge prepared by Kirsty.

"I've stirred brown sugar in it because you are sick," she explained. "We usually have it with salt, but there's a goodly drop of cream in there to add richness for you."

The porridge slipped down easily and felt soothing to Anna's throat. The warmth in her empty stomach was comforting and the headache had lessened to a dull ache instead of a

furious roar.

Anna looked around the room, with the minimum of head action, and saw that Kirsty had lit the fire. She could hear the sound of running water in the adjacent washroom and Kirsty's voice humming as she worked. She came over to Anna and said softly, "I've put a chair in front of the sink for you to have a wash. There are clean clothes there and I will change and wash your bedding. It's a fine drying day outside."

Anna was overcome with gratitude for this kindness from a stranger. To stop herself from crying again she asked, "Don't you have to get home, Kirsty? I am very grateful for your help but I don't want to keep you from your own work."

"Och, Alan will manage for a day or two on his own. He's a grown man and fit as a fiddle. He'll contact the doctor and bring medicine for you later today, as well as finding out how young Fiona and the vet are doing. You've not a thing to worry about, my dear, other than getting well again."

This capable woman reminded Anna more and more of her own mother whose nursing skills were so central to her family's survival in Canada.

Anna ventured to ask Kirsty the question that was predominant in her mind now that all the others had been taken care of.

"Kirsty, do you think I have swine flu?"

"Och, I am sure you have the flu, lassie, but I doubt it's thon swine variety they talk about on the news. We'll see how you go on today. How does your chest feel?"

Anna swallowed and tried a deep breath. She broke into a coughing fit immediately but once she had cleared her throat, she did not feel worse.

"I don't know, Kirsty. I guess time will tell, as you say. I'll have that wash now, I think."

Kirsty's predictions were correct. Anna felt so much better after a wash and change of clothes. When she returned to the bedroom fresh sheets were folded over a duvet Kirsty had unearthed from somewhere, and a tartan blanket on top brightened up the whole room. The pillows had been plumped up and it all looked so inviting that Anna almost succumbed to tears again.

"Just have another wee sleep, dearie, and you will feel better when you wake. I'll have a nice boiled egg and toast for you, if you can fancy it."

Anna obeyed happily. She could not tell if it was the weakness or if she was revelling in a lack of responsibility she had not experienced since childhood, but following Kirsty's orders was quite the nicest thing that had happened to her in ages.

Muffled voices woke her some hours later. For a moment she could not tell if it was another dream, but then she recognized Fiona's tones coming from downstairs.

There was a man's voice also. Anna panicked when she remembered how dangerous it would be for any young person to come in contact with her while she was ill.

She was trying to disentangle her legs from the bedcovers when she heard footsteps on the stairs.

"Stay back!" she croaked.

"It's just me, lassie." Kirsty Matthews' soft Highland voice calmed Anna's fear.

"Don't you worry. I've sent them away. Fiona wanted to tell you she is fine and so is Dr. Moir. They both send their best wishes to you for a speedy recovery."

"Oh, good! That's a relief." Anna sank back onto her pillows. "What did the doctor say?"

"My Alan has spoken to the doctor. He says we are doing everything right at the moment and he will keep in touch but not pay a visit to you, in case it is the swine flu."

Anna visibly tensed up at this information but Kirsty added quickly.

"Now, he does not think you have the swine flu. He says there are a few cases of ordinary flu at the school this week and Fiona might have carried it to you, Anna.

He says, as you are a foreigner, you likely don't have much immunity to the Scottish germs."

"I suppose that could be true." Anna felt better now that she had an alternative to the swine flu nightmare that had been scaring her. "Did the doctor recommend any medicine?"

"Alan brought a prescription for you to help with the congestion and some pills for the headache but bed rest and plenty fluids will do as much good, if you ask me."

Kirsty delivered this verdict with a sniff and a grimace. It appeared she did not trust doctors very much.

"I'll be downstairs making some soup for you, lassie. Fiona delivered fresh vegetables and a nice wee bit of ham on the bone along with new-baked bread from her Granny. Now, lass, sleep and you must call me if you need anything at all."

With this admonishment, Kirsty disappeared through the connecting door to the washroom and Anna was left alone with her thoughts.

It was rather pleasant to be addressed as 'lass' or 'lassie' and seemed appropriate in the circumstances. Anna had no idea of Kirsty's age. She had the clear pink and white complexion of a Scot who spent time out of doors and if she was typical of the elderly women in Scotland, she was an excellent advertisement for their way of life.

When Anna woke again, it was night. The fire still burned brightly and the washroom light was on.

Kirsty must have been busy while Anna slept, as the unmistakable smell of home cooking was wafting up from the kitchen. Anna soon realized she was hungry, and took that as a good prediction of an early recovery. Encouraged by this thought, she found her slippers and robe and made her way cautiously down the stairs.

The sight that met her eyes was reassuring. Kirsty Matthews was washing dishes at the sink and humming along to music on the radio. The kitchen was cozy from the fire's glow and clothes were drying on the wooden frame.

Kirsty seemed right at home in this scene and Anna could not help wondering if Helen Dunlop had been equally comfortable when this was her home for many years.

"Oh, my! You are looking better, Anna dear. Come away in and have some of this soup with fresh bread and plenty butter. I've had mine already but I'll have a cup of tea with you, after I tidy up here."

Now that Anna felt well enough to chat for a while, she asked Kirsty if she had known Helen Dunlop at all. The answer surprised her. Although Alan had not had the opportunity to talk to Helen, his mother had struck up a friendship with her neighbour and, over time, they had confided in one another.

"I wouldna tell this to another living soul, Anna," she said, "but you are family and Helen would want you to know."

Anna sat back with a second cup of tea and listened intently as another part of the Helen Mystery was revealed in the lilting accent of Kirsty Matthews.

Helen's marriage to Harold Fraser was not a happy one. He was older than the young girl and so involved in his family's construction business that Helen had felt neglected and alone from the beginning.

Hearing this, Anna felt a surge of sympathy for the young woman. She, too, had known loneliness in her marriage.

On reflection, Helen had confessed to Kirsty, she did not make a good marriage partner. Her early life had been fraught with pain and she grew up with the suspicion that everyone would eventually disappoint her and probably abandon her.

Helen had never wanted children. She felt she had spent enough time with the Dunlop family as an unpaid nursemaid to their 'real' children, and she was unwilling to take up that role again. This drove another wedge between Harold and his wife.

Harold took solace in drink. He found business acquaintances who also preferred to spend hours at the pub rather than to go home to wives and children, and this became his daily pattern.

Helen grew more and more disconnected from her husband until their large and elaborate home was little more than an armed camp where they both lived separate lives.

Helen felt she had no alternatives.

Applying to the Dunlops for help was unthinkable and, although she had been told she was an orphan, her misery drove her to ask an investigator to track down any remaining family she might still have.

When she discovered her closest family had emigrated to Canada, her despair grew insupportable. The life of secrecy imposed on her by a husband who resented her dissatisfied attitude, and did not want it known outside their home, meant that she had no real friends of her own. The few social acquaintances who only saw Harold's young, trophy wife across the dining room table on rare occasions were never her friends.

Harold's family detested this cold, uncaring wife and made it clear to Helen that they wished Harold would divorce her.

In the end, Harold's death was a relief. After the funeral, Helen was approached by the Fraser family. In return for her silence about Harold's drunken condition on the day of his heart attack, and the consequent accident, she was given the guarantee that she could keep the money from Harold's will that had not been left to his family and their business concerns.

The senior family members agreed to a generous financial settlement for Helen, provided she did not speak to the press, or contest the will.

She left the house and its valuable contents intact, departing the Stirling area forever.

Helen was glad to flee the situation she had been trapped in for so many years.

She left the Fraser name and all its associations behind her. Although she had no place to go where she could feel at home, she was overjoyed at the freedom she had acquired for the first time in her life. She travelled around the United Kingdom as a tourist for a few years, living in hotels and looking for a suitable spot where she could settle down, on her own.

Anna could not wait to ask Kirsty why Helen had chosen the remote area outside Oban.

"Well, now, she said she had grown tired of busy places and curious people who wanted to know her for her money, and were not interested in her as a person. She really wanted to be alone, as she felt she had always been, and this old farm house suited her with its simple style and lovely surroundings."

"Did she spend all her money buying this place?" Anna wondered why Helen had left the fixtures in her house in their basic state and not modernized them for her own comfort.

"I wouldna ask that kind of question," replied Kirsty in an offended tone.

"That was private business, but she did go to Edinburgh a few times and buy some nice things for the house like paintings and ornaments. Personally, I would not have tolerated that antique of a cast iron stove there."

Kirsty threw a baleful look at the black stove taking up so much space in the kitchen.

"I have a fine new Aga at home, myself, but Helen liked the old-fashioned ways best."

Silence fell on the kitchen as the two women thought about Helen, in their different ways.

"It's a sad story," said Anna eventually.

"Now, now!" admonished the older woman. "Helen was happy here for many years, Anna. She told me her story a little at a time and I think it made her all the more content that she had come through such troubles and found peace at the end."

Kirsty nodded and sighed, then glanced up at the clock.

"You've been out of bed long enough, my dear. Off up the stairs with you. I am thinking you are over the worst now, so I will go back home tonight and you will call me tomorrow and let me know how you are doing."

Anna agreed and gave the older woman her heartfelt thanks.

Anna thought she would dream of Helen after hearing this latest episode of her story, but she slept well and when she woke in the morning, she had remembered the decision she had made in the middle of the night before her illness.

She would visit the Osborne Residential Home and find out what they could tell her about Helen Dunlop's final months.

Chapter Twenty-Three

I t was another week or so before Anna felt recovered enough to venture into Oban with Fee again. She had progressed steadily, and received a clean bill of health from the doctor, but she continued, with Fee's assistance, to eat well and rest frequently.

On sunny afternoons she would sit on the outside bench with the tartan blanket over her shoulders and take stock of her situation.

The mantel over the kitchen stove was full of get-well cards from friends and mere acquaintances in the area. A pot of white heather, for good luck and good health (so said the card), was in the centre of the kitchen table. Everyone had been amazingly kind to a stranger in their midst.

Anna would never forget what Kirsty Matthews had done for her, but the serious nature of her illness had been concealed from her Samba friends.

Alina was counting the weeks until Anna's return to Canada and discussions about Anna's future had taken up most of their phone conversations.

The final decisions could not be delayed much longer. Her return plane ticket was prominently displayed on the shelving unit beside the willow pattern dishes and constantly reminded her that time was short.

George provided the address of the Osborne Home, and Fiona drove Anna there on a fine afternoon at the end of the first week in May.

Anna was welcomed into the large Victorian house in its spacious grounds, by a small, elegant woman with curly red hair, piercing dark eyes, and a wary smile.

Anna thought at once that this lady was no fool and this opinion was confirmed when she asked Anna for identification.

Once the formalities had been taken care of, the manager-ess, Catherine Grant, wasted no time in introducing the topic of Helen Dunlop's stay at the Osborne Home until her death, in January, some three weeks before George McLennan's letter arrived in Canada.

The interview lasted just under an hour. Afterwards, Anna walked into the garden to look for Fiona. She found her sitting in an arbour where wisteria vines made a shelter over a rustic bench and the scent of the pendulous blossoms perfumed the surrounding air.

Anna sat down heavily beside Fee.

"What's wrong, Anna? Do you feel unwell?"

"No, Fee, I feel astounded."

Anna could say no more for a minute or two. She closed her eyes and absorbed the sunshine and the rich garden scents, letting them sink into her being.

Fiona waited patiently to find out what sort of event had transpired that could render Anna speechless. Finally, Anna reached into her purse and brought out an envelope.

"You see, Fee," she began, "this whole adventure started with a simple letter and now it ends with one. Along the way there have been other letters to George McLennan and to me, each one adding more information about an amazing woman called Helen Dunlop.

She spent her last months in the nursing-home section of this Residential Home.

She could scarcely breathe from emphysema, but she used what little remaining strength she possessed to weave the web that brought me to this place, with these choices I could never have imagined. We were family members who were never destined to meet, Fee, but Helen Dunlop has given me so much, beyond what even her elaborate plans could have achieved. I will be grateful to her till my dying day."

Fiona had to be content with these enigmatic statements. She hesitated to push Anna further as she was clearly in a serious and contemplative mood.

Anna asked to be dropped off in Oban while Fiona completed her day's driving tasks.

They would get together for a meal later, before the return trip to the farm house.

Anna walked around the seafront to the esplanade and found a stone stairway leading down to the beach. The tide was out and only ripples of water came and went on the sand.

She needed to be alone to think. Few cars passed on the road above and seagulls were the only movement in a blue, sky-and -sea tapestry with the green of the islands to rest her eyes upon.

This view and this town had become so important to her. Oban truly was a gateway to the north of Scotland, an area unspoiled and largely unoccupied. She could not have borne the thought of never seeing all that Scotland offered, but now, she knew that hard choice would not be required of her. The envelope in her purse contained a cheque for the sum of one hundred thousand pounds.

The decision to keep the McCaig farm house was made as soon as Anna had recovered from the shock the cheque had caused. That decision had been delayed by the difficulty Anna saw in how to reconcile the two disparate parts of her life. Now she had the option of relishing the best of both of her worlds. It would take thought and ingenuity to blend her Canadian and Scottish heritages, but the major problems dissolved when the cheque was delivered into her hands at the Osborne Home.

Anna compared her dilemma to McCaig's monument that commanded the skyline over Oban. The town museum and tourist literature described it as a 'Tower', while the local people referred to it as a 'Folly'; a trivial, foolish structure.

It was all in the perception, Anna decided. Some might see Anna's decision to keep the farm house as a foolish idea, doomed to failure, while others (including her Samba friends), would see it as a wonderful opportunity for the new start Anna had needed for so many years.

All that remained was to plan the future. Anna had an excellent example in Helen Dunlop of what forward thinking could achieve. She would dedicate the next week before her return flight, to deriving and establishing these plans. Ideas were already buzzing in her mind but she would reveal nothing until she could transform these ideas into a solid foundation on which to build a future.

The week flew by at frightening speed. Each day found Anna deeply involved in her plans and busy with phone calls back and forth, both in Scotland and in Canada.

Fiona was to drive Anna to Glasgow where the A level examinations were to be held in Strathclyde University. They would stay at the Jurys Inn for several days so that Fee could relax before the two days of exams, and Anna could complete one of her elaborate schemes.

George was privy to some of Anna's ideas as he would be in charge of the money while Anna was in Canada. George was designated her solicitor with a power of attorney for

Scotland so that he could act on her behalf. He held the keys to the farm house and Jeanette had agreed to advise him on matters pertaining to any purchases for the building, as soon as she had recovered from the birth of their child.

On the morning of Fiona's first day of exams, Anna made sure she had a good breakfast and walked with her the short distance to the exam site, not far from George Square.

They had reviewed Fiona's English topics the night before in the hotel and Anna was confident her pupil would do well. She waved with crossed fingers as Fiona entered through the university's glass doors in a crowd of equally-anxious young people.

As soon as Fiona had disappeared from sight, Anna walked back to a hotel overlooking George Square and ordered coffee for three to be served at a quiet table in the hotel's glass atrium. The sun sparkled through the green-tinted panes and lit up the glass table tops. Anna took a deep breath and relaxed. Almost everything was in place now. Just a few finishing touches required her attention.

While she waited for her guests, she took a folder out of her purse and glanced over the rough sketches she had made. Strange, and wonderful, how even fanciful dreams can some-times turn into reality, she thought.

When the two men were shown to her table, Anna recognized one of them immediately. Antonio, known as Tony, was in appearance, a male version of Maria with the same tanned skin, dark eyes and hair. He had the same confident business manner also, as he introduced his companion, an architect with whom he had worked on a number of construction projects.

Anna presented her sketches and photographs of the McCaig Farm House. The architect would draw up plans for the renovations to the building that Anna wanted, and Tony would manage the project while living on site during the summer months when Anna was back in Canada. Both men added ideas to supplement Anna's vision of a lighter, warmer, more spacious home with all-weather amenities.

The simplest of all the ideas would be accomplished quickly. A new drive-way on the east side of the house would lead straight to the barn and allow a car to be parked in there. Anna requested that the structure be made sound with a concrete floor but, if possible, a small roof hole should be left, to allow the barn owls to move in and out.

Blueprints and photographs would be sent to Alina's home for Anna's approval, once she had set up an office there equipped with the latest technology. An on-call tech specialist in the form of James, Bev's son, would create a web site to advertise Alina's new internet craft and knitwear business, linked to a future cottage industry of home workers in Oban and areas in the north of Scotland.

Alina had happily agreed to these plans. Anna would move in with her friend as soon as the sub-let of her apartment had been completed and both women would return to Scotland in the fall to see the final stages of the renovation.

They would also begin the process of establishing the farm house as a registered member of a self-catering, holiday-home company that provided exceptional accommodations for tourists from all parts of the world who came to Scotland for skiing, rock climbing, golf, fishing, sailing and to enjoy the superb scenery in all seasons.

Fiona's training courses in Inverness would occupy much of her time in the next three years, but she would be available in the summer for guided nature tours in the surrounding area that she knew so well. Callum Moir had offered Fiona a part-time position as assistant in his veterinary clinic whenever she was free from term work and her taxi business would continue with a new partner driving during term time.

Anna shook hands with her construction team and watched as they left the hotel.

She could not hear their conversation but she could tell

from their body language that they were enthused about the project she had given them. She had emphasized the importance of retaining the traditional character of the old stone building and providing a focus on the spectacular view of Helen's Hill.

Tony's sons worked with their father and the business included another Italian family related to Maria. They were talking already of holidays in the new McCaig Farm House.

Anna hoped to involve Alan Matthews in her plan. He would represent the farm aspect of the set up. Families could visit the animals on his farm and watch his border collie, Prince, work with the sheep in the fields. Kirsty might even be persuaded to provide a farm house tea to visitors.

Anna's imagination stretched ahead to the future years. All her friends in turn would stay at the McCaig house with Alina and herself. The business would create work for folks in Oban and help promote the Scottish tourist industry.

With both Alina and herself involved, Anna could spend time on both sides of the Atlantic as required. In time, a regular schedule of spring and fall vacations would be possible, leaving the more popular summer and winter seasons for the paying guests.

Anna was excited at these prospects but also at peace with her many decisions.

On her last climb to the top of Helen's Hill, she felt as if Helen Dunlop herself, had overseen all the plans and given her approval.

The house that had brought happiness to Helen in her latter years would be filled with the laughter and joy of her niece Anna, her nephew Simon and his family, and so many others who would appreciate the comfort of her home and the splendour of its setting.

Parting with Fiona was going to be difficult, Anna knew. The young woman was, in many ways, the daughter Anna would have loved to have for her own. It was a comfort to know they would be together again in a few months and that Fiona's life would be filled with exciting prospects.

Looking out at the busy traffic and hustling pedestrians circling George Square's central gardens, Anna was aware that she had unfinished business in the city from which her parents had emigrated so long ago. The reasons for that emigration and the split from their families was still a mystery to Anna and one she knew she must pursue.

Raising a glass of water in a toast, she made a silent pledge to return to Glasgow and track down the real story one of these days. After all, she now considered herself somewhat of an expert in getting to the bottom of family mysteries after the Helen Dunlop saga. It was still hard for Anna to believe that only six months ago she had never heard Helen's name.

As soon as Anna entered the doors of Glasgow International Airport, her thoughts turned to her home in Ontario. Everything in Scotland had been set in motion and now she could return to her birthplace with a clear mind and a new sense of purpose.

Home. From now on she would have to specify which of her two homes she was referring to, but for the present it was lovely to think of summer in Canada.

She could not wait to see Alina, Bev, Maria and Susan. There was so much to tell them; much more than could be conveyed on a transatlantic phone call. Each one of them had played a part in Anna's success and, perhaps, she could at last repay their generosity.

Anna knew for certain she would never again underestimate the importance of friends and family.

In tribute to Helen, or especially, to little Aileen Anne, she would cherish each and every one of them.

. . .

Anna had plenty to think about on the plane, but as they rose over the Clyde and left the verdant shores of Scotland behind, one final conversation re-played in her mind.

Sitting in George McLennan's office that last time, with the cheque in her hand, Anna had asked George if he had known Helen Dunlop had such a sum of money in her possession.

"I have to say, Anna, I was as surprised as you to find out she had this kind of wealth. She did not seem to be living in the lap of luxury, as you know."

"Then, where did all this come from?" Anna waved the cheque in the air as if it could reveal the answer.

George opened a locked drawer in his desk and took out an envelope which Anna immediately recognised.

"That's the letter Helen left for me to pass on to you, George, when I arrived in Oban.

I had forgotten all about it."

"Well there are no secrets left now, Anna, and I am very glad of it. This letter instructed me what to do with the money in your cheque, should you decide to sell Helen's house and return to Canada."

"Are you going to tell me?" Anna's curiosity was aroused.

"There's no need for you to know the details, but I was to retrieve the cheque from Osborne House and dispense small amounts to various people in the town and to the town council for facilities for the elderly."

"But, George," Anna persisted, "did she say where the money came from?"

"I can only tell you what Helen wrote, Anna. Perhaps you should read it yourself."

Anna received the letter in hands which had developed a sudden nervous shake.

These were probably the last words Helen Dunlop had ever written, and the last of the mystery that Anna was ever likely to know.

I have invested money from my late husband's estate for many years
and placed the profits in a safe deposit in a bank in Fort William.
Recently, I have added to this sum by selling sundry pieces of china
and portraits from the farm house. It is unlikely that these objects
would be of value to anyone, other than myself.

When it became obvious to me that I could no longer continue to
live alone, I sold all my holdings and asked the bank to make a
banker's cheque for the entire amount.

This cheque will be in the possession of Catherine Grant,
manageress of the Osborne Residential Home, the place where I
intend to spend my last days.

Should my niece, Anna Mason, decide to sell the property I have left
to her, my instructions to you, Mr. McLennan, are to retrieve this
cheque and disburse the contents as listed on a separate page of this
letter.

I remain, as always, in your debt, sir. You will find enclosed a
cheque for your expenses which can never repay you for the kind-
ness you have shown me and the discretion you have exhibited in all
the dealings we have had over the years.

I wish for you, all that you wish for yourself.
Sincerely,
Helen.

When Anna looked up from the letter, George was
standing at the window. She was grateful that his back was
turned to her as she was in tears thinking of this lonely
woman whose life should have been so different.

Recollecting that moment, Anna could feel the tears gathering
again. The initial sadness was gone, however, and now her
tears were joyful.

Everything had worked out just as Helen had planned.

Anna knew that Helen's legacy was not only the farm
house and the cheque, but also the sense of empowerment
she had gifted to her niece.

If Helen Dunlop could survive the disappointments of her life, nothing could stop Anna Mason from taking charge of her own life and living it to the full.

THE END

The Prime Time Series continues in *Time Out of Mind*, book 2.

Afterword

Prime Time was my first series. I was hoping to find readers in the *prime* of their lives with *time* to read captivating stories, set in real-life locations and featuring women you would like to get to know.

Anna Mason is that woman. She is at a crossroads in her life when she gets a chance to take a new direction and travel to Scotland with the encouragement of her group of faithful friends.

This series is now eight full books and Anna is still going strong with adventures that will transport you to places you might never expect. You will fall in love with Anna, as I have.

Read Ruth's other series, Seafarers, Seven Days, Home Sweet Home, Journey of a Lifetime and Starscopes at retailers everywhere. Also read Borderlines a stand-alone thriller.

www.ruthhay.com

Also by Ruth Hay

Home Sweet Home Series

Harmony House

Fantasy House

Remedy House

Affinity House

Memory House

Journey of a Lifetime Series

Auralie

Nadine

Mariette

Rosalind

Starscopes Series

Starscopes: Winter

Starscopes: Spring

Starscopes: Summer

Starscopes: Fall

Made in the USA
Middletown, DE
28 December 2021

57184695R00165